PRESENCE

For Doug —
All best to
a wonderful neighbor
and friend —
Chris
9/30/99

Christopher Torockio

PRESENCE

Stories

St. Andrews College Press
Laurinburg, North Carolina
• 1999 •

Acknowledgments

Some of these stories previously appeared, in slightly different form, in the following publications:

Aries
Ascent
Cities and Roads
The Dickinson Review
The Florida Review
The Pittsburgh Quarterly

Copyright © 1999 by Christopher Torockio

Library of Congress Cataloging-in-Publication Data

Torockio, Christopher 1968. Presence / Christopher Torockio
Laurinburg, NC / St. Andrews College Press
I. Torockio, Christopher II. Title

St. Andrews College Press
1700 Dogwood Mile
Laurinburg, NC 28352
www.sapc.edu

ISBN: 1-879934-63-9

Typeset in Sabon

First Printing: August 1999

For Halle

The author wishes to acknowledge the assistance and inspiration of Chuck Kinder, Catherine Gammon, Jaimy Gordon, Fred Leebron, Dan Auman and Ron Bayes, who made this collection possible; as well as the talented members of the writing programs at the University of Pittsburgh and Western Michigan University for their dedication and generosity. In addition I would like to express my heartfelt gratitude to my parents, Carmen and Adele Torockio, who have lovingly and unfailingly provided me with all the support I could possibly hope for, in every sense of the word.

CONTENTS

Windup   3

These Things Go Away   15

A Homecoming   38

One Remarkable Thing   61

In Mercer   77

Doe   94

Belong   99

Apart   120

Hepatitis   135

Ice Cream Headache   149

Passing Interest   167

The Farther You Go   189

PRESENCE

Windup

So HERE'S THE THING: Wendy tells me she wants me out of the apartment, ASAP. Big deal; she's said that before. Only this time her announcement comes on the day we find out she's pregnant. With *my* kid no less.

"I don't want my child growing up in your presence," she says theatrically. "I mean it. I want you gone before I get too far into this."

"But what if I don't want to leave?" I ask her. "What if I really want this kid?"

"Doesn't matter," she says, "because you don't. You know it, I know it." We are in the bedroom and Wendy is sprawled on top of our comforter with her ankles locked at the end of the bed, hands folded on her belly, like she's due any day. "You'll quit on this, too. Just like everything else."

Of course she's referring to my dropping out of college. It used to really get me steamed when she'd bring this up, but to be honest I don't even feel the need to acknowledge these jabs anymore. It's that meaningless to me now. I dropped out of school midway through my senior year to become a painter, an *artist*, which, I have to admit, although not to her, was a ridiculous thing to do. I didn't know how to paint. I didn't know the first thing about it really, I just decided that's what I wanted to do. Actually, Wendy was behind me on it at first. She thought, if I ever got good, I could make a lot of money at it. Obviously, neither one of us knew anything about painting. I kept at it for three or four months maybe when we first started really seeing each other, trying to paint landscapes and a portrait or two, and when I couldn't do that, I tried doing some things I figured I would call abstract, and never finished one painting. Then I stacked several hundred dollars worth of paints, brushes, canvases, oils and easels into a corner and got a job selling gaudy furniture in a mall.

Wendy stares at me now with something like venom in her narrow blue eyes. She's working at this. Her aquarium bubbles against the wall by the window, bathed in yellow light. She bought it a few months ago and she cleans the filter every other day. "Besides," she says, "it might not even be your kid."

I smile. "Really?" I prepare my voice for the most patronizing tone I can muster. "Just what exactly are you trying to say, Wendy?"

For a brief moment I think she might break into a smile herself. But she doesn't. "What I'm saying—" she glances up at the tan plaster ceiling then back at me standing there, "is exactly what you think I'm saying."

"You're so full of shit," I say and pull myself up onto our dresser, letting my feet dangle. Wendy flinches and slides her hand along her side, like she feels a kick or something. I think I might laugh. "So, when did this happen?"

"About a month ago," she says.

"Who with?"

"Earl Dezzuti."

"The crippled guy? The one who tries to golf?"

"He has arthritis in his leg, Martin. You're such an idiot."

I'm having trouble believing we're actually in the middle of this conversation. It seems to me the kind of thing you sometimes imagine, and it scares you, even though you know it's impossible. Like when you're in the open air on top of a building or an observation deck or balcony and you think, *I wonder what would happen if I jumped off of here?* The complexity of Wendy's tale is impressive, though, and I almost say so. Instead I say,

"Well that's really something. How old is Earl anyway? He's gotta be pushing fifty by now."

"He's thirty-two, Martin. Just because you're such a child doesn't mean everyone who acts their age is old. Please pack a suitcase."

"How 'bout I marry you," I say.

"Okay."

"What?"

Wendy rolls her eyes up in her head. "Now who's full of shit?" she says. She is an inch or two taller than me and four years older, both of which you would notice right off. We've known each other since she was thirteen and I was nine. Our parents were close friends for a while and one summer our families went on vacation together to the beach in Virginia. My little sister and Wendy's younger brother came along, and the plan was for her brother, Donald, who was about my age, and me to be playmates for the week, while my sister stayed with the parents and Wendy kept to herself in an attempt to meet some other kids her age. Apparently this was real important to her at the time.

Wendy's was the first, well, female body I ever noticed. In retrospect it actually was kind of funny looking—with her white nylon bikini top bunched and drooping off of her like a pair of tents—but when she walked out to the beach from our hotel and untied the knot at her hip, sliding the t-shirt over her pearly stomach and budding chest, I felt a chill. I remember this distinctly because I sat there with sand in my shorts, digging for hermit crabs with Donald as the July sun baked into us like weight, and when she peeled the shirt away—an act which in itself seemed in slow motion—an uncontrollable shiver that had to be visible shook through my body. That image still comes back to me when I see Wendy, under certain circumstances.

So for the rest of the week I followed her around, tracing her footsteps in the sand, trying to look coordinated and walk like a man. Donald told on me, of course, and my father took me aside and explained that Wendy, even though she wouldn't say so, didn't want me tagging along behind her. "You're suffocating her," he said one morning before we went out to the beach. "You don't want her to think of you like that, do you?"

I shook my head no. We were in front of the bathroom mirror and I was slicking my thin, cowlicked hair back with my mother's gel.

"Well then," he said. "There you go. Play with Donald the rest of the time. He's a good little guy."

"I don't like him. He eats things."

My father scratched his crotch pensively then smoothed his mustache down with his index finger. "Things? What things?"

"Stuff you shouldn't eat," I lied. "Bugs and weird-looking stuff that comes out of the ocean." I turned back toward the mirror. My hair looked ceramic, with wide, shiny trenches running through the sides and a patch sprouting straight up at the cowlick. There was a dark line across my forehead where the greasy gel met my skin. "Yesterday he ate bait."

"Bait?"

"Yeah. This old guy was fishing on the beach and Donald snuck up behind him and took a piece of bait out of the guy's bucket and ate it."

"What kind of bait?" He watched my reflection.

"Oh, I don't know," I said. "Shark fins or something."

"Ah." My father reached above my head and removed the comb from my hand. "Well, I'll tell you what. Go on out and play with Donald today. And if he eats any more shark fins, give it a try. Maybe we've all been missing something."

Wendy has always had this thing for fish. In addition to the aquarium in our room, the entire apartment is done up in marine paraphernalia: bottled ships, seascape paintings (another genre I took a crack at), little wooden sailor statuettes on shelves, fishnet hanging from the ceiling, and even a mock porthole on the wall next to the living room window. A while back she wanted to hang a phoney stuffed marlin above the sofa, but I talked her out of that one. It isn't so much a nautical fixation (Wendy gets seasick every time we go out on a boat) but rather an affection for fish themselves and what she once called their "tranquil existence."

I came home from the furniture store one day and the aquarium was all set up, humming and glowing and gurgling away in the bedroom.

"Fish?" I said when I walked in and saw it.

Wendy sat there in the dark, motionless on the edge of the bed, watching the tank.

"We have fish?"

"Yeah," she said, not taking her eyes away. "Guppies actually. Guppies and neon tetras and angelfish—they're my favorite. And see that big one down there on the bottom? That's a plecostemus."

"Plecostemus."

"Yeah. He sucks the algae off the stones and glass. It's very efficient."

"Mm."

Then she turned to me and all at once I saw a cryptic sort of sadness in her face. Sadness and submission and wonder. I didn't realize what it was at the time, although I certainly noticed something—something I'd never seen before—and it made my skin clammy. I formulated this interpretation later, a little at a time, until it finally took shape. "We don't have to keep it if you don't want," she said.

"It's fine. Whatever."

She kept her eyes on me for a moment and then pulled them away and looked back at the tank. This is where I think it started. Wendy regarded me with strained indifference from that moment on. I watched her. There was a castle on the floor of the tank with bubbles rising out of its top window. She gazed at it as if she wished she were in it.

"Shh," she said, though I hadn't even breathed. "Isn't it peaceful." This didn't seem like a question, so I didn't answer. "Watch the angelfish. See how it glides from right to left and into the upper corner, then back down and across? So reliable. So comforting. It's amazing, really."

I held my sport jacket over my shoulder, then flipped it around in front of me and tossed it on the bed. "Wendy," I said. "They're fish."

"I know that. They're fish. They're beautiful fish."

"How much did this setup cost us?"

She didn't look at me. She didn't move. She made no facial expression and no sound, and yet I could see her affection for me deflate from her body and float away down the hall to the living room, where my brushes and canvases hid in a closet beneath the hems of winter coats and the vacuum cleaner, and out the front door. "Please leave me alone for a while," she said finally. "Go out with your friends or something tonight. Just go somewhere and please don't tell me when you think you'll be home. Don't make those promises to me anymore."

I convince Wendy to go out for dinner. I tell her she needs to relax, that we need to calmly discuss this thing and act rationally. I'm so sure she is making up the Earl Dezzuti story that I have to keep reminding myself not to smile, that it wouldn't be tactful. This is a time for maturity, I say, a time for tenderness and level heads. I just hope my MasterCard takes.

Wendy is in the passenger seat of her car. She sits leaning back with her legs slightly apart and her head on the headrest, looking like someone forced to attend the funeral of a despised co-worker, and I suddenly realize the absurdity of us.

I can't help myself. I say, "Want to go to Sammy's Seafood House?" and then wait for a response.

She doesn't offer one, though. She has lost all feeling for me, even the contempt, and I wonder how long this has been the case. "Let's just get this thing over with," she says.

"All right," I say. "Sammy's it is," and press down on the accelerator.

They seat us in a booth next to a painting of an old schooner in what looks like the North Atlantic. At least I think it's a schooner, but I can't exactly say. It's a floating vessel of some sort. You can see land behind it, in the upper left corner. This land is green and brown and rocky and for some reason I figure it is Newfoundland, although I have no idea of this either. Wendy would know, but she doesn't say and I don't ask. I wonder if anyone in the restaurant can see how much I am, suddenly it seems, despised by this woman I'm with. I want to order a fat, fleshy, deep-fried slab of red snapper. Or maybe lobster; something with a head on it. I feel this is necessary. This evening now seems merely academic—it's been coming for a while and now I'm playing it out, like a movie I've seen before.

Wendy flips her menu to the "Land Lubbers" section and scans the beef and chicken options. When our blue-blazered waiter, whose name tag identifies him as *Doug—First Mate*, comes to take our order, I ask for a vodka and tell him to come back later. He writes something on his pad and then turns to go.

"Wait," Wendy says, and he swings back around, standing at attention. "Don't drag this out, Martin. Order something and let's go. I'm tired of this. Get a spine, would you please? And grow up, for Christsake. I'll have the Caesar Salad. No anchovies, please." She looks down at her fingers spread wide on the table.

"She's eating for two," I tell Doug, as though this might clear everything up. "You know what I mean." Then, Jesus, I wink at him. He makes this quick, confused twitch that's kind of like a smile and stands there, waiting, but wanting desperately to leave. I want to explain something to him; I'm not sure he understands. I'm not sure all these people looking at me understand. So I consider telling him about the time, later that week in Virginia, so long ago, when I saved Wendy's life. I consider telling every ridiculing face in Sammy's. And Wendy, too. I want to tell her most of all. It seems to me as good an opportunity as I'm likely to get. I want to explain everything, and see her reaction. And it would be so easy, too. She remembers most of it, I'm sure: how awkward and shy she was, we both were; and how, despite everything, I knew her better than she ever thought someone my age could. And how I followed her, every day, up and down the beach, and she never said anything. How she let me do this, and how, for the life of me, I have no idea why. I held her back. She tried to make friends that week, which was difficult enough, but other thirteen-year-olds don't want to hang out with someone whose got this snot-nosed kid, with his hair greased and flying, on her heels. I ruined her week, no question. But she knows that much. The rest—how I saved her life—I could just tell her flat out. I could say: You know most of it, Wendy, sure, but remember our last night there, when I followed you out to the pier that was down the beach from the hotel. You remember. It was just after dinner and everyone—your family and mine—was going to go play miniature golf. Everyone except you, of course. When I announced that I didn't feel like going either, my father got upset and said you'd end up hating me. But you told him it was okay, you didn't mind. You were so *accepting* then, Wendy. Even though I didn't know it, I'm sure now that I loved you. My father held up his hands in surrender, as if to say, Hey, I tried. Now it's your problem.

I walked down the beach a few steps behind you. The waves were black and white in the dusk and the sand was cool. Once we left the hotel you never acknowledged me. Why is that, Wendy? If you were embarrassed of me, why did you let me come along? Are you still embarrassed of me? Wendy?

The pier stretched out into the sea. Not very far, but far enough so that I couldn't see the end in the darkness. The structure itself looked flimsy to me, almost cartoonish, and the ocean smell was thickest as we climbed its ten or twelve steps from the beach. This is where kids your age came to escape from parents and little brothers. There were only four of them there that night. I remember them well, Wendy, even though you probably do not. The two boys were named Skip and Matt—Manny, I heard Skip call him once—and the girls were Doreen and Carla. You went over to talk to them and I sat down on the edge of the pier, legs dangling high over the surf, to watch for dolphins. I remember that week telling you that dolphins were my favorite fish, and you immediately corrected me. You knew everything then.

I heard parts of that conversation, Wendy. They were going out on one of their parents' boats. Would you like to come along? It was a secret, though. Skip's parents would never let him take the boat out alone at night. But he knew how to operate it fine. No problem. It was just a little motor boat. They'd take it out into the bay, no farther. Hey, who's the little kid? one of them asked. He can't come; he's too little. I didn't hear much more. Then they left. I heard them clomping across the pier behind me, then down to the beach, then nothing but ocean sounds. A moment later I felt your hand on my shoulder. It was windy and my hair was wild, poking out all over and holding there stiffly. I could hear the undertow fizzle beneath us and I wondered, as I still often do, *What would happen if I jumped from here?*

"Any dolphins?" you asked.

I shook my head and my hair rotated but stayed up.

"Let's go," you said. "It's getting cold."

I walked beside you all the way back. You still didn't talk to me, but for some reason, I wasn't ashamed to walk with you this once. We got back to the hotel and the moon was big and full over the water; there were no stars, but the sky was low and wide open. If I weren't so young I'd have recognized the evening as painfully romantic. You went into your family's room and I went into mine and, after patting down my hair and rejelling, I positioned myself next to the window. I was so sure that you'd go right back out to try to catch up with those kids, now that I had been safely returned. But the only movement at your door that night was when your parents and Donald came back from miniature golf. When my parents walked in moments later, they were furious that I was there alone. But I told them you'd been with me, Wendy, that you'd been watching over me.

The next morning we all began packing the cars to leave. I saw you a couple of times in passing, your arms full of seashells and starfish that your father would have to make room for, and you seemed refreshed and happy enough.

We had the television on in our room—the morning news—but I paid no attention to it until, as I walked past the screen, I heard the blond anchorman with pointy cheekbones begin the story about a tragic boating accident that occurred overnight, taking the lives of three teens. Apparently, while cruising along the shores near the harbor, whoever was steering ran the small craft into some rocks, which were marked by a buoy, but difficult to see at night. From there the anchorman let the lone survivor, a boy named Matt, explain the rest in a voice I was sure I'd heard before. He said he didn't know what happened. We just hit something, he said. We weren't paying attention. It was all of a sudden. Thud. Somebody was thrown out, he wasn't sure who, and someone went in after them. He went, too . . . he couldn't remember much—it was so dark—but when he came up the boat was half under and none of his friends were around. Then he felt the rocks against his legs, he said. He didn't know, there were rocks, he didn't know. Then he started crying and I noticed he had red hair. I hadn't been able to tell this the night before. He cried a little more and they cut back to the anchorman with pointy cheekbones who added that the outer edge of the harbor in question also was known to contain very strong currents during that particular time of day and year, and that the police were presently searching for the other teens' bodies but it was expected that they went out with the tide.

I looked at you then, Wendy. You were reaching up onto the roof of the car in your halter, trying to put something else into a suitcase that already had been strapped down.

"Come on, tiger." My father tapped me on the butt as he blew past. "Get your stuff together." Then he stopped and regarded me for a moment. "Nice hair," he said.

I don't know why I never said anything to you then. I was nine, maybe that's why, but for some reason I chose not to. Or maybe it wasn't a choice. Maybe I never even considered it. In any case, I'm telling you now, Wendy, because now it seems important.

That's what I want to say to her.

But now she is staring at the painting of the schooner, of Newfoundland, and Doug the First Mate has disappeared. I'm not sure how long we've been sitting here.

"Are you serious about this Earl Dezzuti business?" I ask her.

"What difference does it make?"

"How long have we known each other, Wendy?"

"That has nothing to do with this."

"How long?"

She takes her eyes down from the painting and grips her water glass like it's a snake. "I don't know," she says. "Sixteen, seventeen years?"

"What happened to us?" I say and then immediately realize that I'm beating this thing to death, that none of this matters.

Wendy looks back up at the painting. I look, too, and it seems to me that the schooner has moved, but I'm not sure how.

"I saved your life," I say.

"No," she says. "You're not even a part of it."

Doug the First Mate cautiously approaches our table now. "Are you ready to order yet, sir?" His eyes dart over to Wendy then back to me.

"Yeah," I say. " I'll have a lobster. And one for the lady, too."

"Martin!" Wendy turns to Doug the First Mate. "I don't want one. I already ordered."

"Two lobsters," I tell him. "Two. And none of this *tails* bullshit either. The whole goddamn thing. You know?"

First Mate Doug scratches this into his pad and retreats from the table. People are looking at us. At me. Wendy is one of them. I can feel her presence. I can feel it but it fills me with an indecipherable, floating kind of dread. I can feel the presence of every person in this room, too, and it's kind of overwhelming.

Finally, Wendy says, "How do you feel?"

"Fine," I say. "Great." Then I say, "Swell."

"You'll never do this to me again," she says.

"I know."

After a time, we are no longer the center of attention at Sammy's Seafood House. Wendy's hand is still gripped tightly around her sweaty water glass. I watch her, and as I watch her I wonder if the way things wind up is a true, reliable account of an entire situation. They say you only need to watch the last two minutes of a basketball game. The last two minutes can take more than an hour. But that's when all the excitement is, when strategy is paramount, when the game's truly decided.

Wendy's nose is the same as when she was thirteen—the same shape, I mean. She has the same forehead, the same delicate hairline. The hair itself is different, though. More coarse; and darker, too. It has an attitude I can't quite explain. I wish I could stop this somehow—apply the brakes. Just rewind and start again. From this afternoon maybe. Or from the day Wendy brought home the aquarium. Or even from Virginia seventeen years ago. That would make more sense. I'm sure I would do things differently, with rationality and forethought. I'm sure of it.

Wendy releases her red knuckles from the glass and looks up at the painting of the schooner again, chin in her hand.

"Where is that, do you think?" I ask her. "Newfoundland?"

She keeps her eyes there. "I have no idea," she says.

These Things Go Away

JEFFERSON BARRETT used to be my best friend before he went and got himself arrested for shoplifting in my parents' store. Well, not really *in* the store. They caught him two blocks down the street with a jar of pistachios, two tubes of toothpaste, a bottle of Stroh's beer and a four-pack of Duracell C-size batteries in his coat. But no receipt.

This event didn't seem to surprise many people in our neighborhood. It surprised me, though. See, my town, which sat along the eastern edge of Ohio at pretty much equal distances from Cleveland, Pittsburgh and Erie, was one where everybody seemed to know the fate of their neighbors far ahead of time. Or so they'd say. The only possible fate awaiting Jefferson, it was universally known (after he was arrested, of course), was prison.

The store itself was perfectly positioned on the corner of South Front Street and Lenzner Avenue in the shadow of two good-sized willow trees that arched out over the street. Each fall I'd spend a portion of my afternoons sweeping the trees' tiny brittle leaves that collected on the sidewalk in front of the glass doors into the sinking gutters at the curb. The location was perfect because this town was not large and South Front, with its stretch of three traffic lights, was the busiest road within twenty square miles. The store occupied the same corner as the middle light and was called Marnme's. My father thought this up. I'll explain: my mother's name was Mary and my father wanted to name the store after both of them. So, Mary 'n Me (my father being "me"): Marnme's.

At least once a week Jefferson and I used to lift a bottle of grape Mad Dog from the refrigerated section and sneak up on to the roof, making like we were cleaning leaves out of the drain pipes. In the winter we'd go down to the cellar, but the dankness and filth all around made this a far less attractive atmosphere. On the slanted roof, though, we could see clear to Pennsylvania on bright, crisp days, despite the fact that the store was only about as tall as a two-story house, a little taller maybe. My parents and I lived upstairs. From up there Jefferson and I had a full appreciation for the sheer smallness of our town, and it made us feel huge. Sometimes we'd go up there at night and watch the three traffic lights on South Front all blink yellow and out of sequence.

"Buckman," he said once, handing the sticky purple bottle across to me, "I'm gonna marry Darla Weege. Have I told you that?"

The sun was going down behind the dry cleaners across the street. My parents were probably cashing out the registers right about then. It was a Friday and my father usually liked to close early on Fridays and go to The Mouse Trap. Actually, Jefferson *hadn't* mentioned this before. "Darla Weege's twenty-nine years old," I pointed out, then took a loud gulp from the bottle and waited for my chest to burn. This seemed to me a significant barrier, since we were not quite eighteen at the time. "Does she even know who you are?"

He shrugged. "Doesn't matter. I think she might know my brother." He was serious about proclamations like this. As far as Jefferson was concerned at that particular moment, he really was going to marry Darla Weege. It was just a question of when.

"I don't know what good that does you," I said. "Your brother's an idiot."

"I know it." Jefferson stood then, bending his one leg at the same angle as the roof for balance, and hobbled like a penguin to the far side, where the willow tree's lower branches rested on the shingles. "All's I said was she knows who he is. The fact that he's an idiot is beside the point."

"You're gonna fall, you drunk bastard."

Jefferson turned and looked at me. He was a thin kid with short hair and a square, jutting chin. It seemed like he had one day's worth of whiskers at all times, only it didn't grow evenly on his face; and he never wore laces in his shoes, which, I believe, above anything else put people in mind of a delinquent when considering Jefferson. He leaned over the edge and glanced at the ground below. On that side of the building there was just a wide, sodded gap for the two trees; beyond that was the record store. "I'll just wait here for Darla to walk by," he said. "Then drop down out of the sky and land at her feet."

"Good plan," I said. "Then she can take you to the emergency room."

He held one foot out over the side. I waited for his shoe to slip off, but it didn't. "What do you know?" he said.

"That your brother and you have a lot in common." I held the bottle out to him.

He looked at it, then down at his feet. "Toss that bugger over here."

I screwed the cap back on, planted my left hand on the roof for support and gave the bottle a sidearm toss. It spun toward Jefferson like a punt, sliced away from him. He reached out beyond the edge and swatted at the bottle, knocking it up in the air a little, and snatched it with his other hand, swaying. He unscrewed the cap quickly and took two gulps. I counted the bobs of his big adams apple. "We shoulda got orange this time," he said.

"I think they're out. They got fruit punch, though, I think. It's new."

Jefferson scrunched his eyebrows pensively, considering this flavor, as if it were a concept worth serious attention. He nodded.

Privately, we both hated Mad Dog.

"Tomorrow," he said, raising the bottle again.

Just then we heard the front door slam closed, the dead-bolt slide solidly into place. The humming from the gold and red neon sign above the door stopped, signifying that it had flickered out. We heard keys jingle and my father say, "For crying out loud, Mary, give me the goddamn things. Here, hold this. You have to jiggle it. Look here. See? Jiggle it and it turns. It's only been like this for five years now, for crying out loud. Another five more and you'll figure it out maybe." We held our breath. The second deadbolt clamped heavily into place, and my parents moved away from the store toward Delila Street. We could have done anything we wanted to them from up there. I thought this and felt the Mad Dog rise in me. My dad's hair was wet and slicked back and he had on his white shoes that my mother hated. Usually he went out alone. The fact that my mother was going along this night made me a little uneasy, although it shouldn't have. Actually, I should have been pleased. On Delila they turned right. The Mouse Trap was just two blocks from there.

The sun was all the way down now, just a dull orange glow seeping above the sloped roof of the cleaners'. I wondered what my parents did at the Trap. I wondered if they got rowdy, loud, if they danced. I hoped when I turned twenty-one I would be gone from this town and not have to go to the Trap and see them there.

Jefferson sat back down next to me on the roof's pointed apex. He leaned back, elbowed me in the ribs. He said, "You know what really yanks my coil?"

I didn't answer him. He turned his eyes away from me and set them toward the western treeline. Thick shadows meshed with the leaves and branches there. Soon the shadows would cover everything. "I'll tell you," he said. Then he said: "That crummy willow tree right there." He pointed in that direction. "And the other one, too. Both of the buggers. The two of them. And you know why?" He waited a moment, knowing I wouldn't respond. He took a swig of Mad Dog, wiped his mouth with the back of his hand. "One word," he said, holding up a finger.

"Their goddamn roots. That's why. They're everywhere, those buggers' roots. They go out under the street, back under old man Winthrop's junk pile, down the block in both directions. Imagine it. Under your old man's store, even. And they wind and curl and strangle everything in their path. They keep going. They don't let anything breathe. You hear what I'm saying? They have a grip like, well, have you ever tried to chop through a willow tree's roots?"

I looked at him blankly, shook my head no.

"Well," he said, shrugging, "neither have I. But I hear it's a bitch and a half."

Those trees had been one of the few things I admired about the town I grew up in. Shops on South Front Street came and went, were torn down, and built up again. Marnme's used to be a real estate office (back when there was a need for a real estate office). The record store on the other side of the trees used to be a strip bar. But the trees were always there, regardless. There was some strange hint of dignity to them, a sense of permanence. Even as a kid I recognized this, and respected it. And for that reason I never tried to climb them. Either one. That and the sanctions imposed by my father which forbade me from "screwing with those trees." People love that kind of shit, he said. It brings 'em in. Surveys proved it.

But I did what Jefferson told me. I imagined it. I imagined roots zigging and zagging below the town like so many veins, searching for something to wrap themselves around and choke the life out of. I imagined the roots as sensors plugged into the lifeline of everyone within reach, fully aware of everything going on in every direction. I imagined them laughing. And then, for absolutely no good reason, I shared Jefferson's hatred for those trees.

"I'm going to Darla Weege's house," Jefferson said then. He stood awkwardly, flexed his knee. "You coming or what?"

This was his way of informing me that my presence would be required. I stood. It was dark now. The crickets were screaming at us, and the roof, for some reason, seemed much steeper than I ever remembered. I thought I might be sick. "What's the plan?"

"No plan," he said, heading for the attic window. "We'll improvise. Improvisation is the key."

I followed, knowing we'd never make it to Darla Weege's house. That most likely we'd snake another bottle of Mad Dog (maybe fruit punch this time?), wander around town drinking and talking about going to Darla Weege's house, then crash back at Jefferson's. His father took off before I knew him, and his mother—a soft, quiet woman with the same jutting chin as her son, whose hair had begun to noticeably fall out—worked the night turn down at Abbott's, a diner on the north end of town.

The upstairs window didn't stick open, never had, so I held it while Jefferson crawled through—butt first, then head, then legs. Once inside, he held it open for me.

"It's a bitch and a half," he said again, to no one in particular.

Let me tell you another thing about this town.

For the most part, there were two groups of people: those who wanted out, and those who wanted to run it. I, of course, was a charter member of the former, and I was active in this role. I sent for information on colleges, started doing this when I was fourteen; routinely checked the Pittsburgh, Cleveland and even Buffalo want-ads just to give myself an idea of what would be waiting for me when that time came. I kept my savings account as plentiful as I could and searched for opportunities to add to it. I never withdrew from it, knowing that if by some chance things didn't materialize for me, I'd need it to start somewhere else, which I had every intention of doing.

I suppose there were others like me, but you keep those kinds of things to yourself, so I never met any of them. At least not to my knowledge.

The larger group were those who wanted to run the place. Now, I don't mean "run" in a political sense, it was more of a quest for social dominance that started with developing a talent for knowing what everyone within the zip code was up to at all times. This did not require any level of skill or practice, just a willingness to observe and to judge. Once this aspect was mastered, you moved on to people's business dealings: which ventures were succeeding, which stores would be closed down within the season, what was moving in to take over the bowling lanes. That kind of thing. When Paul Kearney Jr. opened a Pizza Hut franchise on Truman Avenue in 1982, he was bumped up to godlike status, just like that.

There's more to it, but you get the idea. In the years since, I have been to dozens of towns just like this one, and they are all more or less the same.

Jefferson, though, he didn't belong to either group. He seemed perfectly content just where he was, both literally and figuratively, and I was grateful for this. Somehow, he seemed to keep himself above, well, things, and when I was in his company, I felt above (or at least apart from) them as well.

My parents did not share my views regarding Jefferson, and this bothered me more than it should have. It got to the point, especially with my father, where the mere mention of Jefferson's name would be met with rolling eyes and an irritating throaty groan, which I took as a personal affront to my own character.

"The little rat doesn't even *speak* to anyone," my father was fond of saying. "Just breezes right on by like you're in his way or something. And in my own damn store, no less." This statement was always accompanied by a grandiose sweeping gesture of his hand whenever he said, "breezes right on by."

Unfortunately, this observation was difficult to refute. Jefferson had this way about him. Distant, I guess you'd call it. Unaffected. In fact, sometimes he was like this with me, too, and it left me feeling a little betrayed. I was at times as guilty as the next guy in town to think Jefferson could have benefited greatly from a thorough ass-kicking every so often.

But then, in the next breath, he'd confide in me. It wasn't

always the disclosure of something particularly troubling to his soul or meaningful in the ways of life. Maybe it was something little, something that someone else might have paid little if any attention to, like his opinion of the willow trees. During moments such as this, I felt I understood Jefferson. I *understood* him. And so that served as my standard reply to my father: You don't understand.

We woke just after dawn. Jefferson's mother was scrambling eggs in the kitchen, her wire whisk beating convulsively against the inside of a big plastic bowl. Having just returned from Abbot's she was still wearing the powder blue outfit with the built-in white apron in front. The bow tied across the small of her back hung loosely and vibrated to the quick pulse of her whipping. I rubbed my eyes and watched her through the doorway from my makeshift bed on Jefferson's living room floor. Jefferson sat up on the couch and dragged a hand through his hair.

"You're a dope," he said matter-of-factly. He stretched one fist up to the ceiling and yawned.

"What?" I continued watching his mother whip the bowl of eggs at a frantic pace.

"I gave you an assignment last night. Didn't I ?"

This was true. "No," I said. "You were drunk. You were a drunk idiot last night and I deny all charges."

"Your assignment," he said, "if I'm not mistaken, was to get me to Darla Weege's house. At all costs." He lifted himself uneasily up to the couch and slid a hand into his boxer shorts. "At all costs," he said again. "You're fired."

"I think I hear some life in there," Jefferson's mother called from the kitchen in an exaggerated sing-songy kind of voice. She still hadn't turned around. She was still whipping. After a few seconds of silence she said, "Hello, Peter."

"Hi," I said.

"Eggs coming up."

"Thank you," I said.

"I give you one lousy job," Jefferson said. He reached up on the back of the couch and slid the brown afghan off, then wrapped it around his shoulders. "One lousy job."

Finally Jefferson's mother stopped beating against the side of the blue bowl and moved to the stove, where she poured some of the egg mixture into a skillet. I sat all the way up; it occurred to me that I couldn't remember the last time I'd seen her here. She was almost never home. I watched Jefferson's mother for a moment longer but was embarrassed for some reason and looked up at Jefferson, who was looking at me. I wondered how long he'd been doing this.

"One lousy, stinking job," he said.

"Shut up," I said.

We listened to the eggs crackle for a while and then we heard Jefferson's mother drop into a kitchen chair and sigh heavily. Then I heard other sounds, like she was crying maybe, but I couldn't be sure with all the crackling going on.

"Your mom okay?" I said to Jefferson, quietly I hoped.

He shrugged. "Yeah," he said.

Then she got up. I heard her go to the skillet and stir its contents around. I tried to imagine my own mother, in her Marnme's smock, in the same perspective, but couldn't. I felt for Jefferson's mother right then, although I couldn't say why, and the fact that Jefferson just sat there on the couch with his hand in his shorts, shrugging, made my face and neck burn.

"Go see what's the matter," I said.

He looked down at me and rubbed his cheek with the back of his hand. "You," he said.

I watched his face for sudden movements or twitches. Finding none, I struggled to my feet, kicking the tangled blanket out from between my ankles.

She stood hunched over the skillet, stirring mechanically. Her hair was thin and strawlike and, shamefully, at that moment the only thing I could think of was *I wonder if any of it is falling out into the eggs?* But before I could shake this thought from my mind, she said, "These things go away. You know that, don't you?"

The words struck me oddly. Not their meaning, which I couldn't place anyway, so much as the fact that something had been spoken. I wasn't ready for it. And the only utterance that would come in reply was, "Mm."

She nodded. I heard Jefferson flick on the TV in the living room. It sounded like a western. "I took these eggs from the diner," Mrs. Barrett said. "Don't tell anyone."

I looked up at her. She did not smile or wink. She watched the eggs carefully. It didn't look to me like she had been crying. "Sure," I said. I examined the eggs on the stove and tried to see them differently, scornfully. They were stolen eggs, contraband eggs. I was hungry, though, and realized that contraband eggs were better than no eggs at all. "Sure," I said again, then realized I was standing in her kitchen in my underwear. Then, just as suddenly, a speck of grease popped out of the skillet and landed on my thigh. After a second or two I felt the singe and jumped back slightly, knocking into the kitchen chair. She looked over at me slowly, methodically; her brown eyes somehow displayed a hint of confusion as she looked me up and down. Then she turned back to the eggs and I was no longer a consideration.

"Hey, Buckman," Jefferson called from the living room, and for this I was grateful. I waited a moment then turned and headed out of the kitchen. Jefferson was gone, though. The television blared (it *was* a western) and the brown afghan lay in a pile on the couch where he'd been. I saw that the storm door, which led from the living room out to the tiny cement front porch, was open a couple of inches. I pulled my pants on, walked over and pushed it the rest of the way out. "Goddamn it anyhow," I heard Mrs. Barrett mutter and then the kitchen faucet came on and I didn't hear anything else from in there.

Jefferson sat on the front steps smoking a cigarette. I'd never seen him smoke like this before, under such circumstances. Once in a while, if we were feeling especially giddy, we'd steal a pack of Dorals (since nobody ever bought them anyway) from the checkout isle and smoke them one right after the other, incorrectly taking the smoke into our mouths and blowing it right out for the simple, satisfying knowledge of having gone through the whole pack in one night. But what I saw here was different. Jefferson leaned forward and his gaze was thoughtful. I stepped outside and stood behind him, looking out over his front lawn toward the leather mill.

"So," he said, blowing smoke straight up in the air, far more professionally than I ever had, "you got an analysis, chief? She okay or what?"

I dropped down onto the first step. "Yeah." I forced a chuckle. "I was just . . . you know, I just woke up. I still got jelly-head from last night. She's fine. And I'm fine now, too."

He turned and looked at me over his shoulder. The cigarette was propped between his fingers next to his chin. "No," he said. "She's not." He turned back around and shook his head. "I didn't think she'd be home yet. I figured we'd be gone. I don't know what possessed her to come straight home. She never does. Christ. The one time I wish she'd of stayed the hell away . . ."

I turned around and looked into the house. Mrs. Barrett walked past the kitchen entrance then back across. She wasn't wearing shoes and she looked incredibly gentle. Behind her I could make out a light touch of smoke near the ceiling. I thought of my own mother. Right about then she'd be meeting the meat delivery guy out back of the store. She'd be verifying the quality of the beef and signing his clipboard. My father'd be stamping prices on the newly arrived zucchinis or whatever. Where is that kid? he's saying. You'd think he'd help out once in a while, wouldn't you? He's stamping cantaloupes. My mother shrugs. It's Saturday, Russ, she says. *Saturday*.

"What are you talking about?" I said. "Where'd you get those smokes?"

"I don't know," he said.

Because I thought I should, I sat down next to him on the step. "She's making eggs is all," I said. "She's just making eggs."

Jefferson leaned back on his elbows and flicked his cigarette deftly into the yard. "She's losing it is what she's doing," he said. "She's losing her goddamn cookies. If you've ever wondered what that kind of thing looks like, you're in luck."

"She's making eggs," I said.

He wasn't listening. "Behold," he said. "A woman actually in the process of dropping her goddamn cookies." He held a hand out toward the door. "This is an event, I'm telling you. One doesn't often get the opportunity to witness such a thing as this develop. Usually we see the finished product. But here—here we have the actual transformation taking place as we speak. She's dropping cookies left and right. One right after the other." He looked at me. "You realize what you're in the presence of, don't you?" He kept looking at me.

I froze. I had no idea what I was supposed to do at a time like this. "It's just eggs," I said, stupidly. He kept looking at me and there was a moment of the most intense, brutal awkwardness I have ever experienced. Then I put my hand on his shoulder and he quickly brushed it off.

"No," he said. "Don't."

I looked away. He kept looking at me; I could feel him looking at me. I didn't know why he kept looking at me that way but for some reason I believed I deserved it. I just sat there with my hands on my knees, feeling ridiculous and childish. Then I heard something from inside the house; a scraping, like Mrs. Barrett was rearranging the furniture, dragging things back and forth across the kitchen's linoleum. She stopped and we heard her catch her breath.

"Let's go," she called. "Eggs up. Everything's ready." She sounded like a coach of some sort.

We both stood. "I better head out," I said. "They might need me at the store."

He looked into the house then back at me. He nodded. I went

down a couple of steps and saw Jefferson's pack of cigarettes lying there, the bottom half still in the cellophane. I felt some foul sense of association to see that they were Dorals. I picked up the pack and handed it to him.

The store was empty when I got back. I could hear the lights and the coolers humming all around me. It was cold. Both registers were turned on but nobody was in sight. At the end of one of the aisles three stacks of tomato paste lay on the floor. I took another quick glance around, then walked over and began stacking the loose cans on the appropriate shelves.

When I was done I looked at my watch. It was only eight-thirty. Marnme's didn't really have a precise time when it opened; basically, whenever my father got around to unlocking the door, that's when people were allowed to come in and buy stuff. But eight-thirty was awfully early, so it made sense that no customers were in the place. It was unlike my father to unlock the doors, though. I thought about calling out to make sure someone was around but decided against it. I straightened then took one last careful look around. We were having a special on artichokes, a sign said in my mother's boxy print. Three for a dollar. They were in season. I walked over to the little supply closet by the front door and took out the broom.

It felt good to be by myself, outside, so early in the morning on a Saturday. It wasn't cold out yet, but you could tell it was getting ready to start sometime soon. A lot of leaves were on the sidewalk and I liked the sound they made when I stepped on them. I started sweeping them toward the gutter at the curb, wondering when I'd start hearing from colleges. I'd applied to four over the summer, all out of state.

South Front Street was quiet. Most places opened at eleven on Saturdays. Every now and then a jogger bounced past or someone came by walking their dog.

"Say." I heard my father's voice behind me. "Hopping right

to it, huh? Good man." His head was poking out from behind the glass door. He nodded, impressed. "That you who stacked those tomato paste cans?"

I stopped sweeping. "Yeah," I said.

"Well, you put them on the wrong shelf."

"I did?"

"Yeah. But hey, don't sweat it. Didn't figure to get anything out of you at all today anyway. Didn't expect to *see* you." He paused. "But here you are. And alone, no less. Minus your—"

"Dad."

"Yeah, well. Okay. Whatever." He went back inside.

I finished sweeping the leaves then put the broom away and went upstairs to my room. I stood for a while at the window, which looked out over the lot that housed the two willow trees, and decided I'd had enough of being alone today. So I walked across the hall to my parents room where the phone was and dialed Jefferson's number. I counted twelve rings then hung up. I dialed again. This time, after seven rings, Mrs. Barrett picked up. "Hello?" she said. Her voice was breathy and hollow. I held the receiver to my ear. I kept it there. "Russ," she said, "is that you?" I listened to her breath for a moment longer. Then I set the receiver down and left the room.

I stuffed the flattened bottle of Mad Dog into the back pocket of my jeans. My dad was in the back and my mother rang up a customer she knew. They were talking about the number that hit the night before and my mother told the woman that if she were one who played the numbers she'd have bet just that very one. The woman, whose wide, reddish face I recognized but couldn't place, laughed and said my mother always was a talker. "But I know you, Mary," she said then. "Even if you *did* win a million dollars I'd still come in here once a week and there you'd be. I couldn't imagine you anyplace else other than right there behind that register. And the shock the rest of the town would be forced to endure—" She put a hand to her cheek. "Please. Forget about it."

My mother sorted through the woman's coupons. "Well," she said. "I guess they'd just have to get used to it. If some knucklehead is willing to fork over a million bucks to me, in a heartbeat I'll be telling Russ to pack up whatever he's taking with him if he wants to come, 'cause we'd be gone. Arizona, honey."

The woman picked up her two sacks. "Don't be telling me," she said. "You gotta play the number first."

My father was in the middle of a discussion with Farley Turnbull in the back alley. Farley had no job, and my father sometimes gave him leftover fruit at the end of the day. It was odd to see him this early, though, and most days I'd be interested and stick around to see what was up. But instead I took advantage of my father's diverted attention and headed up the back stairs to the attic and out the window onto the roof.

I stood for a while. I didn't want to sit. A breeze was starting to pick up and I wished I'd brought a jacket. I wondered how long I planned on staying up here. A long time probably, I figured. Cars were beginning to slide past on South Front Street, stopping occasionally, waiting for the light to change. I took the bottle of Mad Dog out of my pocket and unscrewed the cap. I wet my lips and drank for as long as I could hold my breath. When I couldn't drink any more I swallowed two more times then coughed for a little while. I'd barely drunk a quarter of the tiny bottle. My ankles started to hurt from standing at such an awkward angle so I sat down. Then I stood up and walked over to where the trees crawled up against the side of the building. They looked a little thinner, even from just the night before. I figured it must be due to the sunlight showing through the leaves and branches; somehow the space between them appeared greater. I stuck my foot out and pushed down on one of the branches. It gave freely to the pressure I put on it and I was immediately surprised by how flimsy and delicate it was. I leaned out into the tree. The branch bent like rubber under the weight of my foot. I reached out for something to grab onto and I stayed like that for a moment: one foot in the willow tree, one on the roof; one hand around a branch, one firmly gripping my bottle of Mad Dog. I held that position for a long time; I felt myself sway a little. I closed my eyes, feeling the wind blowing in from the Midwest, from further away than that even, and swirling past my face. Then I shifted back onto the roof. I kept my eyes closed. I took the bottle cap out of my pocket and replaced it. The sun was behind me. I crouched down and lay back on the warm shingles, my feet propped against the rain gutter, my head at a raised angle, and I listened to the movement around me, the cars and the people and the air, and I could hear the neon Marnme's sign humming, or at least I thought I could, and I stayed that way, with my eyes closed.

One frigid afternoon during my second semester at NYU, I dropped my books on my desk and saw that my roommate had left an envelope for me lying there next to a plate crusted with spaghetti sauce. I picked up the letter and saw that the return address said, in haphazard, randomly slanting print: J.A. Barrett, Cleveland Heights, Ohio.

I held it in my hand a while. The seal was closed with Scotch tape and the address was written upside down on the envelope. I wondered if this were done intentionally or carelessly and decided it was intentional, then forced myself to smile. Up to then things had not been going as well as planned for me at school. Classes proved overwhelming and, as I had expected but not entirely, the city was as difficult as home was to manipulate, but left me feeling even more lonely when I let it manipulate me.

One of my great fears had been that Jefferson would write or call me before I had a chance to contact him first. I felt it was my move, but I kept putting it off. I didn't know where he was was my excuse. Not that it would've been all that difficult to find out. I just never did is all.

The letter was folded into thirds and then in half so as to fit into a standard-sized envelope. I unfolded the letter, listening to the sounds of the touch football game going on the small patch of lawn outside my closed window. Girls were playing, too. I could hear them laughing.

> *Hey, Buckman:*
>
> *It was a real bitch and a half tracking you down, you know that? I went home a couple weeks ago, see what's going on and all. You know the routine, I'm sure.*
>
> *Darla Weege still lives in the same house, in case you were wondering, but no Buckman (your mark's still there, though—your calling card). Not that any of it really surprised me much. Nothing does anymore, except for one thing. I know how anxious you were to get out of there and all. But I always thought you were a Cleveland, Pittsburgh or Buffalo kind of guy. Isn't that where you had your sights set? Always figured I'd bump into you on the street around here one of these days. New York knocked me for a turn all right. To be honest, something told me it'd be just a little over your head. Guess not, though. Who'd have thought that?*
>
> *My mother lives here, too. With some guy who's not so bad. She found a job in a restaurant downtown. Manager. No shit. Thought you might be interested. Cleveland's okay I guess. I'd be willing to bet that living here is not what you thought it'd be, though. Well, hell, you probably found that out with New York. Wouldn't be surprised if you got it worse even. But that's just me. What do I know anyway?*
>
> *All right. Well, here's the thing, Buckman: This letter is to officially relieve you of any and all guilt. Warranted or not, I know it's there (it always was, Buckman, don't think for a minute that I didn't know), and I just can't let*

you have it any more. It's gone now. These things go away and then everything else comes in and replaces them. That's what my mom says and you know, loony or not, she kinda makes sense this time. Go figure.

Anyway, come to Cleveland sometime if you want. Mad Dog's big here. All the homeless drink it. Not by choice, but they drink it. Ha.

Later, J—

As the sun went down over the rest of the country I stood at my window and watched the football game break up. And then it started to snow. I don't know if one had anything to do with the other.

The Theft, as the event came to be known throughout the more predictable circles of town, happened while I was on the roof. I heard everything: the glass doors swinging open and closed, the wind rustling the willow trees, Mr. Sturgeon trying to parallel park along the curb below, Officer Pullam writing out a parking ticket, the glass doors swinging open and closed again, my mother screaming, "I saw him, I saw him," the glass doors a third time, my father's quick footsteps on the sidewalk, then Officer Pullam's.

Jefferson never ran. I could tell. He continued walking down the street in his coat until my father and Officer Pullam came up on either side of him and each took him by an arm. I listened as they walked him back to the front of the store, my father saying, "See here? Looka here: batteries. What's this? Look at all this here toothpaste. I suppose you expect me to believe you been—"

And Officer Pullam saying, "Okay, okay now, Russ. Just leave everything alone there. Don't upset it. We'll straighten all this out in a minute. Now just don't be touching everything so as we don't know where everything came from."

"Where it came from?" my father said. "It's got my price tag right here. See here? We do receipts, too. Only I don't see any of those on him."

"Just don't upset everything, Russ," Officer Pullam said. "Let's just see if we can't figure all this out." They were stopped on the sidewalk now, in front of the store. I could feel the light through my eyelids.

"I told you already, for crying out loud," my father said. "How many times do I have to spell it out? Good God, look here. The little creep stole a bottle of beer as well."

"Jefferson," Officer Pullam said. "Jefferson—"

"What else you got in there?" I could hear my father feeling around Jefferson. "I always knew this one was just as crazy."

"Russ," Officer Pullam said. "Jefferson . . ."

Then Jefferson called out. "Buckman."

I lay flat.

"Buckman," he called again.

"What the—what the hell you looking for up there, boy?" my father said. "I knew it," he said. "I always knew they both were crazy."

"Is this jar of nuts yours too, Russ?" Officer Pullam said.

"It's got my tag on it, doesn't it?"

"Buckman," Jefferson said. "You knew the whole time. Didn't you, Buckman? You and everybody else."

"Shut him up, Wendell," my father said. "What are you going to do about all this?"

"Depends on what you want me to do about it, I suppose."

I could hear people gathering around now. The glass door swung open and closed again. "Russ," my mother said "Don't, Russ."

I felt the Mad Dog lying on the shingles next to my leg. I needed to do something. I tried to get up, at least it felt like I was trying to get up, but I couldn't. So I tried to lie flatter—as flat as I could—but I felt exposed, on display, and I tried not to hear anything but I couldn't do that either. The sun was directly above me, pushing down.

"Just let him go, Russ," my mother said. "People are watching. Just take the stuff back and let him alone. Come on. The fruit needs sprayed." A moment later the glass doors opened and closed. Then I heard nothing for a while. Some shuffling footsteps, dead leaves brushing along the sidewalk, some murmuring.

I don't know how long I stayed up on the roof after that, but it was a pretty good while anyway. When I sat up my head felt heavy and filled up with something and the light around me was bright and silvery. Once inside the window I stood for a minute, waiting, then I walked down the hall to my parents' room and closed the door quietly behind me.

Everything looked so old and I tried to think of where they possibly could have bought this furniture. I tried to imagine the brown dresser and nightstands on display in some furniture store somewhere, but that was impossible. The room had a sweet smell similar to that of the cellar, but the air was a little lighter and the familiarity frightened me. I scanned the room for something to look through first, then headed over to the dresser and pulled open the top left drawer.

I'm not sure what I expected to find. Proof, I suppose: love letters to Jefferson's mom, receipts for feminine items my own mother didn't own, cologne my dad never wore—anything incriminating. I flipped through socks and underwear, old jewelry and shoehorns and savings bonds from 1961. I found a wig I'd never seen my mother wear, but somehow I knew it was hers; and shotgun shells to an unseen shotgun that I didn't know we owned. I found clothes they hadn't worn in a long time but I was glad they hadn't. I found a bottle of Grecian Formula in one of my dad's drawers, and this made me sad for a moment. I stood there holding the bottle up in front of me and wished to God that I'd just stayed the hell out of their room.

I tried to replace everything as best I could, then went down the stairs and through the store, past zombie shoppers and into the back where I walked out the steel receiving door into the alley, staring at my shoelaces as they flicked out in front of me.

The alley was grey and patches of weeds sprouted out from between the cracks in the asphalt. Adjacent to our receiving door was Mitchelson's auto body shop. Next to the garage door, on the shabby cinder blocks, someone had written "COUGARS '85" in red spray paint and I remembered our high school's football game that would be played that night against our cross-county rival (who were called the Mustangs), and I wondered, had certain parts of this day happened differently, if Jefferson and I'd have wanted to go to the game.

I turned around and walked back in through our receiving door and looked around. Then, sliding boxes out of the way, I reached behind a stack of summer squash in white boxes that had tiny holes in them as if for air, until I felt the wooden handle of the axe my dad kept there, which I'd never seen him actually use. I pulled it up over the boxes with one hand, feeling the heaviness on the other end. When I had it up I held it in both hands across my chest like a rifle and walked back outside, around the house to the sodded lawn next to the record store where the two willow trees stood swaying. When I got to the base of the one closest to our store I stood over it for a moment, staring at the trunk, feeling the weight of the axe head against my palm. I felt the branches above me, reaching out, and I'd never before felt so helpless as this. I raised the axe over my shoulder and struck down as hard as I could on one of the roots partially sticking out above the ground. I'd had every intention of chopping the bastard completely down, slicing all the way through the trunk until it fell hard (in slow motion, I imagined), one way or another; so I surprised myself by chopping at the root. But once I'd begun I kept at it, hacking into as close to the same spot as I could, expecting to see sparks every time the axe came down.

At first I was chopping, swinging the axe back up over my head, and chopping again, all in one quick, fluid motion. But after a couple of minutes my shoulders started to ache and my motion slowed. The sun was starting to go down and a shadow spread halfway across the willow trees' lot. I felt people glancing at me as they passed by on South Front but I would not turn around. I kept chopping. I started to sweat and then I felt something in my chest and I hoped I would not throw up or cry. I kept chopping. Finally I focused on the root itself and realized I'd barely even cut into it at all. There was a tiny notch of cream color where I'd been whacking at it surrounded by the dark brown of the root. People started gathering on the street, peering in between the buildings, and I heard the trees laughing at me. I swung harder and harder until I could not feel my arms. I closed my eyes and struck a flurry of frantic chops, putting my legs into it and I felt as though the veins in my neck might burst and then suddenly, as the blade came down on the root once again, I heard a strange, muffled sound and I tried to pull the axe back up but it stuck a little, and when I looked down I saw that the axe blade was wedged in the ground between two completely severed sections of the root.

I fell to my knees and sat there like that, numb, with my eyes closed, for I don't know how long. I heard the people move away and I felt my heart in my stomach and I just stayed there, on my knees in the grass.

"Well, now you've gone and done it, I guess."

Behind me, my father's voice sounded as though he were on the telephone. Long distance. I picked my head up and tried to summon some feeling in my limbs.

"Well, for crying out loud," he said, closer now. "That's a damn nice tree, you know. Or was, anyway. And not just 'cause it brings 'em in either."

"I know," I said. I felt the blades of grass between my fingers.

He came around in front of me and leaned a forearm against the trunk. All I could see without looking up was his tan cotton slacks beneath the hem of his white smock. "It'll be okay, though," he said. "That little nick won't hurt it. It takes more than that to kill something so strong. It'll survive."

I tilted my head up and looked at him. There was beef blood smeared across the front of his smock, but his face was not that of someone who would have his hands in raw beef. The skin around his cheekbones was loose and the outside corners of his eyes were narrow and tilted down a little. He rubbed his big hands together as if to keep warm.

"Dad—" I said.

He turned and looked out toward South Front Street. I couldn't hear any traffic, but he seemed to be interested in something out there. "I don't know what to say, Pete," he said finally. "I know I should say something here, but for the life of me all I can think of to tell you—that will *mean* anything to you—is that your mother's inside." He paused there for a moment and wet his lips. "She's cashing out. In a minute I'm going to go in there, too, and help her, and then this will be over." He lowered his eyes back down to me. "This . . . episode. And then I hope you'll . . . I hope . . ."

He rubbed his hands together some more and looked up into the upper branches of the willow. I looked, too, trying to follow the line of his gaze through the browning, diminished leaves to the stringy clouds gliding past on the other side; then it hit me that I'd left the bottle of Mad Dog up on the roof, and as my father shook his head slowly from side to side and said, softly, "Well for crying out loud," addressing the words to himself it seemed, I knew I'd never go back up there to get it.

A Homecoming

THE TINY FRONT LAWN hadn't been cut in at least a month. This was obvious. A pair of blue jeans lay in the center, long blades of grass reaching around them, and closer to the house a small hole had been dug. Ivan took this in from his car parked in the slanted driveway. None of it surprised him. He hadn't been back for nearly nine months, his longest time between visits since graduating, so he felt he had no right to question.

He got out of the car and shut the door. Leaves fell from the half-dozen or so elm trees that hung out over the street and he watched them spin helplessly on their way down. He turned back to the house. It didn't seem like anyone was home, though they knew he was coming.

At the front door, which wasn't really in the front at all but on the side of the house, Ivan was caught awkwardly between urges to knock and to just walk right in. He'd never even considered knocking before and he didn't like the fact that the notion occurred to him now. He decided to do both. Twisting the knob with his left hand, Ivan tapped four times with his right as the heavy door swung open.

Inside, the kitchen had a stale feel to it but seemed orderly. There were no dishes and no old food scattered on the counters, no corroded pots on the stove, no glasses in the sink. The refrigerator door was closed. Everything appeared to be in its proper place. But still, it was dirty. There was a film over it. A huge green garbage bag sat propped against the wall by the door, overstuffed. The smell was familiar.

Ivan heard the television going in the living room. "Yo," he called out. "Anybody home or what?"

There was silence for a moment, then he heard giggling. "Yeah," someone said. "Bauer, that you?"

"Yeah," Ivan said, lifting his voice with exaggerated enthusiasm. He walked into the living room, which was much more disheveled than the kitchen. The crack down the center of the brown vinyl chair had grown in length by at least a foot; magazines and fast food wrappers lay strewn over the coffee table and floor, along with plastic cups half filled with tobacco juice. This made him feel a little better about things.

Squib was on the couch, lying flat with his legs sprawled—one foot hooked around the back of the couch, one on the floor. A Chevy Chase movie was on the television. Squib inserted a hand down the front of his sweatpants and turned to Ivan. "Hey, Bauer," he said.

Nice to see you, too is what Ivan felt like saying, but instead he said, "The hell's all *this*?" and held his hands out to signify the general surroundings.

"All what?" Squib said looking around the room.

Ivan let himself fall into the couch adjacent from Squib and put his feet up on the coffee table. "What's going on here?" he said.

Squib shrugged. "Nothing."

"Exactly," Ivan said. "I'm gone a few lousy months and you guys fall apart. Is that it?" He paused a moment, opened his eyes wide. "This *is* Friday, isn't it?"

"Is it?" Squib said and shrugged again. "I lose track. Friday sounds good enough to me. If you say so."

Ivan thought this over and wondered what that was like, not knowing what day it was. Not caring. He'd gotten close to that frame of mind in college sometimes, but not completely. He had to say that there really was never a time when he couldn't remember what day it was. He considered saying something to this effect, but instead said, "Where's McCready?"

Again the shrug. "Julie's I think. He's always over there."

"Julie?" Ivan said. "I don't remember him mentioning any Julie. Where'd he meet her?"

"Cattail's. Couple months ago." Squib was still watching the television. "Says she's just a *friend*." He looked at Ivan, cocked his head. "You getting married?"

"Yeah." He paused. "You knew that. I told you that a long time ago. The last time I was here I was engaged even."

"I thought so," Squib said.

"I *know* you knew that." Ivan felt awkward sitting there. The familiarity of the house disturbed him, and suddenly he didn't know what else to say to Squib.

"Everyone's getting married," Squib said. He pulled his hand out of his sweatpants and tucked it behind his head.

"Really?" Ivan said. "Who else?"

Squib exhaled. "Lenny, Kevin, Hootch. Barry, Calvin. Let's see. Dallas just got married two weeks ago. *That* was a wedding. Christ. Remember the pledge party we had sophomore year at that hall on Euclid? The one where Tollner broke his nose on the side of the bar? Remember that place. Well, Dallas had his reception there." He shook his head. "Lucky they didn't recognize us from that party or they'd never have let us in. I swear, the same two old guys with the bad hats and stubby cigars were still the bartenders. They must be a hundred and six by now." He looked back at the TV. "And Calvin's is next month."

Ivan didn't know what to say. "What's his wife like?" is what he said after a minute.

"Whose?"

"Dallas's."

Squib ran a hand through his hair. "Geez. Okay I guess. I really don't remember, to be honest. We were all . . . Well, no, I guess she was pretty cool. Likes her tequila, I remember that much."

"Yeah?"

Squib seemed to zone out for a moment, like he forgot Ivan was there. Ivan had kept putting off this visit, and suddenly he wished he hadn't come now. When he'd first graduated and moved back to Columbus and started his job, Ivan had returned religiously, at least every other weekend. But now, the longer he stayed away the less he wanted to go back. It was almost as if life in that college town—where so many wonderful, life-establishing memories had taken place that to recall them made him slightly ill with longing—continued on without him and his presence now felt like an obstruction in the flow. "So what's the plan for tonight?" he said.

"Don't know," Squib said. He'd put on weight, Ivan noticed. And his facial hair was strangely arranged—much heavier on his neck and chin. "I think I might have to work."

"Work?" Ivan said. "Well, when will you know, do you think?" He saw himself sitting alone in their empty house for the whole weekend; he felt that for a moment.

"I'm *supposed* to work," Squib said. "I mean I'm scheduled from eight to closing. But I think I feel a case of the flu coming on. Or maybe chicken pox or an Epstein-Barr virus. Something."

"You know you really don't look so hot, now that I think about it."

"I feel like shit."

Ivan nodded. "Rest is what you need."

"Plenty of liquids."

Ivan leaned forward and stood up. "You really should start your recovery program right away." He turned and headed back into the kitchen. "You got any medicine in here, or do we need to make a run to the drug store?" He opened the refrigerator door. "Ah-ha," he said extracting a six-pack of Busch. "Just what the doctor ordered."

"Try the freezer," Squib called from the living room. Ivan could tell from the sound of Squib's voice that he'd sat up. In the door rack, lying on its side, was an unopened bottle of Jim Beam.

"Hey," Ivan said. "The cure-all. You're in luck. What do you keep it in the freezer for?"

"So I know where it is."

This made sense to Ivan so he didn't say anything more about it. In the living room Squib was now sitting on the floor and had cleared some space on the coffee table. He'd also, for some reason, taken off his sweatpants and now wore only his bright yellow boxer shorts. Ivan felt like a part of things. He placed two small juice glasses, with gold and orange flowers printed on the sides, and the six-pack on the table and cracked the seal on the whiskey. "Where's Schuster? He and McCready should be here."

"Why?" Squib said.

Ivan sat down on the floor. "I don't know. I just . . . It seems like they should be here, like we should all be here. You know?"

"You gonna pour that or what?"

Ivan poured a healthy shot into Squib's glass. Squib picked it up and downed the shot in one quick movement.

"I think the Schuster's losing it anyway," Squib said after a few seconds. He pointed to his own temple and made a face. "Like once a month he'll do something that you just have to shake your head at. He's got this new thing now where he comes home drunk and shits in the sink. Done it twice now; once in the kitchen, once in the bathroom. I found the first one. I come down one morning and go to get a drink of water or whatever and there it is, you know. Just this big shit sitting there in the sink. So naturally I wonder where this came from and I look around and there's Schuster passed out in the chair over there in his underwear. And I swear to you," Squib raised his right hand, "I absolutely swear to you that the look on his face was the look of someone who had just taken a shit in the sink, if you can picture that." He set the glass down. "Don't ask me how that could be, but you'd know it if you saw it."

Ivan leaned back against the base of the couch. "On purpose?" he said, trying to shake the mental image.

"Nah. He was wasted, didn't have a clue. Denied it both times even." Squib picked up the bottle and poured another shot. Ivan noticed it was much bigger than the one Ivan had poured. "You're up," Squib said.

"Wait a minute." Ivan leaned forward. "So, what did you do? I mean, once the crime had been discovered?"

"Come again."

"Once you found the shit in the sink."

"Oh. Well, I mean, what do you think? We made him clean it up is what we did. I think it's a pretty standard household rule: You shit in the sink, you clean it up." He looked at the TV. "Drink that."

Ivan lifted the glass and held his breath. It occurred to him that maybe he wasn't ready for this just yet. He wondered if he should try and do the whole shot or split it into two. Doing it all at once would be very difficult and perhaps quite messy, but two times didn't particularly appeal to him either.

"You want a nipple on that?" Squib said, not altogether jokingly.

Ivan caught a whiff of the whiskey and balked for a moment, then dumped it into his mouth. When he suddenly realized it wouldn't all fit, he was caught between swallowing what was in there and forcing the rest, and as a result he did neither. He felt Squib watching him as he tried to negotiate his horribly botched shot. It took him four swallows to get it all down and a ridiculous coughing fit ensued. He gathered himself and wiped away some sweat that had embarrassingly formed on his forehead. "Whoa," he said.

"I'm not going to have to run you to the emergency room, am I, killer?" Squib said.

"I've never had it cold like that before," Ivan said, then immediately wished he hadn't.

Squib poured another. "That must be it," he said, smiling.

It went like this for a while, Squib pouring shots of varying amounts, sliding the glass between them on the coffee table. They never used the second glass. After the first couple of shots, they started going down a little better for Ivan and only occasionally did he wonder what in the world he possibly could have missed about all this.

Then someone kicked open the front door and walked in.

"It's just McCready," Squib said, craning his neck to see through the doorway.

Ivan heard McCready toss his keys on the kitchen table then open and close several cupboards. He and Ivan had lived together for two years of college before Squib, Schuster, McCready and Ivan all had rented this same house together for their senior year. Finally a cupboard door slammed closed a little harder than the others and McCready said, "Who ate my fucking noodleroni?"

"You did," Squib said, pouring. "Wednesday night, after 'Tail's. You wouldn't remember. You made a big production out of it. Very entertaining."

McCready opened and closed the refrigerator, much too quickly to have actually seen anything inside, Ivan thought, then walked into the living room. "Bauer," he said. "Oh, shit. I forgot you were coming this weekend."

Squib picked up the glass and started it to his lips. "His car's right outside, shithead. Where'd you think that came from?"

Ivan could sense the whiskey starting to go to work now. He wanted to say something to McCready that would instantly place them back on familiar grounds. He felt that it was needed. "McCready," he said, but then stopped.

"Here," Squib said holding out the glass. McCready reached down and took it. Ivan saw that the shot was much larger than any of the others they'd done, but McCready tossed it back as if his throat was not a consideration.

In his wrinkled white shirt, blue cotton pants and matching blue tie, McCready looked to Ivan like the manager at a Midas muffler place. His clothes hung loosely on him and his dark hair had thinned noticeably since the last time Ivan had seen him. It occurred to Ivan that if he hadn't known McCready and had passed him on the street, he'd think he was much older than he was. "How long you here for?" McCready said.

"The weekend." Ivan lifted himself back up onto the couch, away from the Jim Beam. The important thing, he thought, was to pace himself. "Why you dressed like that?" he said, nodding toward McCready.

McCready looked down at himself. "Oh," he said. "I haven't changed since work. Went straight over to Julie's. I quit today anyhow."

Nobody said anything for a moment. Then Squib nodded and said, "That's why you were home so early."

Ivan thought maybe he missed something. "You quit today?" he said. "What for?"

McCready made a motion for Squib to refill the glass. "Sick of it," he said. "You ever been forced to spend eight hours a day with a pack of raving idiots?"

Ivan almost said, Yes. Every day. But he held it back.

"I just had enough," McCready went on. "Tell you what: if I can't do any better than that, then I just might as well chuck it. Blow my brains out." He put an index finger to his head and cocked his thumb.

Squib watched the television. He didn't seem to Ivan to be interested.

"So, what are you going to do now?" Ivan said.

"I'm going to have another one of those if Stupid over there will fill up that glass. Hey, Stupid. We're not keeping you up, are we?"

Squib, without taking his eyes from the television, sat forward and poured a generous amount of whiskey into the glass McCready held.

"I'll be right back," Ivan said, then got up and walked around the corner to the bathroom. He took a leak then pulled back the shower curtain and examined the tub. Someone had cleaned it recently and Ivan wondered which one of them it had been. The curtain itself even looked new. There was no scum or flaky white crust along the bottom. He shut the curtain then and thought about what he was doing. "What are you doing?" he said. He was looking at himself in the mirror over the sink when the bathroom door flew open and McCready came in, his dress shoes clicking on the tiles.

"Need some help in here or what?" he said moving past Ivan.

Ivan made like he was fixing a contact. "All set," he said. He looked at himself, tried to appear relaxed, natural.

McCready glanced at Ivan's reflection in the mirror. "You getting married?" he said.

Ivan turned. "You, too?"

"What?" McCready began to unzip, paused.

"Do you guys really not remember me telling you that? Really? You don't remember giving me all kinds of shit about it last time I was here? All the talk about bachelor parties and hookers and honeymoons and—and wallpaper? You really don't remember that? Or are you just fucking with me?"

The incredulous expression on McCready's face made Ivan sorry he'd said all this. "Shit," McCready said. He'd stopped his zipper half way. "Forget it, man. Forget I brought it up. Christ." Then he looked down.

Ivan laughed, ran a hand through his hair and turned away from the mirror. He laughed some more. "You guys," he said. "Chipping away at that short-term memory, huh? Pretty soon you'll have it licked."

McCready shrugged, smiled. "We do what we can."

"You really quit your job?"

McCready nodded, zipped back up. "Yeah. I'll get another one."

"Squib's been looking since graduation, hasn't he? For a, well, for a *real* job I mean."

"That's Squib."

Ivan thought about this, decided it was true, and reached for the bathroom door.

"Squib don't know his balls from his belly-button," McCready added.

"That's true," Ivan said.

"So," McCready said, "what do you do in Columbus anyway?"

Ivan released the doorknob and turned back around. Out the tiny square window over McCready's shoulder, he saw a cat leap up onto the splintering picnic table he had helped steal from one of the Metroparks and put on their porch for no particular reason. Ivan had the feeling that the cat had been there before, frequently. "Marketing," he said.

"No," McCready said. "I guess what I'm saying is: What do you *do* in Columbus? You know? There's a difference."

Ivan didn't answer. He watched the cat. It was tan with black and reddish patches. It lay down on its side and picked its head up. It looked back at Ivan, or seemed to. He thought about what he'd have been doing this weekend if he hadn't forced himself here. It was a little thing, a weekend. Two days. *One day, two days.* What difference did they make?

"There's no difference," he said.

"All right," McCready said. "Look." He put his hands on Ivan's shoulders and guided him down to the side of the tub, then slid himself up onto the edge of the sink and thought for a moment. "Listen," he said finally. "Here's the thing: You know me better than anyone, right? We've been through—Well, Christ, we've been through a lot of shit, me and you. A lot of shit . . ."

This came as somewhat of a surprise to Ivan. Truth was, he didn't feel like he really knew McCready at all anymore. There was a time when he did, but now his recollections of those times felt like accounts of other people, stories he'd heard told to him and wished he'd experienced himself. Ivan turned back toward the window. Two brown leaves fell past outside, one following the other's path exactly. The cat was asleep now. *We're sitting in the bathroom*, he thought. *We're sitting in the bathroom and we're talking.*

McCready leaned in, rested his elbows on his knees. "So, I guess what I'm saying is this: I've had it."

"You've had it," Ivan said.

"Yeah."

"I think maybe you gotta be little more specific than that, Mac. You pretty much lost me."

"Okay." McCready looked up at the ceiling and took a breath. "Here it is. I'm checking out. Pulling up anchor, bailing out, whatever. You asked me why I quit my job. Well, there you have it. I'm outta here. Tomorrow afternoon. Tomorrow morning maybe, depending on how I feel."

Ivan examined his friend's face, tried to remember what life had been like living with this person, and what it would be like living with Leah; he experienced a flurry of very distinct yet ambiguous feelings all within a two second span, then it occurred to him to ask: "How many of those Beamers've you had?"

McCready's face went sour. "You're not listening to me, Bauer. I want you to come-with. Understand? Columbus . . ." He shook his head disgustedly. "Fuck that. There's nothing doing in Columbus." He was using his hands a lot now.

"I'm getting married in three months, McCready," Ivan said. "We just went through this."

McCready shifted his head a little and raised an eyebrow.

"What?" Ivan said. "Why don't you take one of these guys along? Take Squib. He's certainly not going to miss anything here."

"Ah, none of these puds'll come." McCready was getting increasingly annoyed, and Ivan wondered what exactly was behind all this.

"Where you gonna go?" Ivan said. "What are you going to do?"

McCready slid down off the sink and looked into the mirror. He poked at his thinning hair. "I'm tired of all the planning," he said. "All the scheming—what job I should have when, where I should be when I'm thirty, forty, fifty. You know: status." He took a breath. "I have insurance now. *Insurance*. Disability, pension, dental, all kinds. And what the hell for? I'm not ready for that shit yet." He smiled at Ivan in the mirror. "I'm very immature for my age, you know. I've been told that."

"Yeah," Ivan said, nodding. "I've heard it."

"There you go." McCready's voice had a hint of finality in it. He turned and rubbed his hands together as if trying to start a fire.

"Where're you going?"

McCready opened the door. "Living room."

"No. I mean tomorrow."

"Oh. I'm thinking New Orleans. For starters anyway. New Orleans then . . . Hey, wait a minute. Don't *you* go getting logical on me now. I gotta change out of these clothes." Then he made a quick left turn out of the bathroom and clopped up the stairs, leaving Ivan propped stiffly on the side of the freshly disinfected tub, fingers gently brushing along the porcelain.

They sat around the coffee table and drank. McCready appeared not to be plagued in the least by his recent decision, in fact his mood and demeanor struck Ivan as exactly the same as he'd always remembered: high-strung, flighty, perfectly content to do most of the talking. And Squib—who'd called his boss, shortly after Ivan emerged from the bathroom, to reveal the sudden appearance of "this nauseating, shooting pain" in his stomach that he thought might be food poisoning but probably was just one of those twenty-four hour deals —didn't appear to have much interest in anything. Ivan drank what was handed his way and released a strained, blurted laugh whenever one seemed called for. The Jim Beam was half gone, but Ivan didn't feel drunk. He felt rather outside himself in a way he couldn't quite identify.

A single lamp lit one corner of the living room in a dull yellow glow that made Ivan think vaguely of disease. Every few minutes the phone rang and McCready answered saying, Yeah, we're just sitting here drinking—Squib, Bauer and me. Yeah, yeah, he said, and then hung up. It occurred to Ivan to wonder where

Schuster was, but he didn't ask. Then, as McCready finished swallowing the last of an enormous shot, he set the juice glass down on the coffee table and looked at Squib, then Ivan. "Okay," he said, "let's go out now."

Squib scratched himself "Where?" He reached for the remote.

"Who the hell cares where? Put some pants on."

Ivan closed his eyes and felt his chest rotate a little. Even in the darkness he still could see patches of that cursed yellow light seeping through his lids. He imagined the situation he was in. He imagined Squib lying on the couch and McCready sitting there across from Squib, elbows on knees, ready to go to New Orleans in the morning. He saw this clearly, saw himself there, too—there, but not there as he used to be. He asked himself: Do I need this?

"Bauer?"

Ivan opened his eyes and saw McCready, standing, peering down at him, eyes wide but steady, the sickly yellow glow wrapped around his head from behind like a halo.

"Need a nap?" McCready said, then turned to Squib. "How 'bout you? I won't let you leave without pants. I'll beat the living shit out of you before I let that happen. I have at least *some* respect for the rest of society."

"I'm not going," Squib said.

"Like hell you're not. This is an occasion." McCready bent over and refilled the glass.

"What occasion?" Squib said. "What exactly constitutes an 'occasion' to you?"

"Shut up."

"What about Schuster?" Ivan said.

McCready held the half-filled glass above the middle of the coffee table so whoever wanted it could take it. "Forget him," he said.

Ivan looked over at Squib. "What did you skip work for? I mean, if you were just going to sit here anyway . . ."

"I didn't feel like going to work," Squib said.

Ivan didn't know what to say. He looked up at McCready who still stood holding the glass out, only now he glared at Ivan accusingly. Ivan took the glass and held it under his chin. Staring across the room at the sick lamp he thought about this precious ache that'd been growing in him for these people and this house and this town with its streets and shops and bars beyond these cracked, postered walls. He used to consider all of it his own. He wondered if the ache would ever end; and, if it did, he wondered if that would be a good thing.

The whiskey had no taste now. As Ivan swallowed he felt his head inflate with heat, but he couldn't taste anything.

"Bauer," McCready said, taking the glass from Ivan's hand. The tone was congratulatory. Then he turned to Squib. "Get up *now*. I'm in no mood to beat you senseless."

Squib shifted in the sofa. It was the slightest movement but there was a decisiveness to it that frightened Ivan a little. "I said I'm not going."

The movie Squib had been watching went to a commercial and the volume seemed to jump several decibels. McCready stared down at Squib for what, at least to Ivan, felt like a long time. But Squib made no acknowledgment of this. Finally McCready said, "All right. Well, fuck you then. Come on, Bauer."

Ivan had been sitting on the sofa with his hands pressed flat against his thighs for so long now that this apparent call to action gave him a jolt that immediately and embarrassingly brought more sweat flowing down his back.

"I'll drive," McCready said and moved a hand around in his pocket, searching for keys.

"There's an idea," Squib said, not flinching.

"Let me make a quick phone call," Ivan said. He thought for sure he was going to get up as he said the words, but he didn't. He just sat there looking up at McCready who looked back at him.

"What, you gotta get an update on your stocks or something?" McCready said.

"I just want to check something," Ivan said. "Something else," and this time he did pull himself from the sofa. "Give me one minute." He let his knees steady underneath him for a moment then walked toward the kitchen with what felt like big, loping, uncoordinated steps. In the dark kitchen he put his hands on the counter and closed his eyes. The movie came back on in the other room and Ivan heard McCready laugh and say what at first sounded like, "Drop the menu for me," but couldn't have been. It didn't make any sense. So Ivan picked up the phone, stared at the receiver to let his eyes adjust with the dark, then dialed Leah's number.

The ringing on the other end sounded distant and strangely acoustic, like those old-fashioned rotary phones. It was more of a buzzing sound than an actual ring. After a moment someone picked up.

"Hello." The female voice on the other end was breathy and hollow, as if just having been viciously awakened out of a death-like sleep. And it wasn't Leah's voice but that of her roommate.

"Oh," Ivan said. "Nancy. I need to talk to Leah. Could you put her on, please?"

"Ivan?" She paused for a second or two, regrouping. Ivan pictured her down in Columbus, standing in the center of her dark bedroom, pulling her eyelids open with her fingers. "Ivan, she's not here. She went out somewhere." There was another pause. "What time is it anyway?"

"I don't know," Ivan said, then suddenly wondered that same question himself. "Why didn't you go out, too?"

"What? I have to work in the morning. Sunday, too, actually. Ivan, where are you?"

There was more laughter from the living room, then Squib told McCready to fuck off. Ivan dropped heavily into a kitchen chair and looked out the window at his car in the driveway beneath the streetlight. "I'm . . . I'm not home right now. I was just checking in. I didn't think you guys'd be in bed yet."

"What time is it?"

"My friend, McCready, he's going to New Orleans in the morning."

"I like New Orleans."

"No. I mean he's going to New Orleans for good. He's not coming back. He's driving down there in the morning and he's staying there. At least for a little while. Then he might go somewhere else, but not back here."

"Ivan, honey, I'm kind of tired."

"I'm sorry. Tell Leah I called, okay?"

"Um. Yeah."

"Maybe you should write it down. Write it down now and leave it on the table so she sees it tonight, when she gets back. Tell her I called tonight."

"All right. I will."

"It's important. It's important that she sees it tonight."

"All *right*."

He waited as Nancy turned the light on in her bedroom and found a piece of paper on which to write the message, and as she walked out to the darkened living room to place the note on the table, unobstructed. Then he thanked her and apologized again for waking her and gently placed the phone back in its cradle.

When Ivan turned around he saw McCready standing in the doorway, smiling, leaning against the frame, arms folded, with the yellow haze of light and television sounds filling the space behind him. From his position on the sofa, Squib belched significantly. McCready turned his head and took in the scene. When he turned back around the smile was still there. His eyebrows twitched slightly, signifying the recognition of some shared private knowledge.

"Well?" he said.

McCready couldn't find a radio station he liked. Continuously leaning forward to examine the dial, he poked furiously at the buttons with his index finger while trying to keep the car in at least one of the lanes using just his instinct and left hand. This bothered Ivan. He remembered these urban streets as being heavily patrolled by city police, especially on weekends, especially late at night. And the fact that McCready was hitting the tail end of every yellow light at every intersection wasn't helping any.

"Why don't you let me do that, Mac," Ivan said finally.

McCready gave one last poke then sat back in his seat. "Last few years, man, radio's gone to hell."

Ivan set the radio dial to a station he recalled thinking was pretty good, then sat back and looked out the windshield. They were on Chester heading into town and these urban outer sections of the city were exactly as he remembered them: dark. Even though streetlights rose from the sidewalk every hundred yards or so, it was still dark. The big round bulbs atop the posts seemed to give off a circular glow of a few feet and then abruptly stop, as if encountering something impenetrable. It reminded Ivan of London, though he'd never been there. Or a big lollipop. On one side of the street—Ivan's side—windowless warehouses sat like huge, decaying carcasses; the other side was taken up by fast-food joints, liquor stores and check-cashing outlets. Beyond that were east-side neighborhoods.

At the corner of Chester and East 11th McCready hit a light that wasn't yellow anymore but red. He stopped, even though Ivan could tell he was considering alternate options. Once the Oldsmobile was at a complete stop McCready pulled a beer from his jacket pocket and handed it over to Ivan, then he took out another and cracked it open for himself. Ivan tapped the top of the beer with his finger a couple of times, then held it in both hands. "Where're we going anyway?" he said.

"Someplace significant." McCready seemed to consider his words for a moment, then took a long swallow from the beer. "Like I said, this is an occasion."

"So what place would be of sufficient significance to suit this particular occasion?"

McCready made a face as if choking on his beer. "Listen," he said, eyes still straight ahead. "You're going to have to knock that shit off. I hear that kind of talk again and I'll have no choice but to dump you here and leave you for dead."

Ivan did not respond. In fact, he wasn't sure *how* to respond. He sat silently and waited, then McCready turned toward him and laughed a short, two-pitched laugh that seemed to say, *That's a joke, in case you were wondering. It's just the way I am. Remember?*

After a few blocks buildings started getting taller and the warehouses started fading out as they advanced farther into the city. And it wasn't quite so dark, as if the air had thinned, allowing the streetlights to properly function. They didn't speak now. Ivan fingered his unopened beer; McCready drank his—in big, cheek bulging gulps—and watched the road, wrist bent over the steering wheel, hunched forward. Then Ivan said, "You been saving money or anything? For tomorrow I mean; for New Orleans."

McCready tilted his head, considering this. He took a swig of beer and swallowed. "No. Not really. I got two hundred and nine dollars in my checking account. That oughtta get me there well enough." He drained the last of his beer and set the empty can on the floor. Ivan, remembering the unopened beer he'd been holding in his lap, popped the top and handed it across to McCready who accepted it without reply.

Ivan wondered if Leah was home yet. He had no idea what time it was since McCready's Oldsmobile did not have a functioning clock and the idea of lifting his hand to glance at his watch gave Ivan a fluttering in his stomach he didn't like. He figured McCready was heading to somewhere in the Flats. They were in the heart of downtown now, heading slowly west. The last time Ivan had been to the Flats he'd also gone with McCready, as well as with Squib, Schuster and a couple of other guys. That was about nine months ago. They stayed till two-thirty when they were told to leave and when they finally stumbled back in to the house and began wrestling childishly and eating whatever they could find, the phone rang and someone thrust the receiver at Ivan. The possibility that Leah might call him at all during that weekend, let alone that time of night, had never occurred to him and it took him a moment, upon hearing her voice, to pinpoint exactly what was happening. She told him she didn't want to be a pest but she'd been missing him and just wanted to hear his voice and blah, blah, blah; and when he said good-bye and hung up the phone he took much abuse, especially from McCready. Ivan thought now about that last visit and, although he had to admit that the phone call had made him feel a little ridiculous in the presence of his friends, he couldn't help wondering whether Leah considered calling him tonight, or the possibility that *he* might call *her*; and what exact elements of their lives had changed in the past nine measly months. Then, for no good reason, Ivan wondered how many weekends that added up to and decided it wasn't all that many.

At a stoplight on the corner of Chester and Ontario a black-bearded homeless man wearing a knit cap emblazoned with a Cavs logo hobbled out of the darkness and came with considerable effort over to the car. McCready instinctively rolled down his window and held out a five dollar bill along with the rest of his beer. The man silently accepted both then returned to the shadows of a bank made of dark opaque glass. As they pulled away from the intersection Ivan saw the big green sign for the on-ramp to Interstate 77 South and, completely aware, told McCready to stop the car.

McCready pulled over to the curb next to a hydrant and flicked on the hazards. "What?" he said.

The on-ramp was to their immediate left. They could get to it with a hard, tight U-turn. Ivan sat back and consciously took in all that was visible out the windshield: diagonally to his right between two buildings was the stadium and beyond that a swatch of the lake; diagonally to the left, next to the I-77 on-ramp was a vacant area where a building had recently been demolished; straight ahead was the bridge to the west suburbs. Behind him, out the back window which he could not see through without significant effort, was the place where he had gone to college, his youth. Ivan turned and regarded McCready who sat patiently, tapping the steering wheel with both thumbs. "You know what I'm doing on Monday?" he said finally.

McCready stuck his lips out, shrugged.

"Well, at nine I have a meeting with my whole department where we talk about what we need to do that week; then I have to have about a thousand mailing labels made and sorted by zip code so we can stick them on brochures and have them sent to—"

"Brochures?"

"Oh, they're quite fascinating. I'll send you one for leisure reading. They tell in great, elaborate, *painful* detail about our new line of little rubber stoppers for all different kinds and sizes of tubing. We call them tube plugs—pretty ingenious, huh? Anyway, once I have the labels I go into this empty office—it's empty 'cause the guy who was in it got laid off—and stick all the labels on the brochures and take them down to the mail room to be sent out to all our top customers. Then, if all goes well, in a couple of months we sell a whole shitload of tube plugs. Oh, but that'll be a joyous time. The accountants will have woodies for weeks."

"Well, sure."

"We're talking serious bucks. For somebody, anyway."

"Good news all around. Here's to it." He tilted his head back and took a long drink of beer.

"But wait, that's just the morning. In the afternoon I get to meet with Leonard Kettering. He's the lead engineer for the new line of motor operated valves. I'll talk with him for a while to try to determine an appropriate market for them. Then we'll develop a strategy. Not that day, of course, but we'll set a meeting eventually. Maybe we'll have a meeting to determine when the meeting will be. Yeah, everyone's real excited about these new MOVs—that's what we call them around the office, you know: MOVs. Then I'll go home and watch TV and . . . well, you get the idea."

McCready nodded. "Sounds like a full day."

"Go to hell."

McCready shifted his weight in his seat, unfazed. "Look," he said. "I understand what you're saying. Believe me, I do. But I want to be absolutely up front about this: I don't *care*. It just doesn't make for very good tragedy these days. Not in my book anyway." He turned away. "Sorry. I guess I'm not very sympathetic tonight."

Ivan found himself suddenly confused, and a little pissed off. "But, what about everything you said? Back at the house? All of that . . . that . . . "

"What about it?"

They both sat staring out the windshield. The stoplight up ahead changed from red to green. After a moment McCready turned back to face Ivan. "Hey," he said. "Aren't you getting married?"

As McCready finished speaking, a police car pulled up next to the Oldsmobile and slowed to a near stop. The chubby officer in the passenger seat looked right into Ivan's eyes, then appeared to shift his gaze to McCready, who never pulled his attention from Ivan. After a few seconds, just as Ivan began to feel his pulse pounding in his head and throat, expecting to see the cop car stop completely and the red and blue lights to begin flashing, the officer turned to the driver, said something, and the cruiser continued down Chester. After traveling two blocks it made a right-hand turn.

Ivan swung back to McCready, who showed no apparent concern. "Okay," he said. "Let's go."

McCready leaned to his right, put a hand behind his ear. "What's that now?"

"Let's go. Like you said before: I'm coming with. That's what you wanted, right? But we gotta go right now, before I change my mind. None of this tomorrow shit. Make the turn and let's go." Ivan pointed toward the I-77 on-ramp and waited for protestations from McCready of not being ready, not having any clothes with him, and other things that didn't have an opportunity to formulate in his mind.

McCready looked where Ivan's finger was pointed, then reached down and flicked off the hazards. "We'll need to get beer in Akron," he said, and pulled out onto Chester where he made a wide turn that took the Oldsmobile onto the shoulder on the opposite side of the road, then to the on-ramp. The engine roared violently. "And gas. We're at about half now."

Ivan refused to let anything surprise him. He sat back and closed his eyes. He let the car take command. He listened to the tires and the road humming all around him. He felt the strain of acceleration as the on-ramp became the interstate, and the relief of the engine settling into the highway, gliding, creating its own individual space. He liked having McCready there, driving him, in control of what they're doing and where they're going, not having to make any decisions or worry about what came next. He was pleased that only McCready was there and not Squib and Schuster; that would dilute things too much, spread the experience too thin. He kept his eyes closed for a while. He was going to New Orleans. McCready began poking at the radio again and this time Ivan didn't let it bother him. He decided he'd never felt quite this way before and it was something he'd always remember—something distinct and relevant; even more so than the time Tollner broke his nose against the bar at that pledge party sophomore year, or anything else. This was a memory in the making, he decided, and held onto that thought for as long as he could. He made it work for him. Then suddenly he wondered if McCready was aware of an obvious possibility: that, while they passed through Columbus in a couple of hours, Ivan might very well ask to be let off at Leah's apartment. For a moment he was concerned that this would upset McCready, that he would hold it against him, that he would think less of him in some way. Then he decided that no, McCready was aware of what was going on, and of that possibility. He also had an appreciation for the moment, for the potential memory.

Then, before the previous thought even had a chance to exit his mind, Ivan felt the car veer smoothly to the right and begin a leisurely descent. They had left the interstate.

Ivan opened his eyes and looked straight out the windshield before him. All he saw was black, nothing, with the gold glow from the Oldsmobile's dashboard seeping into his vision from the left. He was moving, he knew this; cornfields undoubtedly whipped past his window, but he couldn't see any of it; he had no proof. He heard himself say, "McCready."

"No highways," McCready said. "Not on this trip. I hate highways. We're taking the back roads all the way." Then, as if answering a question not yet asked, he added, "Figure we'll just drive south till we hit swamp."

Feeling a strange combination of dry-mouthed uneasiness and security, Ivan closed his eyes again and was just about to begin planning the most appropriate method for retrieving his car (wondering if that were still somehow possible) from the house the next day, when he heard his friend give the radio a forceful poke that sent a rattle through the dashboard. This time McCready found a song he liked on the first try and sat back, releasing a long breath.

Ivan knew the song, too. It was familiar.

One Remarkable Thing

WEBER LIVES in a third floor apartment in the Coventry section of Cleveland; the east side of town. On the street level of his building there is a club called Hoyle's that doesn't close till four a.m. where a lot of them hang out. They wear used clothes by choice and combat boots and rings through their faces and they talk loudly while waiting on the sidewalk for cabs. They talk about art by artists with exotic-sounding names and politics and lovers and music that Weber's become accustomed to hearing about, but has never actually heard.

Sometimes, if the weather is all right, he sits out on his tiny balcony and listens to them, but he doesn't want to give the impression he's listening so usually he stays inside and listens while trying not to hear. Also sometimes, if he is feeling particularly strange, he turns out the lights in his apartment and sits cross-legged on the floor with five or six candles going in his living room, and pretends he is part of their conversation. He pretends he fits in with them, that they accept him and listen with interest to what he has to say about topics he knows nothing about. He sits in the shadows thrown from the candles and pretends he's waiting on the sidewalk with them to go wherever it is they go next, after Hoyle's. He does this more and more lately and this is what he is doing when he hears her voice on the street below his window.

The voice itself is what hits him first: that nervous, excited quality it has when she is turned on about something, when she is in a good mood; high-pitched and urging. It takes him a minute after immediately recognizing the voice before he can focus in on what she is saying. He sits rigid on the floor, as if he is hiding, keeping his head down. He tries not to breathe. In his hand is the remote control for the television which is tuned to channel 9, a channel that does not come in and shows only silvery, vibrating static on the screen. The volume is set on mute. He hears her voice clearly but he cannot comprehend any words; then he hears several other personless voices, and then hers again. She is disagreeing with someone about something, but it is a pleasant sort of disagreement. She giggles between exchanges and speaks with a teasing, goading air. He can tell she doesn't know what she's talking about, but the others don't seem to mind. It's like nothing he's ever heard on the street under his window before. Every few seconds a car drives past blaring its radio and drowns her out, and in that short time he cannot decide whether he hopes that when the car finally passes she'll still be there, or she'll be gone. And then, as he is trying to come to a decision on this, he realizes he hasn't heard her voice for . . . well, a while at least.

Then new voices float up from the street, new but familiar: one is low, monotonous, pensive; another jumps around all jittery-like, tightly wound, rattling nonstop, perhaps on something other than fresh air; then there's a loud one, rude, fist-clenching (Let's find a fucking place to *dance*, man); then some fluidity. It is demure, theatrical, capable of breaking into poetry recitation at any moment. Weber recognizes each one. Some of them he even gives faces to.

He has this thought sometimes, as he is having it now, sitting on the floor watching the television snow: he ties a rope into a noose, good and tight, then attaches one end to the radiator against the wall and the other, the loop end, around the neck of—what? A mannequin of some sort? His duffel bag stuffed with sheets, and shoes sewn to the bottom? He's not exactly sure, but the length of rope is just right so that when he throws whatever it is out his window the rope will catch sharply and hold so that the feet dangle just inches from the sidewalk in front of Hoyle's. He wonders if that would shock them, then shakes his head no as if trying to convince someone who is not there. Probably not. Probably, in order to elicit any kind of effect, the rope would have to be attached to his own neck.

Lying back on his floor, hoping to hear her voice again but knowing she is gone, he shakes this morbid thought from his mind. He didn't use to have these kinds of thoughts. It must be the shadows, he tells himself. The way they flicker across the walls. What else is he supposed to think?

He gets up to blow out the candles. Standing in the center of the room, on the cold, hardwood floor where the area rug used to be, he thinks of the thorough decline in appearance and atmosphere the apartment has undergone since she left. They are not simply the same rooms without her stuff in them. There is something else—something tangible—missing and this absence, the awareness of it, is capable of sending shivers through his limbs. He figures this is normal, that this happens every day to many people, but such knowledge serves as little comfort. He just cannot get over the radical change in the raw *spirit* of these small, plain rooms.

Cautiously, he steps out onto the balcony and peers over the flimsy railing. He remembers their moving to this part of town— this apartment—because it would keep them young, she said. Below, the people are coming and going, just the tops of heads above long black coats, quieter now, murmuring. The street is wet and shiny and he likes the soft sound the tires make as cars move past the blinking yellow light at the corner. If he went down there, what would he say? How does *she* know what to say? Has she always known? His neighbors come and go continuously, in taxis and on foot. He's going down, he decides. He's going to change clothes and wet his hair and go down to Hoyle's and meet some of these people whom he feels he knows. He stands there looking down for two more minutes, gripping the railing; he can't feel the tips of his fingers. It starts to snow lightly, and then when one of them—a tall girl with long, perfectly straight red hair and sickly green eye shadow—glances up at him, he takes three steps backwards and pulls the door closed. The thin pane of glass at his eye level is frosted over on the outside.

When his alarm wakes him at six-thirty he feels rickety, hungover, though he knows this is impossible. His mouth is dry and the little strip of light coming in under the shade from the window cuts brutally through his eyelids. He doesn't care if he's late for work. He doesn't care if he is fired and never has to go back. He turns onto his side away from the clock and pulls the covers up over his ear. Today, he decides, he will begin learning to paint. He will become a painter, an impressionist maybe, and he will convert his apartment into a studio. He feels himself drifting off, the light inside his head fading, everything losing itself into darkness; he senses his breathing becoming more composed and rhythmic in his chest; and then, suddenly, he jerks alert and sits up straight, eyes wide and darting. If he doesn't go to work, if he gets fired from his job, he'll have to stay inside the apartment; and it will still be his apartment, not a studio. There will be nowhere for him to go. He swings his legs over the side of the bed and leans forward, massaging the inside corners of his eyes with thumb and forefinger.

They used to set the alarm a half-hour or so early every morning so they could just lie in bed together, consciously. During those thirty minutes, the pillows were extra cushiony, the comforter thick and luxurious, their bodies warm and sensitive and alive. There was a lot of touching and petting and interlocking of legs. Sometimes they'd doze off, but not really. He always *felt* awake, always knew where he was and whether or not she was asleep and how much longer they could lie there before they had to get up. She used to like to lean her head way back across the pillow so he could kiss her neck, and when he did she would press up against him.

In the bathroom, he showers, standing under the hot water for much longer than he has to, shifting his weight from one foot to the other, until he feels the water begin to lose a little in temperature. Then he washes quickly and steps out of the shower. I should shave, he thinks, but the mirror in the bathroom is covered with steam so he decides to skip it. *Maybe I'll grow a beard?*

He takes the bus down Mayfield Road to Chester and into town where he walks one block to his office building. It has stopped snowing overnight but the wind has picked up, blowing in off the lake into his eyes. He buys a newspaper from the grey-faced fat man in the lobby, steps onto the elevator with three people he sees nearly every day but does not know, and gets off on the fourth floor where his darkened cubicle is waiting for him around the corner. He sits down and for the first time notices that from his desk he cannot see a window.

For three hours he posts invoices for valves and O-rings into an electronic ledger on his computer screen. He hears people who work near him moving throughout the office, talking to one another, talking about each other. He intentionally does not glance at his watch. Sitting back in his chair, staring at the neutrally colored felt that covers the collapsible walls of his cubicle, he imagines the people who actually use these valves and O-rings. He imagines a man, maybe two men, in a plant or factory wearing hardhats and white jackets. They are installing an O-ring onto—what? All he sees is a big steel machine. It makes a lot of noise. In his mind he hears a screeching whine and something that reminds him of a foghorn. But what if these people, for whatever reason, ran out of O-rings? What if an O-ring broke or malfunctioned and they went to wherever they kept the spares and there weren't any left? He figured the people in his mind's factory would be very upset. There would be a panic. The whole deal would be awfully important to them. Then he thought: *But what if I just didn't enter any more invoices?* and it disturbed him to realize that, simply, his company would be missing partial records of how many valves (sizes 0.5 through 3.0) and O-rings they'd sold, and how much they'd made on them. He would be fired, and then someone else would sit in this cubicle and enter the invoices for valves and O-rings. That's all.

A bald man named Efrem stops at Weber's cubicle then with a manila folder in his chubby hands, and leans against the frame of the cube. Weber doesn't know Efrem, but he knows his name, simply because of the name itself: Efrem.

Efrem's face is set in seriousness, lips squeezed together, outlined in white from the pressure. He wants to know if there has been any word regarding a purchase order submitted by Cleveland Electric Illuminating Company. There had been a discrepancy in terms, Efrem says, and we are only supposed to bill them for a portion of the invoice. "And that's what I need to know so I can close the books for the month," Efrem says. "Which portion?"

Lowering his eyes to Efrem's chin Weber understands that Efrem views this situation as critical. He imagines Efrem in a hardhat. "I'm not sure," he says, scratching his neck, trying to convey concern, and Efrem, without looking, pats his chest until he locates a red pen in his shirt pocket. Weber watches Efrem and wonders what made this man choose the red pen out of all the others in his pocket. *Why does he need to carry around so many damn pens?*

Exhaling in frustration, Efrem opens the manila folder. Inside, he makes some marks on one of the pages there. "Aren't they part of your customer base?" Efrem wants to know. This is very important to him.

Weber closes his eyes for a moment, then opens them. He tells Efrem that yes, Cleveland Electric Illuminating Company is one of many meaningless names that appear on what people insist on calling his customer base list, and therefore his responsibility; but no, he has received no word regarding what portion of the purchase order in question he is to seek payment for. He says these words in an attempt to sound like he knows what he's talking about, then swivels his chair around and turns his back to Efrem, as if he's getting back to work. *Go away now.*

Efrem clicks the cap back on his pen, says he needs that information by the end of the day, latest. Efrem is nobody's boss, but obviously would like to be.

Weber puts a hand to his stubbled cheek and hears Efrem move away and shuffle down the row of cubicles. The air here smells of old carpeting.

It has been snowing off and on all day, a wet, blowing snow that stings when it hits the skin, and the people on the bus are damp. Thick humidity hangs in the air here and reminds Weber of a quarantined area. Very few people are sitting together but there is one person in nearly all of the seats; it looks as though everyone is making a concerted effort to proportionally space themselves out amongst each other. As he is walking down the aisle, glancing from side to side, a woman in a fur coat too big for her stands up quickly and scurries (Weber pictures a large rat) for the door. Her two plastic bags, each drawn together at the top, bang against the seat backs as she goes. Weber drops into her vacated seat.

The bus lurches once and pulls into traffic. Weber slides to the far outside part of the seat and sets his briefcase on the inside. He rubs his palms on his knees trying to draw the wetness from his skin, but it is no use. The window to his right is fogged, blocking his view of the mouse-colored streets and buildings of Cleveland, leaving just the back of some man's head sitting in front of him to look at. This man's hair is jet-black and shiny, almost blue, and seems to have something of a part going down the back. Weber has never seen anything like it.

At the next two or three stops several people get on the bus but nobody gets off. Then, once they are out of the city, this trend begins to reverse: people get off and very few get on. With the windows all foggy like they are, Weber has no idea where he is. He feels as though he is in a spaceship. At the corner of what Weber thinks might be Mayfield and Overlook the bus whines to a stop and the door opens. For a few seconds nothing happens. Some of the people sitting around him look at each other. Weber rubs his palms against his knees. Then one of them climbs up the steps and scans the bus for a seat.

The hands are buried in the pockets of a black overcoat and the eyes shift casually.

Weber stares at the blue-black hair in front of him, focusing particularly on the rear center-part. Then he stands and stretches, raising his hands to the steel roof of the bus and flexing his legs. He isn't quite sure what it is he's doing but he stands there like this, waiting, waiting, and when the man in the black overcoat gets to Weber's row he looks at Weber and after a moment says, "Excuse me."

The man in the overcoat slides past. He nudges Weber's briefcase with the back of his hand, just slightly, and sits down on a small section of the seat against the window. Weber, still standing, rubs his muggy palms across his thighs several times before he too sits. He looks straight ahead. *There are plenty of other seats.* The ends of his toes are cold. The bus whines, spitting out a wad of exhaust that Weber imagines seeping into a lung, and starts off again. This person sitting next to Weber, his skin is pasty white—white but natural somehow—and his hair is long and straight. It is styled to look that way, not long for the sake of being long, and not at all unkempt. The earring dangling from this person's ear is a symbol of some kind: a narrow oval with a straight line cutting diagonally through it. It looks heavy, metallic. Weber wishes he knew what it was a symbol for. Also, he doesn't want to admit it to himself, but Weber thinks maybe he has heard this person's voice before. *Excuse me.*

Weber now has no idea where he is. Cleveland; he knows that much. But the windows are so completely fogged with the breath of the passengers that nothing can be seen outside. Again, Weber feels as though he's traveling aimlessly through space.

His palms are still wet but he resolves not to wipe them anymore. This person next to him is calm; this person knows where he is, where he's going, what he's going to do when he gets there, all that. Then the man with the earring, inexplicably, begins to hum. Weber's first instinct is to try to place the song but, having failed that, his thoughts quickly revert to the notion that this is quite an odd thing to happen and Weber can't help himself: he turns his head and looks this person right in the face.

The man lifts his eyebrows to Weber. "Like the Cure, man?"

Weber has never heard of the Cure but assumes it is a musical group. "A little," he says. "Their old stuff is better."

The man nods. His earring bounces a little, in perfect conformance with the movement of his head. "I hear you. It *is* different, I'll give you that. But I like the new stuff myself—from *Disintegration* on. That's just me now. 'Fascination Street.' Killer." He shrugs. "Hey," he glances down at Weber's tie then back up at his eyes, "haven't I seen you around before?"

Weber shifts his eyes from side to side. "At Hoyle's maybe," he says.

The man taps his forehead three times with his fingers. "That must be it," he says. "That place sucks now, doesn't it?"

Weber shrugs. "It's okay." He wonders where the hell he is. His stop must be coming soon.

"Used to be 'coffeehouse' was just the feel of the place, you know?" the man observes. "It was always pretty laid back, granted. But it was cool. Now what you got are these nimrods going in and having their cheesecake and a spot o' tea." He says 'Spot o' tea' in what Weber considers to be a pretty good British accent. "It's a whole new crowd." He stops and waves a hand in dismissal. "These yuppies—where the hell do they come from anyway?" he says then bites his bottom lip, perhaps believing he may have somehow offended Weber. "Well," he goes on, "you know the place. You know what I'm saying."

Weber sits back in his seat. He wonders if *she* is part of this new crowd that's bringing Hoyle's to its knees, and he's not sure if he hopes this is the case or not. The bus driver grinds the gears heavily and pulls off to the side of the street. Weber figures this is close enough.

"This is my stop," he says to the person next to him, standing, swaying with the sudden movements of the bus. He takes hold of his briefcase.

The man stands next to him. "Yeah. Mine, too. At least I think it is. Can't see shit out these windows." He smiles at Weber. "If not I'll just pound it the last block or so."

"But," Weber says, "it's snowing."

"'Right."

As it turns out, Weber has picked the correct stop to get off at. His apartment is just around the corner. He turns nonchalantly and begins heading up the street. The wind blows right into his face, wrenching his tie from his overcoat and flicking it over his shoulder. Weber feels uncoordinated. *Why is it that the wind always has to blow right into you no matter what direction you're headed?* After ten seconds or so he hears, "Hey. You're not going to Hoyle's *now*, are you?"

Weber slows slightly, suddenly remembering that his apartment and Hoyle's basically are the same place, but decides to keep walking and not look back. He hasn't gone more than a few yards farther when he hears quick patting footsteps coming up behind him. He quickens his pace as much as he can without being too obvious. The earring moves up next to him. It's all he can see to his right, in his peripheral vision.

"You going up to Hoyle's?"

Weber keeps walking. "Yeah," he says. "Just thought I'd stop in for a minute."

"By yourself?"

"I live around here," Weber says, hoping this will make some kind of sense.

"Well, hell," the man says. "I'll go with you. I'm supposed to be at work, but . . ."

"Oh, don't miss work on account of it," Weber says. "No

big deal, really. Maybe I'll just skip it and go home."

Out of the corner of his eye Weber sees the earring shake back and forth. "Nah. I don't feel like going to work anyway. I work right there." A finger points to a little shop across the street. It is called Interpose and the glass in front is completely covered over on the inside by randomly arranged posters of bright swirling patterns and solid blocks of various colors. Weber has never been in the shop and has no idea what they sell, but the front windows always have reminded him of the Partridge Family bus. As if the man walking along with him has just read Weber's mind, he says, "We sell what you might call knick-knacks," and smiles. "Ceramic water bongs and shit like that. Handmade. But I can get another job just like it tomorrow. No big deal. Yeah, I'll hang with you a while at Hoyle's. Hey—" Weber senses the motion next to him slow just slightly. He thinks maybe this person will stop and turn around. "Is Hoyle's even open yet? What is it—like five-thirty?"

"It's open," Weber says. He wonders what exactly it is he's doing.

"All right. Whatever you say, chief. You oughtta know."

They pass by the bank and the Fine Indian Cuisine restaurant and the Record Exchange where a lot of them buy their CDs, used. Weber has gone in once or twice himself and bought CDs, just so they'd have the little RECORD EXCHANGE stamp on them. She took most of them when she left, though. Traffic is heavy with cars passing through Coventry from downtown on their way to their homes in the east suburbs. Weber can see his breath; he hears the soles of his shoes scuffing across the cinders on the sidewalk.

Then, before he can figure out the curious sequence of what's just happened, Weber is sitting at a square table in the center of Hoyle's. Wet feet squeak over blue and black tiles. There are more people here than Weber would have guessed, coming and going. Weber wants to observe, to see if he recognizes any faces, if he was on the money with any of his preconceptions of them, but instead he stares straight ahead, at Morris, who this person he is with has since identified himself as. Morris orders two vodkas and begins talking. He speaks with such a brisk, rapid-fire delivery Weber wonders when he has time to breathe. He tells Weber about his future former boss at Interpose who used to be the mayor of Ashtabula, Ohio, and who now sits in the back room of the shop all day testing the water bongs; his older sister who has skin like rubber—you can stretch it and twist it and pull it several inches from the bone like chewed bubblegum and it snaps right back; his roommate who will only eat the organs of chickens because they are the tastiest ("You know, the gizzard, liver, neck, kidneys"); an ex-girlfriend who never slept— she "rested," but never actually slept, and is to this day the most vibrant person he's ever met. "Irritating as hell; but *vibrant*." Every minute or so Morris picks up his glass of vodka and takes a gulp, holding it in his mouth a moment before swallowing. He tells Weber that every person he's ever known has one truly remarkable thing about them, and what he enjoys most is discovering what that thing is.

Yeah, Weber thinks. *And then telling complete strangers about it.*

A three-piece band is setting up in the corner. Weber sees an electric guitar, a violin and a set of bongo drums and he wonders what kind of music this band could possibly produce given their oddly limiting assortment of instruments. At the bar is a woman wearing a plain yellow baseball cap with no logo on the front. Thick auburn hair spills out the sides of the hat and around her shoulders and Weber thinks she is beautiful. Through all the muffled talking and clinking glasses, he can hear the long tracks of cloudy lights humming above his head.

"I'm thinking of quitting my job, too," he tells Morris.

Morris spits an ice cube back into his glass. "The hell you wanna go and do that for, man?"

"You just did it," Weber says, not by way of explanation but in defense. He's not sure how it sounded, though.

"Yeah, but look at you," Morris says, indicating Weber's tie. "I'd venture to guess you got a real job. I'd also wager there's not a single water bong in your entire office." He smiles. "That's one sure sign of an unreal job: water bongs on site."

Weber loosens his tie and unbuttons his top button, hoping this act will send some kind of message, although he's not sure what. He runs a hand though his hair half expecting it to feel as long between his fingers as Morris's looks. Morris tilts his head a little to the side, looking at Weber as if wanting confirmation of his water bong theory. Weber takes a sip of vodka.

"Well, there you have it," Morris says after another moment. "You can't quit that job. Shit, I don't think you're *allowed* to quit that job, sounds like to me. The jobs I have," he shrugs, "they expect me to quit after a couple months. So forget about it. There's no comparison here."

Weber sets his glass on the table between them and rubs his damp palms on his knees. He says, "People I've never seen before sell these little metal things to other companies and then I mark down how many little metal things these people have sold to other people—I've never seen *them* before either—and how much money my company's made on them. That's my job." He picks up his glass and holds it beneath his chin. "And I'm not even very good at it."

Morris nods. "And . . . "

"And there you have it."

Morris leans back. He laughs in loud convulsive bursts for a moment, drains his glass of vodka then motions in the general direction of the bar for another. He laughs a little more. Then he stops and begins humming again. This time Weber doesn't look at him. The woman in the yellow hat is not at the bar anymore. Weber turns and sees her sitting at a table against the big picture window that looks out onto Coventry Road. She is sitting with another woman and a man. He wonders what the deal is with that. *How does that all fit together?*

The three band members sit down on stools in the corner and

pick up their instruments. One announces that they are the scheduled Happy Hour entertainment. Then they begin to play. Surprisingly, they sound pretty good to Weber. The tune has sort of a melancholy, twangy, swaying kind of cadence. The guitarist is getting a lot of feedback which, coupled with the violin, is a sound Weber can't remember ever having heard before. He imagines a field of tall, tan grass. He imagines these three musicians standing in the middle of this tan field with their instruments; the season is autumn and a breeze blows in off the plains. It seems the most unnatural combination ever, yet somehow it feels perfectly right to him. Morris keeps humming, even though the tune is not even close to what the band is playing. The woman in the yellow hat turns her head slightly and looks at Weber, and instead of continuing her gaze through to some other direction or object, she keeps looking at him. Weber closes his eyes. He keeps them closed for what feels like a pretty long time. He concentrates on the music, on the tan field. Focusing on the whine of the violin, he wonders what his one remarkable thing is. Whatever it is, he figures it's probably not something positive; most likely it's not even something interesting. For a moment he considers asking Morris if he knows what it is, but instead he opens his eyes. The woman in the yellow hat has turned away. She chats casually with the man and woman across the table. It might be a cup of tea in front of her. Weber stands quickly and slings on his overcoat.

"What gives?" Morris says. During the time Weber's eyes were closed Morris received a fresh vodka. His lips shine with it.

"I need to go," Weber says. He looks around haphazardly and tries to picture where she sits, or stands (or dances?) when she comes in here. Then suddenly he wonders if she'll come in here tonight.

Morris shakes his head, as if simply negating Weber's statement. "Not yet. These guys are good," he says, indicating the band. "The guy on the bongos is a regular customer." He points a thumb over his shoulder. "Down the street, I mean."

"Gotta go," Weber says, buttoning his coat, feeling fully exposed in the middle of Hoyle's. "I'll catch you next time. Here." He makes a motion with his hand indicating the surroundings. "I'm in here all the time."

Morris nods. "Fair enough." He takes a significant drink from the glass, and Weber wishes he'd wipe his lips with the back of his hand. Then Morris looks up at Weber and nods again. But it's a different kind of nod; one of confidence, of just-realized wisdom.

"What?" Weber says.

Morris leans forward and rests his elbows on the table. "Deliberate," he says.

Weber just stares.

"That's your one thing. You're very deliberate. Calculated, maybe. No—deliberate. That's the word I want. And that . . . deliberateness—that leads to other stuff. I'm not sure what yet, but definitely remarkable things. Give me a little more time, I'll get it. But, yeah. Anyway, you're very deliberate."

"You think?"

"Ah, maybe not. Never mind. I'll see you later." Then he turns and fixes his full attention on the band. The bongo player is in the middle of a bizarre sounding solo. Weber pushes toward the door through the people who have recently wandered in, keeping his eyes down. The floor is wet and slick from the buildup of more and more people moving about.

On the sidewalk, several of them stand together, waiting, talking, laughing. It's snowing again. Weber stands among them for a minute or two, stamping his feet on the concrete to keep warm. He is waiting for a taxi to pull up to the curb and let her out. She'll be dressed a little differently but on the whole she'll look the same as he remembers. She'll toy with the driver a little as she hands a tip through the open window. He hears her laugh and then realizes that Morris is wrong, that probably the only remarkable thing about him is the love he once had for her, still has for her. He doesn't know about this "deliberate" stuff; he's not sure what that means. He thinks Morris might be crazy. What he does know is that if she were to pull up in a cab and step out onto the curb, he would probably look at her and start to sweat. He would look for a place to hide, a tiny crevice to force himself into, a way to disguise his pathetic anxiety. Then, finding nothing to serve as sanctuary, his heart would swell and explode on the spot, literally bursting through his chest. Now *that* would shock them, he thinks. *That* would be remarkable.

But she does not pull up in a cab, and he finds that he is disappointed, and a little relieved. He turns toward the street-level door of his building and takes a few steps, feeling stares that he knows he's imagining. He doesn't particularly want these people to see him disappear up the stairs to his apartment; he thinks that somehow he'll be giving a piece of himself away that he'd rather keep. But he doesn't want to stand on the wet, cold sidewalk any longer either, gripping his briefcase, listening, waiting. He realizes that he feels more alone here than he does upstairs. As he puts his key into the lock he tries to determine which way the wind is blowing now. It's coming from the right he decides, from north to south, not directly into his face anymore, and as he leans his head back, looking up through the falling snow at the underside of his own balcony he holds perfectly still, hoping to feel it shift.

In Mercer

DIANE TOLD ME THIS:
When she was fifteen or so, she used to help out some evenings at the restaurant where her mother worked as a waitress back in Mercer, Pennsylvania. She'd clear and set tables, fill water glasses, wash dishes, whatever. It wasn't a particularly extravagant restaurant from what I understand—on the second floor above a bar, serving steaks and burgers and pasta—and she had to wear a brown polyester uniform with wide shoulder straps. Sometimes kids she went to high school with would come in and she'd have to fill their water glasses.

Her father'd died a couple of years earlier and she worked at the restaurant simply because she had the time, and the minimum wage she earned helped with her mother's bills.

But all that's background anyway. This is the part she told me once that now I can't forget: A small, thin man of about fifty used to come in about every other week, sometimes more frequently, and sit in a corner booth by himself. The man had one thick, bushy eyebrow that traversed the entire width of his forehead and was missing the top half of one thumb. He always ordered a small salad, cheese ravioli, and coffee. Every time. Diane never waited on him or took his order (that wasn't her job), but she noticed he always left a little bit of everything when she removed the dishes from his booth after he'd left. He seemed like a nice enough man to Diane and it bothered her that he always came in by himself. He didn't even bring a newspaper or anything; he just sat there and ate, eyes forward, chewing methodically, until it was time to get up and leave.

It also bothered her that some of the women who worked there began to make up stories about him—made-up stories based on assumed fact, as they huddled together behind the double swinging doors that led back to the kitchen. Rhonda, who was about thirty, said she'd lay odds he kept his wife locked in an apartment somewhere to knit and vacuum and whatever while he went out to dinner. "He's got a creepy stare," she said. "His eyeballs don't move when he orders or when he eats. They're like frozen in his head."

But Jean, a heavy, older waitress who'd retired twice and came back both times when her husband got laid off, disagreed. "He's been in prison," she said, nodding. "There's no question about that. He's been in prison for some sort of sicko crime. Nothing *violent* necessarily. I wouldn't say that. Just sick. Public perversion or something. Exposing himself at the playground."

More or less the same conversation took place—a conversation to which neither Diane nor her mother contributed—every time the guy came into the restaurant. (Incidentally, Diane's opinion of why this guy became such a center of the waitresses' attention was that, more likely than not, if you lived in Mercer you knew everybody else who lived in Mercer, you knew their stories; and the fact that this guy *had* no story to speak of bugged these women to no end.) Diane's mother, whom I've since met, does not talk much, regardless of subject. She listens, and smiles occasionally, but she does not speak unless spoken to and even then her words are few and softly spoken and accentuated by a tug on her wiry, greying hair, a lock of which usually becomes somehow wrapped around an index finger.

In any case, one night the guy comes in and waits patiently by the door until the hostess seats him in a booth against the wall, his back to the rest of the square, dim room. It is early December and snowing outside. The guy struggles out of his tweed blazer and jiggles it lightly above the worn carpet, shaking the excess wetness from the fuzzy surface. Then he folds the jacket and puts it on the inside of the booth next to him and fixes his eyes on something straight ahead. He does not pick up the menu.

Diane, having already filled the guy's water glass and attempted a smile that was not returned but not altogether ignored either, is fixing the place-setting at a table across the room when her mother approaches the guy's booth to take his order. A muffled sound of shattering dishes is suddenly heard from behind the swinging kitchen doors. It lasts for quite a while, stray plates spinning on the floor at different pitches. Then nothing. Silence. Diane shakes her head, lays down a fork. When she is finished with that table she looks up and sees that her mother is still standing at the guy's booth, hip locked and pushed out to one side. Diane can only see the back of the guy's head but she assumes he's speaking since her mother is doing a lot of nodding and raising her eyebrows. Rhonda passes behind Diane's mother with a tray of loaded plates and pauses—not at all inconspicuously—to check out the situation at the booth. After delivering the meals to another table she walks, swinging the empty tray at her side, over to Diane.

"You better keep an eye on that," she whispers.

Diane glances down and adjusts the positioning of a paper placemat. She does not look back up. "Why?" she says and immediately realizes she should have said *what?* but it is too late.

"I'm just saying," Rhonda says, shrugging. "Just some friendly advice is all." Then she heads back to the kitchen.

As soon as the doors swing closed, Diane's mother scratches one last thing into her pad, smiles while turning her eyes from the guy, and quickly follows behind Rhonda. Diane notices a recently vacated booth and moves to clear it. It's nearly seven o'clock and the restaurant is beginning to fill up, so she needs to make sure there are as many available tables as possible.

*　　*　　*

Twenty minutes later Diane's mother brings the guy's meal. By this time the waitresses have been talking among each other and practically have themselves worked into hysterics, to hear Diane tell it. Every time Diane's mother walks by the booth, the guy stops her. Can I have another glass of water? My fork fell on the floor, can I have a clean one? You know, on second thought, I think I'll have the creamy Italian. So when she finally brings the guy's food, she has quite an audience. The other waitresses try to look busy in other parts of the restaurant, within earshot. Even a couple of the patrons have begun to take notice.

Diane wants to say something. And she wants to smack Rhonda. She wants to push Jean, knock her over on her back like a fat, pathetic sea turtle. But from her spot in the far corner, standing next to her cart piled high with a load of dirty dishes, Diane watches, too. She has a pretty good angle. Her mother sets down a plate. The guy smiles, looks up at her, says something, chuckles. Her mother sets down another plate—a smaller one—above and to the right of the one already positioned. The guy looks down at it. His head moves in odd directions, his shoulders bounce. Diane's mother smiles, looks away, rubs her chin with the back of her hand. She takes a step backward, then, when the guy says something, leans down slightly to hear him. It looks to Diane as though her mother does not want to get too close to the guy for fear of catching something he has.

The waitresses watch. Conversation seems to fade into a murmur. Most likely it doesn't, but it seems like it. Diane shifts her gaze and notices a couple she's seen before but does not know across the room. Jean is standing at their table, notepad positioned at her chest. When her customer begins to speak to her, Jean puts up a hand to shush him. Rhonda and Nikki, the hostess who is new and Diane does not know very well, are standing together by the kitchen door. They no longer attempt to disguise their interest in the booth either. One woman at a table in the middle of the room, who apparently has taken notice that something is going on, turns her head completely around to see.

As Diane's mother takes another tiny step toward the guy, who now is apparently making some sort of reference to his food that he thinks might interest her, Diane picks up four dirty plates and a glass and begins walking toward the kitchen. She looks around. It seems as though all eyes are fixed on that booth. When she arrives at a point she judges to be pretty close to the middle of the room, she slams the dishes down onto the floor.

Unfortunately, she hasn't factored in the carpeting, which, although thin, serves as enough of a cushion to prevent the destruction of all but the glass and one plate, and causes practically no sound whatsoever. Some people do turn and look at her, though, as she bends down to pick up her mess, and the hot realization hits her that she has not really created a distraction for her mother so much as negotiated a temporary annoyance for the spectators, and significant embarrassment for herself.

She haphazardly picks up as many of the broken pieces as she can carry and rushes toward the kitchen, cutting through everyone's field of vision to the booth and feeling as though she were in some kind of dangerous line of fire. In the kitchen, she throws the pieces in the trash and stands there. The air is warm and wet. Ray and Ned, the cooks, stand behind her, camouflaged within a cloud of steam. They are preparing something and don't seem to notice her. She stands there, breathing strangely, squeezing at bunched-up sections of her uniform. She has no idea what she should do next. It occurs to her that maybe she didn't really smash the dishes, that maybe she just imagined smashing them. It's a possibility. It has that kind of feel to it.

The door swings open behind her and without turning around to see who's there she knows it is her mother. But still Diane does not turn around. Instead she stands facing the big, square trash can, slightly hunched at the shoulders, chewing on a fingernail.

Her mother goes to the shiny, metallic island in the center of the kitchen that separates Ray and Ned from everyone else and claims a plate of pasta that Ray has just set there. She puts the plate on her round tray. "Go clean up your mess," she says in a hollow tone. Then she adds, "People are talking."

Diane does not move. No course of action she can think of seems appropriate. Of course she'd planned all along to clean up her mess, but now she thinks maybe she won't. Maybe she'll walk right out the kitchen door—the one behind Ray and Ned that exits onto the alley—and go home, or go somewhere else. And maybe, just for good measure, she'll take the plate of pasta from her mother's tray and smash it, too, on this hard, tile floor *before* she heads out the door. Maybe she'll give Rhonda that smack she's been meaning to give her, *then* leave. Any of these choices seems to Diane like a good possibility, and she makes up her mind to follow through on at least one of them. But when she silently spits a piece of fingernail into the trash can and turns around, she sees that her mother is not—has not been—looking at her either. In fact, she's staring past the tray held at her waist, staring straight through the tray to the floor, but she's not really staring because her eyes are closed. Her eyes are closed and she's holding perfectly still, like she's trying to blend herself into the thick, hot, sticky air.

"I miss your father," she says.

Now, this is where the part I don't quite understand starts. I don't understand it and don't think I ever will. Instead of breaking anything or smacking anyone or running out the back door or even *saying* anything to her mother, Diane turns and walks back through the swinging doors to the hazy reddish-lit dining room where, in front of those same curiously blank faces, she kneels down and picks up the unbroken dishes, piles them carefully across her forearm, and carries them, past the faces, past the thumbless guy in his booth, into the kitchen.

Ned looks up. "Your mum left," he says from behind a wall of steam.

Diane puts the dishes down in the big sink. She doesn't say anything.

"She went out the back," Ned adds, and points. Then he

says, kind of incidentally, "You gonna leave those pieces in the sink like that?" then looks back down at what he was doing before Diane came in. Ray, pounding on a mound of pizza dough, pays no attention. The smell here is a mix of garlic and disinfectant.

Diane still says nothing. She finds a damp rag and goes back out to the dining room to wipe the carpet she stained with spaghetti sauce and gravy. She works the rag across the carpet with both hands, scrubbing up and down. She is on her knees and, although her attention is focused on the stains, she can see the thumbless guy's shoes across the room. Brown shoeboots. Ug-ly. People have left the restaurant since last she noticed. She hasn't looked around, but she can feel it. Fewer eyes on her. Nikki the hostess stands by the door. She glances at her fingernails, pushes back a cuticle. Diane figures that tables probably need to be cleared, but the carpet is her first priority. The waitresses can clear some tables. It won't kill them, God knows.

When the carpet seems to her as clean as it's likely to get, Diane stands up. Her shoulders are stiff and her left foot is asleep. She gets a tray from her cart and clears the three tables that have no people sitting at them. Nobody is watching her anymore, and nobody is waiting for a table. There is no hurry, she knows, but she feels rushed. When the tables are cleared she wipes them down with the same rag she used to clean the floor. Rhonda walks by with somebody's bill, but doesn't say anything.

The thumbless guy is still sitting at his booth staring at his empty dishes. He's been there for nearly two hours. Diane figures she better take care of him since it's become obvious that neither her mother nor any of the other waitresses are going to. She approaches the booth from behind him. When she reaches past his left shoulder and picks up a plate, the guy jumps a little, makes a noise kind of like a hiccup, and looks up at her.

"Ah," he says.

Diane reaches past him for the butter dish. "Excuse me," she says.

The guy clears his throat.

"Can I get you anything else?" Diane asks.

The guy shakes his head no. Suddenly Diane has an urge to get him talking. She wants something from him. She feels he owes her.

"How was everything?" she says.

He puts his palms on the table.

"Everything okay?" she says.

"Good," he says. "Real good."

Diane stands watching him, waiting. She decides she'll stand there as long as it takes for him to say something else. Something meaningful. She'll *make* him talk to her. The guy glances from his hands to Diane back to his hands. His single eyebrow twitches. Then he says, "That's the first veal I've eaten in pretty near ten years."

Diane can't take her eyes from the guy's mangled thumb against the tabletop. "Is that right?" she says.

"Yeah. Stomach problems."

"Is that right?" Diane says, then immediately realizes she's already said that. So she adds, "Stomach problems, huh? Well, that's a shame." But the guy's already turned away from her, tuned her out. Diane, in a sudden loss of motivation, gives up on the guy and takes the dishes she's already collected from his table into the kitchen. Rhonda is waiting for her there. Diane nearly slams into her on her way through the double doors.

"I hope you know what he had," Rhonda says. "There's no bill, you know. Your mother's got it. And if she expects the tip—or any tips from tonight for that matter, well, she's just . . . she's—"

"Veal," Diane says. "He had veal. First time in ten years."

"Say again."

"Nothing. He had veal. All right?"

"What kind of veal? It makes a difference."

"Marsala," Ray says.

Rhonda looks back sharply at the cook for a moment. Ray, eyes down, scraping the burnt bottom of a cake pan, pays Rhonda no attention. She keeps her eyes there for a few more seconds, though. "Fine," she says and walks out of the kitchen. As the door swings back and forth, settling into place, Diane notices that the thumbless guy is no longer at his booth. She can see the stain on the carpet, too. She wishes for something then. Or maybe for the absence of something. She's not sure what, but she wishes for it as hard as she believes she can.

When the restaurant closes and everything is picked up and wiped down, Diane puts on her coat and gloves and heads downstairs without saying goodnight to anyone. At the bottom of the narrow, wooden staircase she stops, looks at her watch. It is ten forty-five. She pushes open the door and steps out onto East Butler Street.

It is still snowing and the sidewalk is covered. She has about a fifteen minute walk home. She turns right onto Pitt Street and heads toward the blinking yellow light at the intersection of Pitt and East Market. The courthouse is brightly lit in big, gaudy, red and white bulbs, decorated for Christmas, which is in three weeks. This is really the only time that Diane enjoys her surroundings. The stillness of the deserted streets and sounds of the cold permeate her. She feels as though she is moving through the model of a small town, being watched by something larger. As the frigid wind brushes her cheeks, she is putting together a script of what she wants to say to her mother when she gets home. One thing she will say is that she's decided she must quit working at the restaurant. She'll get another part-time job. She wants her mother to know she hasn't lost her senses. She knows what is important, and she doesn't expect her mother to carry the entire load. But she simply cannot continue working there, with those women. She just can't. Tomorrow, after school, she'll check out the possibilities at Iasly's on 62; maybe the Agway store out toward Grove City, although getting back and forth would be difficult. Or the mall in Hermitage—they probably need extra help for the holidays—but the same problem applies there as well.

In any case, she'll explain it to her mother.

And she'll let her know that she understands.

Then she'll make a case for *both* of them quitting the restaurant. What's the benefit? she'll ask. What benefit is gained by working there that couldn't be gained working anywhere else in the county? We have enough problems without having to worry about the petty provocations supplied by a bunch of bitter barmaids. Diane smiles. She likes the way that sounded in her head and decides she *has* to remember those exact words if she is going to make an impression. Look what it made me do tonight, she'll say. Smashing—or trying to smash (which is even worse)—dishes on the floor. Pathetic. That's not me, she'll say. (Although, maybe, she thinks, it is.)

Her feet make a funny crunching sound on the fresh snow. She clears her mind and listens to that sound for a while as she passes the hardware store and the Mercer Grill. She can smell stale beer and grease from the burgers and she makes a mental note *not* to seek employment there. She turns down Second Street, a brick road off the main section of town that leads to her and her mother's apartment, and immediately—in the dark, enclosed alcove in front of the door to Mitchell's Pharmacy—she sees the black shadow of a man standing with his hands disappearing into the pockets of his sportcoat.

Diane stops. The crunching sound from the last step she's taken seems to hang in the air for a few seconds, and it takes her that long to make the connection of the figure in the pharmacy doorway to the thumbless guy from the restaurant. At the moment she does make the connection, the figure says, "Evening."

A warm, swelling feeling spreads inside her. It starts in her chest and moves out into her fingertips. She knows this should frighten her, and, actually, it does. But it seems too much like a dream for her do anything other than say, "Well, hello there," before she can stop herself. Her voice is not cheerful, not frightened, not anything. It's just words. She swings around to face him straight-on, arms folded in front of her. Then she notices the guy's tweed blazer. "Aren't you freezing?" She's not sure what it is she's doing, but she knows, whatever it is, she shouldn't be doing it.

The guy takes his hands out of the pockets and blows on his fingers. "It is a chilly one," he says.

Diane turns away. "Excuse me," she says, and starts off again down Second Street.

But now she can't hear the crunching noise beneath her shoes. Her mind feels compressed, cloudy.

"Miss," she hears behind her, but she keeps going. A few seconds later the thumbless guy is walking alongside of her, hands back in his pockets. "Miss," he says again. "Miss . . ."

She stops. "What?"

"Um . . ." The thumbless guy, caught off guard by her abrupt stop, had continued on another step or two. When he finally stops as well, he seems flustered. "I, ah—if it's all right, I'd like to walk you home."

"I was on my way home the whole time. Without your help. I do this a lot actually." She starts walking again, but she doesn't even get past him before he is back alongside of her. Now both of them are making the crunching noise—an odd, haphazard rhythm. The snow is coming down pretty steadily and the guy's shoulders and head are covered with it.

One thing about Diane I should mention here: she's a beautiful girl—no question—although there is nothing about any one particular feature, or group of features, that you would single out as being beautiful. She doesn't carry herself well and she's uncomfortable with things like what to do with her hands at certain times or what facial expression is appropriate when. Neither is an attractive trait, of course, but taken all together, well, I keep seeing her there on Second Street in Mercer, with some thumbless guy in a sportcoat following after her, and her knowing she should scream or hit him or at least run, but kind of wanting to hear what he has to say, and I wonder what she did with her hands. Probably she put them in the pockets of her coat, even though she was wearing gloves—just stuffed them in. That's probably what she did with them. And, I don't know, there's something beautiful about that.

"That woman," the thumbless guy says between deep breaths, "the waitress that took my order tonight—she your mother?"

Diane slows down. She doesn't stop, but she slows down considerably. "Excuse me?" she says. Diane is a sweet, sweet person. She is not an intimidating or overbearing presence. So when she is the slightest bit reprimanding or abrupt, the impression made is greatly magnified. That's another thing about her.

The thumbless guy stops, trying to catch his breath. Diane wants to keep going, but something about the way the surging cold, grey cloud billows from the guy's wheezing mouth makes her stop and wait for what he has to say.

"I . . . I was just curious . . . if the woman who took my order . . . is she your mother? Because . . . if she is . . . well . . ."

"What are you asking me?" Diane says, louder than she normally talks. The man is bent over, hands on his knees, looking up at Diane from under his big eyebrow. Diane can see her apartment building at the end of the street. The porch light is on. "You want me to tell you who my mother is? I'm supposed to point my mother out to you—to some guy from a bar that never speaks . . . that never speaks and . . . and—" She can't think of how she'd meant to finish the statement, can't think of how the speaking frequency of this guy has anything to do with why she doesn't want to tell him anything about her mother, so she adds, "Until now, I mean. That's what you're asking me, right?" Diane means to start walking again but doesn't. "I think you got a piece of bad veal, mister. That's what *I* think."

"Well," the guy begins to regain his breath. The cloud from his mouth is not as solid now. "I guess if you put it in those terms . . . I was just asking because I think she is an awfully nice lady." He releases his knees and stands up straight. "And I just thought that, as shamelessly juvenile as it sounds, you could, perhaps, tell her that for me." His eyebrow does a squiggly, jerky kind of movement, and then he looks down at his feet.

"What other terms are there?"

The thumbless guy does not move. It looks like he's freezing, although he does not shiver. "None, I suppose."

Diane takes her gloved hands out of her pockets and holds them at her sides. "Yes," she says. "That's my mother. The one that waited on you. But she doesn't work at the restaurant anymore. She quit tonight."

The guy looks up, meets Diane's eyes. "That is too bad. Truly. She is—was—different from the others, somehow."

"Of course," Diane says dryly. "That's why she quit."

"I wonder if I could impose a little further?"

Diane stands looking at him, watching his eyebrow for clues.

"I wonder if it'd—" he begins and then stops. "Please," he says in a new, calmer, tone. "Let me walk you home."

Diane looks toward the porch light. She imagines it going out, but it doesn't. It stays on. They live on the second floor of a two-story house, above a young couple and their three-year-old son. She thinks about making a run for it. Then, for no reason in particular, she thinks about how she has been pressuring her mother to get a cat. But her mother won't allow it, even though the landlord lives all the way up in Meadville, because it's against the terms of their lease.

"Okay," she says.

The thumbless guy does a movement with his body that makes Diane afraid he might extend his arm for her to hold onto, as if she was his prom date. But all he does is start walking, slowly, cautiously, waiting for her to pull even with him. When she does her hands are back in her coat pockets. "It's just up here a block or two," she says. "It's not far."

They pass by Diane's cousins' house. And her friend Jennifer's, which has a wraparound porch. Everyone she knows lives either down the street or around the corner. Sad, kind of. But just then she thinks of something her father once said to her. She couldn't have been more than seven or eight at the time. He told her about the tornado of 1968 just before she was born, and about how, with Mercer getting hit so hard by the draft and consequently so many young men overseas in Vietnam, there were not enough hands to efficiently clean up and repair the damage. Mercer itself did not fair too badly, but less than a mile outside of town to the north and west it was bad. Houses demolished, crops and livestock wiped out, power lines taken down, wells sucked up and torn apart. A lot of people were hurt or killed and the hospitals in both Sharon and Meadville were grossly overcrowded. So here's what Council did: Being the county seat, the town of Mercer contained the county jail. Council voted to request that all of the so-called "violent" criminals—those doing time for more serious crimes—be moved to one section of the jail (there were not many that fit this description because most serious offenders were shipped off to larger, better equipped prisons in Pittsburgh or Cleveland). Inmates doubled, tripled up on cells, which left many empty. Then—almost unbelievably—some inmates were released on eight-hour furloughs to help with the cleanup effort around town. And the empty cells were sterilized and converted into semi-private hospital rooms. At the end of the day the inmates, most of whom were serving short sentences for public drunkenness or disorderly conduct and didn't particularly mind being in jail for a couple of weeks, returned to jail for the night, sometimes sleeping four or five to a cell. All this went on for close to a month. That's what Diane's father told her. Whether or not it's true, I really couldn't say.

But what's more, Diane remembers how when her father finished telling that story, he looked down at her sitting beside him in their big old Buick as he drove them somewhere that, unquestionably, was not very far away, and said, "Something I've always liked about small towns: the shit doesn't always necessarily rise to the top. It just kinda gets mixed in with everything else till you can't hardly tell the difference. I think that's a good thing."

Diane glances over at the thumbless guy walking next to her—head down, blowing into his cupped hands—and wonders how this guy works into her father's scenario. Of course at the time Diane had not the foggiest clue what her father was saying to her; only that he'd said the word "shit" in a way that made her feel grown up, as if it conveyed something more than just what she assumed to be its standard definition. But now she thinks maybe she's finally got her hands around the crux of her father's meaning. She says, "What's your name?"

They're almost to her apartment. She can see inside the windows now. The guy looks up, turns to her. His cheeks are red and windblown, as if his face has been freshly slapped. "My name is Duane," he says. "Duane Ish. I live on Sycamore. Well, a tad *off* Sycamore actually."

"I see."

Duane leans his head back, thinking.

"Don't you want to know my name?" Diane asks.

"I already know your name. I apologize."

"My mother's name is Ruth."

"I know that, too."

Neither speaks the rest of the way, which perhaps is less than a minute. When they get to the front of Diane's apartment they stop on the sidewalk and look past each other. Duane shuffles his feet and Diane just waits because there is something inside her that wants to wait. The snow has tapered to flurries but the wind has picked up a little. Diane looks up at their front window and is relieved to see that her mother is not standing there, looking out. She can see the lamp on the endtable, glowing through the sheer white curtain. It looks warm inside. Finally Duane clears his throat. "I wish I had a car," he says.

Diane wiggles her gloved fingers inside her pockets.

"If I had a car—a big one, a Lincoln—I'd come by here one day and pick your mother up and drive her off someplace. Florida maybe. Fort Lauderdale." He coughs. "I wish I had a car," he goes on. "I wish that when I came by for Ruth she'd be expecting me. I'd have a dress for her in the backseat hanging on a hook. It would be pink. She'd see it and start crying she'd be so happy. She'd slide over and sit right up against me while I drove us to Florida. And she'd love me and laugh all the time. I wonder how that happens? I wish she'd never seen my thumb."

Suddenly he seems to remember Diane. "Oh, Jesus," he says. "Oh, Jesus, I'm sorry. Forgive me. I . . . Oh, Jesus."

Diane stares at the stubby bush in the Espositos' yard. With the snow all around, it looks as though it's floating, wavering from side to side. When she looks at Duane, which she does without planning to, she at once realizes that she's never before seen such a sorry-looking sight. He is shivering now. His face is splotchy, red and white; snow is caught in his eyebrow. His thin, wet hair sticks up at the sides and his narrow shoulders are pushed forward and together. The tips of his fingers, all except for the one thumb, poke out and look as if at any moment they might be completely gobbled up by the sleeves of a tweed sportcoat too large for him. His teeth chatter silently.

"I'm going in now," Diane says and steps away.

"Please," Duane says and she stops, facing away from him, facing her house. "I know I don't deserve it. But if you could, like we discussed earlier, mention me to your mother. Not mention me the way I am, but, perhaps, the way I . . ."

It keeps snowing and Duane stands there searching for words that he has to know are not going to ever be relayed to Ruth. He keeps searching, though. Shivering and searching. Finally he lets out a long breath and says, feebly, "Just tell her. Okay?"

Sometimes, here, on static, black nights, Diane would sit at her window in her bedroom, listening to the hushed road sounds from I-79 in the distance, and think about the times her father had taken her to Shenango Lake when she was little. They'd rent a rowboat and spend the afternoon paddling around the huge expanse of water, in and out of inlets, feeding the ducks and feeling the warm sun on their faces while her mother went shopping in Pittsburgh. And sometimes they'd fish. Or pretend to. They never kept any they caught; it was just for something else to do. They'd drop the line through the shiny, soft water and

Diane would imagine the hooked piece of cheese falling and then catching, suspended, held by the invisible line and bright red bobber. And sometimes, when the fishing would get slow, she'd toss little bits of cheese overboard and listen to the *poink*. She'd imagine the yellow cheese, surrounded by the black water, dropping in slow motion. And, in her mind, it never hit bottom. It didn't exactly *disappear*, but it was gone all the same.

That, I understand.

"Sure," she says to Duane. "Sure," and heads hurriedly toward her front door, through the falling snow.

Doe

It's raining and my wife is staring out the window on her side of the car, watching streaks of water run down the outside of the glass. She's not speaking to me and I think I know why. I won't let on, though. I never do anymore.

She lets out a long, exaggerated sigh, designed specifically to make me glance over and examine her, maybe ask her what's wrong. But I won't bite. I flick on the radio and start pushing buttons in search of a basketball game.

"What did you think?" she says. "About the movie, I mean. Did you like it?" She's still looking out the window. I can see her reflection out of the corner of my eye. I don't think she's blinked.

"It was okay," I say, still twisting knobs. "A little unrealistic, though."

She nods as if this was the answer she had been expecting. "It was sweet," she says.

"I guess."

She turns and looks at me; I can feel it. I imagine her face and the positioning of her lips and eyebrows. The tightening. These things are strategically planned, every movement charted and preconceived for maximum effect. I know what she wants from me, but I don't know, either. And if she got it, I still don't know if she'd be satisfied.

I give up on the notion of finding a game and tune the radio to a music station. At a red light she sighs again, recrosses her legs, and looks out the window. I have no idea what she sees.

The light is red for a long time, it seems. When it turns green and I pull back out into traffic, my wife flips her hair with the back of her hand and faces forward.

"It's not so unrealistic," she says. "Just because people show a lot of affection and are tender toward each other, that doesn't mean it's not real. They were in love, that's all. That was real. From then on, you can't explain it. It doesn't *have* to be real then."

"Lisa," I say. I'm trying to sound attuned to what she is saying. "It's a movie. They make it that way so people will go see it. It probably took them twenty takes for each scene to find just the right amount of mushiness."

I have chosen the wrong word. Immediately I realize this.

She clicks her tongue and turns back to the window.

"You know what I mean," I say.

I wish I smoked. This would be a good moment to light a cigarette. Instead I change the station on the radio even though the song playing is one I like. I wish we had kids, or a pet even. Something to talk about. Lisa looks at her nails.

"That still doesn't make it unrealistic," she says. "That has nothing to do with it."

"Sure it does," I say. "People just don't act so goo-goo over each other. They'd make each other sick in one afternoon."

I don't know why I'm doing this. It would be so easy to simply reach over and pull Lisa across the huge expanse of front seat between us and put my arm around her. I could kiss her on the cheek and tell her, Sure, Honey, it *was* sweet. I can be that way, too. I don't do that, though. I imagine myself doing it, but I don't move. I think maybe I'm defending myself.

It's still raining but not as hard now. I turn the windshield wipers down a notch and make a left turn up a steep hill that winds through a green, wooded area on the way to the town where our apartment is. Thick rows of pines line one side of the road and on the other is a field with tall yellow grass and a ranch-style house in the distance where the land is flatter. I can't see it, though. It is dark and the green has been enveloped by black. I drive this route a lot. It seems like movies have become our sole diversion. We are at a loss to come up with anything else.

Lisa isn't saying anything now and it's my guess that she won't for the rest of the ride. When we get home she'll hang up her coat, then go into the bedroom where she'll change into a sweatsuit and get into her side of the bed. I don't blame her for this. There is a gap through the center of our bed almost as wide as the one between us now, in the front seat of the car. It is a three-foot strip of cold sheet usually separating our backs. When we were first married, our apartment was furnished with two small single beds that we mashed together. Sometimes they would slide apart and maybe one of us would fall through the crack. We'd always laugh about it and once or twice we even slept together on the floor between the beds. Lisa loved this. I often wonder what would happen if our bed now were to split down the cold center seam, if that were possible. I keep thinking, it really wouldn't surprise me if that happened.

Lisa runs a hand through her dark hair. She's thinking about the movie, I know. It was an action-adventure-comedy kind of thing and, of course, the hero and heroine end up together. There were two scenes that sparked the conversation we're having now, or were having. One was a, well, sensual love scene I guess you'd call it, and the other was just *cute*: the two characters rolling on the carpet, nuzzling, sharing food, giving piggybacks—a collage of sappiness.

We were holding hands—we still do that sometimes—and I could feel Lisa's fingers tighten, her palms clam up and go damp during these scenes. Then she'd shift in her seat, uncomfortable, squeezing my hand.

She shifts now, too, in the car's leather seat. Although not as steep here, the hill is long and we're still ascending. Rain shadows from the yellow streetlamps streak Lisa's face and make her look evil. She is not evil at all, though, and I almost find humor in the fact that the idea even crosses my mind.

"Do you want to stop and get something to eat?" I say.

Her elbow is resting against the door and she is holding her chin in her hand. I think about touching her leg, or maybe her shoulder. I should. I should touch her face with the back of my hand. Something.

I'm thinking this. I don't actually move to touch Lisa, but I'm thinking it, and in that split second something, an animal, leaps into the road. I see it—I know it's there—but I'm not looking at it because I'm thinking of touching Lisa's thigh, and I really don't even make an attempt to hit the brakes. The car plows through the animal. I don't feel anything but I hear it. It is an exploding sound that erupts underneath the car and blasts upward, passing through us and then the roof, mushrooming out into the rain. The car hydroplanes slightly and then stops. I'm still looking at Lisa's leg.

"My God, Tom," she says. "You hit it. Didn't you see it?"

"No," I say and turn to look out the rear window.

"The poor thing," Lisa says.

I open the door and get out of the car. It is still raining. I can see it falling through the beam thrown by the headlights. I can't feel it, though; not really. The first thing I do is check the front of the car. The fender is badly dented and most of the grille is caved in. I think it might need a new radiator, other things. Lisa pokes her head out of her window. "Go check on it," she says.

I walk back down the hill past the car. I've never actually been on the hill, not on foot. It seems different, unexplored, like I am the first human to set foot on this rainsogged soil. I keep walking, looking, walking farther, until I realize that I had continued driving a considerable distance after hitting the animal before I stopped. I turn and look back at the car. It is a long way off. Finally I see a matted down section in the high grass off the shoulder of the road.

It is a deer—a doe—and it's very dead. I know this immediately, even before noticing the animal's disfigurement: the broken legs (how many, I don't know); the collapsed midsection; the twisted, wobbling neck with its head overlooking its back; the bottom jaw turned inside-out. I knew the animal was dead even before seeing the injuries that caused its death. But now, having seen them, I begin to cry. I murmur for a moment or two, feeling it in my stomach and my throat, and then I am bawling, howling even. I don't know why, but I am standing there, thirty years old, and I'm moaning and sobbing, wailing violently in the rain. I try to stop but my resistance only turns the crying into snorting, croaking sounds. It's stupid, but I can't stop. I am on my knees now, crying harder, blubbering. My face is wet and I can't see; everything is black and shaking. I want to laugh, I try to, but I just cry.

Then I feel Lisa's hands on my shoulders. I don't know if she's there or not, but I *feel* her, standing behind me. She squeezes my shoulders and rubs my neck and smooths out my wet hair.

I reach my hands back to touch her.

Belong

THEIR WORK BROUGHT THEM. Her work, to be specific, but that didn't make any difference really since one was as good as the other and the result was the same. They both had been looking for new jobs out of town, as their life in Cleveland had become not so much dull or tedious or difficult, they told themselves, but simply too familiar. They just needed a change.

He came home from the gym one afternoon in September and she was waiting just inside their apartment door. He almost walked right into her.

"How do you feel about the south?" she said.

"I don't know. South of what?"

"Just south. *The* South. Georgia, to be exact."

"Well, I guess I feel fine about it."

She opened her mouth to speak, then stopped short and scrunched up her eyebrows. "Really?" she said. "Good."

It just as easily could have been him who found a job out of town. But it was her and they'd had an agreement so it was settled, a point of order. And that really was fine with him.

"It's fine with me," he said.

They went out that night to celebrate. At a seafood restaurant in the Flats she explained the details of the job—she'd be a staff case worker with the Madison County Department of Social Services, a field for which she was trained and which she had been trying to work her way into for some time—and how she came to hear about the opening (through a friend of a former classmate).

"Danielsville, Georgia," she said. "That's where we'll live."
They toasted to Danielsville.

The waiter brought a second bottle of champagne. Later, when the MasterCard was rejected, they tried the VISA.

Within a week, the transition was complete. They committed to a one-year lease in the town's only apartment complex, situated on a patch of exposed orange clay and shaded by pine trees, about a mile from the Oconee River. Two bedrooms, one bath, beige walls, no pets. The kitchen cabinets were worn and warped and did not close all the way. The water, the cost of which was not included in the rent, tasted funny—heavy and slick—and they could hear everything that went on in the next apartment when someone over there was home, which wasn't often.

During the days, she went to work and he kept his eyes open. That was her phrase as she headed out the door: "Keep your eyes open." He was on the lookout for opportunities. He had a college degree, common sense, and vague experience. Surely he'd find something here, some way by which he could make a contribution to their lives. There was a time limit, though, he knew that. Their MasterCard was maxed out. So was their Discover and one of their VISAs. Sometimes, when she was at work, he'd sit on the sofa and look around the apartment and try to figure out what they had to show for their debts. A decent stereo, that was one thing. And a funky, black metal wine rack they got at Pier One. And . . . what? He wasn't sure how it happened, but one afternoon—their eleventh day in Danielsville—he started crying and was unable to stop for more than an hour.

When he finally finished he laid a cold washcloth over his eyes until the swelling went down, then went to the Food Lion and bought stuff for chill. He had it waiting on the table when she came home from work.

"Can you believe those people next door?" she said hanging

up her jacket. He stepped out from the kitchen, holding a dish towel for no particular reason, and watched her. "They have that little boy home by himself all afternoon and all night—until one in the morning anyway. Can you believe that?"

"No."

"You made dinner. What a sweetheart."

He went into the kitchen and returned with two beers. "It's getting cold," he said, setting the bottles down. "We might as well start."

She looked at her watch and it occurred to him that it probably was too early to eat dinner.

"Sure," she said. "Okay."

She made a big deal about the food—how good it was, how she couldn't remember the last time she had chili. He didn't tell her that he charged the groceries he'd bought and that they probably could have gone out to a fairly nice dinner for less, had a fairly nice restaurant existed in this town.

At a point when neither had spoken for several minutes, she raised the beer bottle to her lips and held it there. She said, "That little boy next door—I told him if he ever was alone at night and he got frightened or anything that he should just come over here. I told him just to knock on the door."

"When was this?"

"Just now. On my way in. I saw him in the hallway."

"Oh."

"Both his parents work second shift at the meat packing plant."

He didn't say anything. What occurred to him suddenly—a notion that seemed to suck the air from the open space in his gut—was that, very soon, he'd have to start looking for work on "second shift" himself. It was a very real possibility now.

He watched her jab three or four times at the food he'd made, then set her fork down beside her plate. She didn't look right. Nothing about her did. Her brown hair didn't look right against the stark, beige wall behind her; her skin, the color of it, the tint, didn't look night in the fuzzy yellow glare of the ceiling light; the vest and blouse she wore, which he'd seen a hundred times, didn't look right. It didn't look right *here*. He imagined he was looking across the table at an artist's rendering of his wife, only the artist had inserted her image into the wrong setting. He was almost about to remark on this when she said, "I'm thinking of filing a report. At work."

He had no idea what she meant by this, and it brought on a sudden flutter of panic. "A report," was all he could say. It wasn't even a question. Just words.

"Yeah." She got up from the table and walked over to him. She shifted his chair with him still in it—and sat down on his lap. "He's only eight years old," she said. "He told me, just now. Can you imagine, a boy that age, coming home from school every day to an empty house, having to fix dinner for himself, do his homework by himself, get himself ready for bed, and going to sleep—alone. What's more," she said, "it's illegal. It's neglect."

He was still holding his fork. "And you're going to file a report?" he said, following her now.

"I'm thinking about it."

"Geez."

She looked down at him. "You don't think I should?"

"I didn't even know there was a little boy next door. What's his name?"

"Andy."

"And you invited him over here? Whenever he wants?"

"Yeah." She got up from his lap and began collecting the dishes—their dishes, wedding gifts. They didn't look right either. "He won't though," she said. "I don't think he understands how lonely he is."

Andy came over the next night. His knock startled them. They looked at each other across the room for several seconds before she finally got up from the sofa and went to open the door.

"Well, hello there," she said, taking a step back. "Come on in."

Andy shuffled into the apartment cautiously, as if on the lookout for snipers. His wide eyes shifted back and forth beneath the uneven bangs of classically orange hair. He wore a black t-shirt emblazoned with the words EVENT STAFF. No shoes—just white socks.

"Say hello to Richard," she said, closing the door.

"Hi," the boy said. "How tall are you?"

Richard, for some reason, stood up. "I don't know," he said, looking down at himself "Five-ten or so."

"Yeah, *right*," she said, heading toward the kitchen. "Would you like something to drink, Andy? Pepsi?"

"Okay. "

"Maybe I'm more like five-nine," Richard said. "How tall are you?"

"Four-one and three-quarters," Andy said, then lowered himself onto the edge of the sofa. "I'm shortest in my class but for one kid."

Richard hadn't planned on replying to this, but after waiting through several seconds of silence, he decided he probably should. "That's all right," he said, still standing. "You're a late bloomer."

Andy shrugged. "Yeah." Then he said, "What's that lady's name?"

Richard finally sat back down in the adjacent chair and picked up the *Sports Illustrated* he'd been reading. "What lady?"

"The one in the kitchen."

"Oh. That's Sarah."

Andy leaned back. "Sarah." His feet barely reached the edge of the sofa. He sat there and looked around the room. He looked over toward the TV, which was off, then he leaned over to his left and picked up a framed picture of Sarah and Richard—a wedding shot—from the endtable. He examined it for a moment, then glanced up at Richard, comparing.

Sarah returned carrying a big plastic tumbler full of Pepsi, ice clunking against the sides. Richard let out a breath. She positioned a coaster on the coffee table and set the cup down on it. "That was our wedding," she said.

Andy still stared down at the picture, which featured the newlyweds in the traditional wedding cake-in-your-face pose. "That cake looks good."

Sarah giggled, plopped down onto the sofa, leaned in so she could have a good look at the picture, too. "I don't even remember," she said, and giggled some more.

"My momma and daddy had a wedding," Andy said. Richard, now, noticed a much thicker southern drawl in the boy's voice than he had before. "But they didn't have no cake."

Sarah took the picture from Andy and placed it back on the endtable. "Would you like to watch TV?" she asked.

Andy nodded.

"All right. There's the remote. Go ahead and put on whatever you want."

The boy picked up the remote and held it in his hand. Then he aimed it at the television. When the screen flickered and flashed to life, Andy lowered the remote to his lap. After a minute Richard recognized the show—a courtroom drama that had been popular several years back. For whatever reason, though, Andy made no move to change the channel.

"This is what you want to watch?" Sarah asked.

"Yeah," Andy said. "This is good."

"Well, all right," Sarah said.

So the show stayed on and Richard went back to his magazine article. Sarah asked questions. Have you finished your homework? Did you take your bath? Have you had your dinner? Andy had successfully accomplished all of these tasks but let it slip (unwittingly, Richard guessed) that he was having trouble in math.

"Why don't you run next door and get your math homework," Sarah suggested, "and we'll go over it."

Richard cringed, and was about to say something—something joking and dismissive and accompanied by a chuckle—but Andy stood up, said, "Okay," and headed for the door.

"Are you sure you should be doing this?" Richard said, once Andy was out of the room.

Sarah pinched the bridge of her nose. She closed her eyes. "That poor kid," she said.

Richard got up and went to the coffee table. He picked up the remote and began scanning channels.

"You could help me here, you know," Sarah said. She was leaning back now, as though exhausted from having run a long distance. Strands of hair stuck haphazardly to the sides of her face.

"Help how?" Richard said. He kept flipping channels.

"I don't know," she said. "Show a little support."

"Support for who? Look, Sarah, I just think we have enough problems without sticking our noses into someone else's."

"Richard, it's my job."

His knees did a funny wobbling thing. He wasn't sure if this reference to her job wasn't in some way a stab at his not having one. She sat looking up at him, arms folded above her head as if in some bizarre surrender. "I'm only say—" he began, but then stopped when Andy pushed open the door and came back into the apartment—noticeably more at ease this time—with a textbook under his arm. As he approached the sofa, he smiled.

"All right," Richard said. He was still standing at the coffee table, remote in hand. Sarah sat forward. Briefly, expertly, she touched his leg.

As she took her hand away, Andy slipped through the space where it had been, between Richard and Sarah, and settled himself back on the sofa. He opened the book across his lap, noisily flipped through some pages. "We're doing money," he said. "Learning how to make change."

* * *

Andy's bedtime was nine, or so he said. At ten it was decided that he should leave a note for his parents—so they would know to stop by and get him when they got home—and sack out on Sarah and Richard's sofa. Richard didn't think it was such a good idea.

"This isn't a good idea," he said. He was sitting on one end of the sofa, Sarah on the other, and Andy lay stretched out between them, mouth open, snoring lightly from the back of his throat.

"He's so innocent," Sarah said. She reached down and stroked Andy's red hair with her fingers.

"Innocent of what?" Richard said, much louder than he had planned. "Just what exactly is the crime here, Sarah?"

She removed her hand and looked across the sleeping boy at her husband. "Where have you been?" she said. The question, he immediately understood from her voice, was to be taken literally. She wanted to know where he's been.

"Sarah," he said. "We . . . we have so many bills."

She squeezed her eyes shut for several seconds. When she opened them she said, in a harsh whisper Richard found particularly disturbing, "This boy does not belong. Anywhere. Weren't you listening to him? Did you hear anything he said? No friends. When can he ever see them? No one's allowed to come over when his parents aren't home, which is always. And of course he can't go anywhere. Not to mention that he only sees his parents—either of them—for a few hours on the weekends. This is an eight-year-old boy and tonight is the first time he's gone to sleep on a school night with an adult in the house in who-knows-how-long. This is his life." She leaned back into the sofa and closed her eyes again. For a moment, Richard thought she'd fallen asleep. But then, her eyes still closed, all lines gone from her forehead, she said, "That won't happen to our child— if we ever get around to having one. Our child will belong." Then she opened her eyes and looked over at Richard. "Do you hear me?"

* * *

The knock woke him. Sarah, who had to get up at six, had gone to bed, leaving Richard to wait up for Andy's parents to get home. It was one-fifteen. An infomercial for some sort of cooking apparatus that to Richard looked like a medieval torturing device was on the television. The two hosts were very enthusiastic about its many features.

Richard did not get up. He watched the infomercial, watched the man in the apron extract two triangular sandwich wedges from between the metal plates, and Richard found that this actually succeeded in making him hungry.

When the second knock came he got up from the sofa. He leaned over Andy and gave a soft poke to the boy's shoulder. "Hey, Andy," he said. "Your mom's here, buddy. Or someone anyway."

The boy stiffened, as if being struck by an electric prod. He lifted his head, eyes struggling to open but only able to form slits, and looked around. One sock dangled limply, the top elastic gripping the middle of Andy's foot.

"Let's go, pal," Richard said, then went to the door. When he opened it he found a woman's clenched fist in mid-backswing, preparing to knock again.

"Oh," the woman said, and held her fist in the air by her ear. Richard thought it looked like she was cheering for something. "Hi."

They both turned and looked toward Andy, who sat on the sofa, clenching the cushions next to him, looking perplexed.

"Oh, my," the woman said. She was only about five feet tall, light freckles from forehead to neck. Andy was definitely her son. "Did he just barge in on y'all?"

"No, no," Richard said. "We were just hanging out. That's all. Come on in." He turned to Andy. "How are you doing over there, champ? Think you can pull yourself together?"

Andy just stared at them, dazed.

"He's been asleep for a while," Richard said.

The woman walked over toward the sofa. "Come on, Andrew," she said. "Get up now. We'll get you over to your bed." She took Andy by the arm and pulled him up. "Get a hold of yourself now, Andrew, for goodness sake."

Richard guessed the woman to be about thirty. Her navy blue shirt, he noticed, had dark stains on it that he hoped were not blood from the meat-packing plant. The image of her in such a place did not work in his mind. He couldn't see her there, packing meat, or whatever. He wished there was a way to say this to her, but he shuddered at the thought of how the words might sound. He swallowed.

Andy's mother knelt down. She fixed his sock, smoothed down the hair around his face. "Let's go, sweetie," she said. "Take Momma's hand."

Andy did as he was instructed. As they brushed past Richard to the open door, the woman turned in Richard's direction, lowered her eyes to his throat, and flashed a brief, self-conscious smile before leading Andy, math book under his arm, out into the hallway. She said nothing. Richard stood with his hand on the doorknob. He waited until he heard keys jingle and deadbolts unclamp before gently closing his own door.

"What'd she say?" Sarah asked as Richard slid into bed next to her. The room was dark and Richard had tried to be quiet, but he realized that it didn't matter. Sarah had been awake all along.

"Not much," Richard said.

Sarah shifted around next to him. "Well, did she seem embarrassed or anything?"

"No. Not really. I don't think so." He found that suddenly he was not very tired.

"Did she say thank you? Did she at least *thank* us for taking care of her kid tonight?"

Richard thought, staring up at the ceiling. His eyes were open but they might as well have been closed. He couldn't remember the woman saying thank you. She didn't even introduce herself, now that he thought about it. "Yeah," he said. "I'm pretty sure she did."

Sarah exhaled loudly, shifted again.

"Honey," Richard said. His next words were going to be, He's not even our kid, but something stopped him—a realization of sorts, but one he could not identify. A sudden burst of ambiguous clarity overcame him and frightened him and he knew the thing for him to do was to reach across and pull his wife over to him and hold her and try to soothe her, to administer to whatever it was that needed soothing. But he didn't. He felt incapable of even that and he lay next to her, trying to quell the awful fluttering sensation in his stomach. At some point, he hoped, he would forget all this.

He'd soon find that the awful feeling in his stomach would diminish a little each night, after each time he turned Andy back over to his mother.

"Okay, Andy," she'd call from the doorway. "Time to come on home now."

But Richard didn't feel right about anything. This routine had gone on for more than a week, and still the woman hadn't introduced herself. (Her name was Nicole. They knew that only because Sarah, fed up with Richard's continual failures, finally asked Andy.) It was on this same night that Richard slid into bed, settled himself, and realized that his stomach was absolutely still. No fluttering or twisting sensations. Nothing. Then, as if it had been intentionally withheld from his memory until that moment, he thought of their debts, and the fluttering returned with a rush, with renewed intensity.

"Oh my God," he said out loud.

He found their debts to be the root of all problems. The fact was, it occurred to him, they could not get by. They could not have children. They could not be happy. Not until their debts were gone. And this he now found to be his own fault. He closed his eyes, opened them. The ceiling was grey. Shadows from the streetlamp across the street stretched diagonally to the far corner above the dresser. Even if he got a job tomorrow, he thought, they could only keep up. But there were no jobs anyway. He'd already applied for several jobs for which he believed himself to be overqualified, and did not even receive an interview. Probably, he thought, those jobs were going to nephews, or brothers-in-law. That was probably it. Sarah coughed and turned over, put her back to him, which he found to be appropriate. He reached across and touched the warm skin at the back of her neck, and suddenly his stomach constricted and he understood with absolute certainty that he would never in his life have a career, an occupation that defined him, and for some reason he decided that this was all he really wanted out of life. If he could have that, well, then maybe he could be happy. But the problem was he couldn't imagine it. He couldn't imagine ever being able to say "I'm an accountant" if someone were to ask, or, "I work for IBM," or, like his wife, "I'm a social worker." He could not imagine a set of circumstances that would ever allow him to speak in such a way. The facts were that he had a college degree in liberal arts and experience selling radio advertising airtime and coordinating the details of customer meetings for a uniform rental company in Solon, Ohio. He believed he was qualified to do just about anything, which meant almost nothing.

He figured that in the time he had been lying in bed the interest on their credit cards had cost them about ten bucks. Tomorrow, he decided, he'd go down to the meat-packing plant and take whatever they offered; then he turned onto his side, pulled Sarah tight against his chest, and tried to let the rhythm of his own breathing fall in with the calm, measured cadence of hers.

The next day he waited for her to come home but she didn't. At six Andy came over, and at six-thirty she called and said that, obviously, she was going to be late.

"I'm working on a new case," she told him, "and I want to make sure of a few details before I submit it for investigation tomorrow."

"Oh," he said. He stood in the kitchen. Through the doorway he could see Andy sitting on the sofa, ankles crossed, watching television. "I got a job at the meat-packing plant," he said. "I start tomorrow."

She didn't answer. He reached out, turned on the faucet and let the water run for a few seconds, then he shut it off. "Sarah?" he said.

"I heard you, Richard. It'll help."

"Yeah. That's what I was thinking."

"I have to go now," she said. "I want to get this done. Otherwise I'll think too much about it and I won't—" She stopped.

"What?"

"Nothing. Just . . . I'll be home in an hour. Maybe two. Is Andy with you?"

"Yeah."

"Okay. Good."

"Sarah," Richard said. He heard Andy's giggles coming from the living room. "Don't."

"Don't what?" Richard suddenly noticed she was whispering. "Make sure he gets something to eat," she said. "I'll see you in a couple of hours." Then she said, "All right, bye now," and hung up.

Richard went into the living room and stood over Andy. A sitcom was on television and Andy waited for an exchange between characters to end and the audience laughter to begin before looking up. When he finally did, Richard said, "You hungry?"

Andy shrugged, looked back to the TV, then up at Richard again.

"All right then," Richard said. "Get your jacket. We'll eat later."

"Where we goin'?"

"Just come on," Richard said. "You'll like it."

"I *won't* like it," Andy said matter-of-factly.

"How do you know?"

Andy shrugged again.

"Come on, Andy," Richard said. "You're my pal, aren't you?" He went over to the TV and shut it off. Andy's eyes shifted up to Richard. "I need you to help me with something very important. Think you can handle it?"

Andy's eyes widened. He thought for a moment. "What?"

But Richard wasn't quite sure himself. He went back into the kitchen, to the basket by the toaster where he kept all of their bills, and took the stack up in his hand. He felt his stomach bottom out, just completely empty itself of all weight and feeling. What are you doing? he thought.

"What are you doing?" Andy called from the living room.

"I don't know," Richard said. "I mean, I'm just getting something. Are you ready?" He came back into the living room, the fat stack of bills in his hand.

"Yup," Andy said, standing. "I'm ready. Ain't Miss Sarah gonna come?"

"No. Just us. Just the men." Richard opened the door. "Let's go."

They descended the two flights of stairs and went out the front door. The night air was chilly and Richard immediately remembered he'd forgotten to follow through with his instructions for Andy to get a jacket. The wind was calm, though, and Richard's skin adjusted quickly to the chill. And Andy didn't seem to mind. The boy settled into a trot to keep up with Richard's hasty steps and every now and then belted out a few bars of "I Guess I'll Go Eat Worms."

They headed up the gravel driveway to the streetlamp and when they reached the main road they turned right. After two minutes or so the glare diminished behind them to the point where no light was produced. They kept going, high, dark grass alongside, an occasional car or pickup speeding by on its way to Athens, until finally Richard admitted to himself what he suspected all along to be true: they were headed to the Oconee River bridge on Route 29, and when they got there, all of their bills—his and Sarah's—were going to commit suicide.

"What'chu laughing at?" Andy said. His breath was a little short but otherwise seemed unencumbered.

"I wasn't laughing," Richard said, thinking Andy looked even shorter than usual from this angle.

"Yes, you were," Andy said, then laughed himself.

"You think that's funny," Richard said, and Andy laughed harder.

They kept on, up a slight grade, past Frederickson's Angus Farm, another half-mile past that. Andy never asked where they were going; he didn't seem to care. He sang another verse of the worms song that didn't make any sense (Richard believed he was making up the words as he went along now) then rambled on about how when he got his growth spurt he'd be the best athlete in his school.

"What's your sport?" Richard asked.

"All of them."

"Yeah. But which is your favorite?"

"Football. I got great moves," and then he demonstrated a couple of them on the gravel shoulder of the road, cutting and juking away from imaginary tacklers.

"Not bad," Richard said.

"My daddy says I'm gonna be the next Hershel Walker. He was at Georgia, you know."

Richard reached over and cuffed the boy playfully behind the head. "You weren't even born yet, you little squirt."

"I've seen him, though. On television." Then he slipped out from under Richard's hand and orchestrated some more exaggerated, awkward, hip-turning moves.

Richard watched as he walked, smiling for some reason he could not quite identify, until something occurred to him suddenly. Andy would be small his entire life. It was a certainty to him now. Richard felt bad having this knowledge but at the same time he knew that the sooner Andy accepted this fact, the better off he'd be. Things very rarely work out the way you think—or hope—they will. Just holding on, believing that somewhere down the road things will magically get better, did no good. New jobs, a new place, a new beginning, were supposed to solve all of Richard and Sarah's problems. Well, he thought, they haven't. He felt worse than ever, and he suspected Sarah did, too. And right now she was at her new job figuring out how to "help" this boy who Richard had coerced into helping him do a stupid, stupid thing. But life doesn't always work itself out and Richard had decided that something had to pay for such an injustice. Starting with these goddamn bills.

A car's headlights appeared in front of them. As it approached Richard noticed that the car nearly straddled the center line and was, possibly, drifting toward them. He took Andy, who was in the middle of an intricate spin move, by the shoulder and pulled him farther off the road, placing himself between the boy and the oncoming car.

"What?" Andy said, then swung around and watched as the car—a big, late model American job—sped past. "Whoa, " Andy said. "That boy musta been drinking."

"Maybe," Richard said.

"You didn't have to grab me, though. He'd of missed me. Watch this." Andy then ran out ahead and launched into a three-sixty spin followed by some sort of lunge that resulted in the boy depositing himself onto his back in the high grass beyond the road shoulder.

Richard stopped walking. "Nice one. You all right?"

"Yeah." Andy picked himself up and returned to the roadside. "I just tripped on a rock is all. A damn rock."

"A damn rock, huh?"

Andy looked up at Richard. "Yeah," he said, and turned away as casually as he could.

"Okay," Richard said.

They started walking again and before either of them said another word they came to the little arched bridge that traversed the Oconee. A sign announced, "Bridge Freezes Before Road Surface."

"They's cottonmouths in this river," Andy said as they took their first steps onto the bridge.

Richard brushed his fingers across the stack of bills he'd stuffed down the front of his pants. "Good."

"Is this where we was headed?" Andy asked.

"This is it."

Andy tried to peer over the bridge's paltry concrete wall, but he was too short. When they reached the middle of the slight arch Richard took hold under Andy's arms and lifted him onto the flat, wide top of the wall. Andy turned and dangled his feet over the outside edge. "I coulda climbed," he said.

"Sure," Richard said. "I know."

"What're we doing?"

"Performing a ritual of sacrifice. Here." Richard took an envelope from the front of his pants and handed it to Andy. From the white light of the moon Richard saw that it was their Discover Card bill. Minimum payment, $106. "Go ahead. Toss 'er in."

Andy examined the envelope. "Sacrifice," he said. Below them, Richard could hear the wet, moving sounds of the river, but when he looked out over the edge all he could see was blackness.

"Sounds like the water's moving pretty fast," Richard said, though he had no idea if this were true, or what it meant.

Andy looked him over skeptically, holding the Discover bill up around his ear.

"Go on," Richard said, and Andy let go of the envelope. They watched it flutter partway down and then disappear. They kept looking over the edge, as if waiting for a splash, for several seconds, and then Andy turned to Richard.

"Good," Richard said. "Ready for another?"

Andy shrugged. He didn't look to be having as much fun as Richard had anticipated. In fact, he looked a little distraught, maybe even like he might be sick. Richard held out another bill. VISA. "Let 'er fly, tiger," he said.

Andy swallowed. "I don't want to."

"Why not?"

"I just don't."

"You have to have a reason, don't you?"

"Yeah."

"Well, what is it?"

"I don't know."

"Fine," Richard said, and held the bill out over the bridge's wall himself.

"Don't," Andy said. "Don't," and he leaned out, stabbing at the envelope with his hand. Richard pulled away and Andy's momentum carried the weight of his little upper body out beyond the edge of the wall. He gave a quick, bleating squeal, and flailed his arms in a swimming motion to try and catch his balance. After a moment of dumb confusion, Richard grabbed the boy by the shirt with his free hand and settled him again.

But Andy was shaken. His eyes were so wide they seemed to Richard to be making noise—high-pitched screams similar to the one Andy had just released—and his freckles seemed brighter, glowing through the darkness. He was breathing quickly.

"Take it easy, pal," Richard said, and touched the boy on the shoulder. "It's okay. You're not gonna fall."

Andy was stiff beneath Richard's hand. "I wanna go back home now," he said. "My momma's home."

"No, Andy. She's not. It's only eight o'clock. She won't be home for another five hours."

Andy wet his lips. He looked up the road in one direction and then the other.

"Don't you wanna help me with my ritual?" Richard said.

The boy shook his head. "No. I don't like it."

"All right then. We won't do it."

"I think my momma might be home now."

"No, Andy. I told you."

Andy slid around so that his legs now dangled off the inside of the wall. He braced himself with his hands and looked down, evaluating the drop. Then he said, "Could you help me down?"

"Sure thing." Richard stuffed the VISA bill down the front of his pants with the others. He lifted Andy down and they stood on the side of the road for a minute or two. Richard looked up. No stars. When he looked back down he found Andy with his head tilted back, checking for whatever it was he believed Richard had been searching for. "Okay now?" Richard asked.

Andy kept his head back. "Yeah."

"What're you looking at?"

Andy looked down, gave his head a shake as if knocking out cobwebs. "I don't know. Nothin'."

Richard meant to say something reassuring, like he should have said to Sarah a few nights back, something fatherly, something an older brother might say. Exactly what, he wasn't sure, but before he could say anything at all a set of headlights appeared from the north and he froze. The car continued toward them and after it emerged from a curve in the road a couple hundred yards away, Richard recognized it as Sarah's Nissan. He thought of the bills stuffed down his pants and suddenly he recognized in himself an unaccounted-for urge to destroy the evidence.

"Just stay there, Andy," Richard said. "It's all right." As soon as he spoke the words, though, it occurred to him that there was no reason why anything *wouldn't* be all right, and that his saying this probably put it in Andy's mind that something wasn't. "It's just Sarah."

Andy took a step forward, toward the road surface, and watched the headlights creep closer. He held up a hand and waved. The car slowed and when it got to within fifty yards or so, its high beams flicked on, illuminating everything. Richard and Andy shielded their eyes and turned away. The car pulled over to the side of Route 29, just beyond the far threshold to the bridge, and stopped. But its high beams stayed on.

"What in the world . . ." Richard heard his wife say. Then he heard the car door slam closed and Sarah's footsteps crunching in the roadside gravel. "What's going on? Richard? Andy, are you okay? What are you guys doing out here?"

Richard, face turned away from the car, touched the bills in his pants, wishing he'd tossed them all.

"We were doing a sacrifice," Andy said. "That's all."

"Excuse me?" Sarah said. "Richard?"

He turned toward her but couldn't see anything except a gold burst of light, a fuzzy aureole around the outer fringe of his vision, and the black, human form of his wife off to the side. He tried to zero in on this shape but the longer he looked the more it lost focus. "Did you do it?" he asked. "Did you make the report?"

"Richard," she said sharply.

"Did you?"

She didn't answer right away. Richard tried to make out what she was doing but he couldn't. He knew all he had to do was move a little to one side so the light wasn't directly in his face but he was conscious of the fact that he chose not to. He also knew that she had a perfect, well lit view of him. There was no way he could hide, and this suited him fine. He waited. Finally she said, "Yes, I filed it. Well, I have everything typed up, ready. I'm going to file it in the morning. What's this 'sacrifice' stuff?"

"I was going to offer up our bills to the Oconee River gods," he said, and made a motion with his head toward the far side of the bridge's protective wall. "But Andy stopped me." When she offered no response, he added, "Tomorrow morning I start at the meat-packing plant."

"I know," she said. "You told me. People do that, you know."

"Yeah, I know they do." He turned and searched the glare until he found Andy standing a few steps off to his right, near the wall, watching the conversation that was taking place, a look that Richard first identified as terror, then revised to simple worry, on his face. "I know they do," Richard said again. "Both of Andy's parents do." He reached down the front of his jeans then and took out the stack of bills. With the aid of the headlights he shuffled through it, noticing each company name and address, taking mental note of which ones were overdue. Then he went over to Andy and held the stack out to him. "Here," he said. "Hold onto these for me. Before I do anything else stupid."

Andy took them. "Okay," he said.

Richard knelt down beside the boy. He put a hand on his back, feeling the tiny, brittle bones of his ribs and spine. "Remember what you said to me when I was about to throw those into the river? Right before you nearly fell in yourself. Remember that word?"

Andy blinked, and Richard silently mouthed the word. "I think Miss Sarah needs to hear you say that to her now. She needs to hear it from you."

Andy looked into Richard's eyes for several seconds, revealing nothing. Half of the boy's face was lost in the shadows thrown from the headlights, but the other half had regained its original color, freckles dancing. He blinked twice more, then turned toward the source of light.

Apart

I WAS CUTTING THE GRASS when I remembered something that happened to me when I was eleven. This was on a Saturday and my allergies were getting ready to really kick in.

I'd been allowing these moments to happen more and more lately—brooding on things over which I no longer had any control, that is. This was becoming a source of tremendous disappointment to me. There was a time in my life when I considered myself to be pretty strongminded, focused. In college, when a psychiatrist came into our psych class and tried to demonstrate the "powers of the mind" by putting a bunch of us under hypnosis, I was the only one (there were seven or eight of us up there in front of the class) who wouldn't give. I gave him a fair shot at it, too—I closed my eyes, tried to picture myself floating in water, clouds and all that. But he didn't even come close.

That day seemed a long way away now. Ancient history.

So I guess I shouldn't have been surprised when I felt my wife shaking me by the elbow, trying to snap me out of whatever I was in while I stood there behind the Toro. She tilted her head at me and made this twisting motion with her wrist, meaning for me to turn the motor off.

"What in the world are you doing?" she said, nearly laughing, once we could hear each other.

"I just remembered something," I said.

"You did?" She leaned in toward me, like I was just the oddest thing she'd ever seen. The sun behind her was reflecting off the drain pipe running along the roof of our house. It made her blond hair look blistering white.

"Yeah," I said. "I remembered something my mom said right before she left us. Left my dad, I mean."

My wife pulled back a step. She wanted to laugh. She wanted me to say something silly so she could slap me in the arm and tell me, showing all her teeth like she does, to quit screwing around and finish the lawn so we could actually do something, seeing as how it was Saturday. So I felt bad for having told her the real reason she caught me standing in our front yard like a statue behind the lawnmower. I'd only cut about three strips. See, I'd never really been much into household maintenance, lawn care and all that. I'm allergic to grass clippings for one thing. I once sneezed seventeen consecutive times. "It was in *her* voice, too," I added.

"What was?"

"The thing I just remembered."

"So, are you saying you'd forgotten this?" She exhaled loudly. "Until now, of course."

"I guess not," I said. "I just kind of re-remembered it." I knew this sounded just as stupid to her as it did to me.

She made a sour face, squeezing her eyes up into her forehead. "How do you just re-remember something like that?"

"I don't know. It just happens."

"Well . . . stop it," she said.

"Okay." I bent down then and gave the cord on the mower a tug. When the motor roared back to life and I straightened again, I saw Laura walking across the lawn to the front door. I thought about what I had told her as I marched back and forth across our yard. It's activities like this—mowing the lawn—that have always provided the perfect forum for what I shamelessly consider my most profound thinking. In the shower is actually my favorite. Laura's caught me in there many times, just standing under the gradually cooling water, pruned and late for work. I memorized my marriage proposal speech in the shower. But mowing the lawn is a similar sort of mindless, necessary activity that allows the same warped focus, and I even thought how when I finished mowing the grass I'd have to take a shower.

But these thoughts came to me in between images of my mother, standing over my brother and me, a green garbage bag full of clothes slung over her shoulder, on one of her stops at the house "to pick up her things." Usually we were in school and weren't around for these stops. We'd come home each day and a little more stuff would be gone. But this time we were home. I'm not sure why. We must have had a half day or something that she wasn't aware of, but I can't really say. The point is: we're standing there, right? Larry and me. We're in the kitchen and Larry's got a glass of lemonade and the three of us are all looking at each other like, Who the hell *are* these people? and afraid one of us'll make a noise in our throats that we'll all be ashamed of. It was that awkward. Really. Finally my mom (who was wearing these black cowboy boots I'd never seen before—brand new they looked like) pipes up and says, "If you come across anything I missed, just put it aside somewhere and I'll pop by later and pick it up." (*Pop by!*) Then she smiles, and Larry and I nod like buffoons, eager to help out.

All this was bad enough, but it's not what snuck up and hit me broadside while I was cutting the grass. The thing that came to me and accomplished what that college psychiatrist could not, was spoken a couple of minutes later, just as my mother was walking out the door for what would be the last time. She stopped and turned to us in front of the open door. A breeze blew in rustling her Hefty bag, and a painfully bright red orange sun shone over her shoulder. What she said, very cheerfully, like a hotel concierge, was, "Call if you need anything."

The true lunacy of the words didn't register with me then. In fact I remember at the time figuring, Sure, okay, I'll just call if I need anything. I can do that. I never did, though, and in the middle of that third strip of lawn those words made a little more sense to me. They presented themselves for what they really were:

nothing. I had my mother's words figured out from all angles while I cut that grass. Now, if I'd had to actually explain my enlightenment to another person, I'm sure I wouldn't have been able to; but, man, from behind that lawnmower it was elementary. I was in tune, you know?

The front yard I cut in straight, horizontal strips starting down by the road and working my way up to the front door as usual; then I tried something new with the back yard. I cut a swatch around the entire outer boundary of the yard (kind of a warning track) then worked my way inside the perimeter in a swirling pattern, like a zamboni would. About halfway through I noticed my eyes had stopped itching and I hadn't sneezed in a while. I kept at it until I was maneuvering the mower in quick, tight circles in the middle of the yard, and the loop finally closed in around itself.

When I walked into the kitchen from the back porch, Laura told me she wanted to go to the polo matches. I wasn't quite sure how to react to this and in response, unintentionally, I made this airy sound from my nose like a horse.

"I'm serious," she said. "It doesn't start till four. We can make it if you don't take one of your epic-long showers."

"The polo matches," I said. I wanted lemonade (I'm not sure why since I don't particularly like it) and started opening and closing cupboards looking for a can of mix. "Do we have any lemonade?" I asked, looking across a shelf.

"Have we *ever* had lemonade?" she said.

I swung the cupboard door shut and turned to her. She had put on a blue sundress. Very pretty. Her hair was pushed back behind her ears and she looked too clean to touch. "The polo matches?" I said. There were tiny clippings of grass stuck all through the damp hairs of my forearm.

"It's culture," she said and leaned her elbows back on the counter. "These kinds of things go on, you know."

"Lots of things go on," I said. "Gang warfare *goes on*. That doesn't necessarily mean we have to be there to watch."

She picked at her dress with two fingers as if it were statically pressed against her legs. The dress hung loosely, perfectly, the hem just above her knees.

"The polo matches," I said. "All right. Give me ten minutes." I headed down the hall.

Upstairs, I wanted to take a quick shower. Though I tried not to, quite consciously fought it in fact, I started thinking about something and I couldn't get it out of my head: I wondered how you can love someone, and then not love someone. Water pounded my shoulders and I wondered when it is that you begin noticing this change, what that feels like. I wondered what it would take for me to not love Laura anymore, for my feelings toward her to deteriorate to the point where I didn't want to be around her, and wanted her out of my life. Then I tried to imagine that this was happening. I pretended I had just realized that Laura and I had grown apart and I didn't want to live with her anymore. I tried to plan how I'd break this to her, how I'd comfort her when she cried (I assumed she'd cry) but it really wouldn't bother me because of course I didn't love her anymore. This scenario made me feel devious, though, and embarrassingly immature; and besides, I figured it might be a little too neurotic, even for me, so I stopped and thought about my parents some more, how I'd never been able to shake how disgustingly pleasant the whole process of their divorce was; in fact I used to wonder if it wasn't simply an extension of the marriage itself. There was no arguing that I knew of, no talk of affairs or money problems or insensitivity. When Larry and I finally worked up the nerve to ask about it our father told us Mom just wanted to try living by herself for a while. I told Laura this once, and we laughed about it. Lives change, people change, and we should have understood that on a more realistic, adult level, but we thought my parents' actions had been nothing short of ridiculous. Borderline absurd. We hadn't talked about it in a while, though, and suddenly I wondered if she still thought so.

I felt the water in the shower get slightly cooler and listened to the exhaust fan purr steadily above my head. Usually Laura would have stuck her head in the bathroom by then to hurry me up, and the fact that she hadn't yet unsettled me for a moment. It occurred to me that maybe she was only kidding about the polo matches. I flicked the water off with my foot and stepped out onto the cool yellow tiles.

In our bedroom I stood by the dresser, speculating as to what one might wear to a polo match. There might possibly be a dress code of some sort that I wasn't aware of, and I figured that whatever I chose to wear would be severely inappropriate. Even as I pulled a pair of khaki shorts from the drawer and unfolded them, I knew they were the wrong thing. I put them on anyway and moved over to the window. Laura was standing on the back porch, hugging herself as if it were cold. She was facing away from me, out toward the lawn I'd just cut, and I wondered if she could see the pattern of the grass as I could from up here. I also could see a tan bare patch in the yard near the top of the slope where the sun hit it directly. I wondered if she'd given up on the polo matches due to what must have been my lengthy shower or if she simply felt like standing out on the back porch. Certainly there was nothing wrong with that. But there was something about her, the way she clasped her own arms around her like a kind of embrace, that led me to speculate otherwise. At that moment I tried to guess what she'd do next. I closed my eyes and decided that when I opened them she'd be . . . what? I held them closed, sensing the orange haze from the afternoon sun as it filtered through my head. When I open them she'll be . . .

Damn, I thought. *I should know this.*

As I opened my eyes I conceded to myself that I had no idea what she'd be doing and then immediately saw that Laura had taken off her shoes and was walking around in the backyard, slowly, dragging her toes through the grass as she went, following exactly the circular, swirling pattern I had just cut. She was still holding herself around the shoulders, looking down at her feet.

As she made her way toward the center of the lawn, I slid the window open and leaned my head and arms out. My hair was still wet. The warm sun found my forehead and a breeze blew past from the Harrisons'. Laura did not took back at me, she did not look anywhere except down at her feet. Her blue dress actually glistened. Really. It *glistened*. She made smooth, meticulous, gliding turns; tight collapsing circles, still clutching her own arms. I wanted to say something witty to her, yet at the same time I felt a strange hesitance to disturb her.

"Maybe you should take over the lawn care duties from now on," I said then. "Looks like you got all the moves out there." When I finished I cringed a little. She stopped sharply and, without taking her hands from her arms, looked up over her shoulder at me. Her eyebrows scrunched for a moment and I thought, *What in the world did we buy this house for?* My hair was wet. My hair was wet and I was wearing these stupid, stupid shorts—these goddamn khaki shorts—that, even though she couldn't see them, seemed all the more ridiculous in the presence of her blue dress.

But I knew I shouldn't feel this way. I shouldn't be embarrassed by my shorts in the presence of my wife. I backed away from the window and slid it closed. As I heard it suck cozily against the base of the frame, Laura turned back around and, facing the line of pine trees separating our lot from York Avenue, gently rubbed her upper arms with open hands.

She was sitting on the edge of the porch when I came outside, her toes skimming back and forth across the grass. I walked up and sat beside her. Our shoulders touched and, just above the ground, our bare feet swung in a hypnotizing sequence that made me have to catch my breath. Without taking her eyes from the center of the pattern I'd made in the lawn, she said, "Okay, so what's this thing with your mother?" She leaned back and supported herself on her hands, elbows locked.

"I don't really want to talk about it," I said. If I'd known this was coming I'd have prepared more thoroughly in the shower.

"Sure you don't," she said. On the other side of the trees, someone was playing basketball. We could hear the sound of the ball bouncing on the driveway and a heavy, echoing clank when it hit the rim. Laura said, "Why haven't you ever told me before? I mean, if it's important. Is there some sort of reason I should know about? Something I've done?"

"Are we still going to the polo matches or what?"

She paused. "Yes," she said. Then, "Yes. Yes, I think we are. Absolutely."

"She told me to call if I needed anything."

"Your mother?"

"Yeah. 'Call if you need anything,' she said. Just like that." I leaned back even with her and breathed in through my nose. I remember thinking right then and there that this should be one of those moments you always remember. A moment that defines something. But what would I remember? My khaki shorts? Laura's blue dress?

"Did you ever call?" Laura said. She had not taken her eyes off the grass. The spot she stared at might've been the exact center of the lawn, if someone took enough time to do the math.

"No," I said. "I never did."

The phone started ringing inside. I jumped a little and glanced at Laura, but she never budged. "Well, did you ever need anything?" she said. "That makes a difference, whether or not you needed anything."

The phones kept ringing and I didn't know what to do. I could hear each of them: the one in the kitchen, the one upstairs in our room. They rang and rang—the answering machine must not have been turned on and this worried me a little. Laura kept her eyes to the grass, waiting I guess. I must have been waiting, too, because I sat there next to her, trying to follow her gaze across the back lawn, to see what she saw, until there finally was no sound coming from inside the house.

* * *

We went to the polo matches. Even as I searched for a place to park the car at the far end of this huge, tree-locked field of flattened tan grass, I was having trouble believing where we were. A local community group held these things a couple of times each summer but that was about all I knew about them and I'd never known anybody who'd attended one. It was difficult to tell where the actual matches were taking place. We were late and therefore the only ones presently driving around aimlessly trying to figure these things out. Had we been on time, Laura informed me, twice, we could've just followed the flow. Laura sat up with her ankle tucked underneath her and craned her neck, trying to see between trees and parked cars. "Over there," she said, pointing. "I think I see people."

I tried to find what she pointed at, but I didn't see anything but trees. "How about horses?" I said. "Do you see any horses?"

"No horses," she said. "Not yet. Just pull up next to that car there. The van."

"I'll block the path behind it if I do that." Branches hung out over the edge of the parking area and paths led in different directions. One of them must've led to the polo grounds, but we had no way of knowing which.

"What difference does it make?" Laura said. "Everybody's already there."

So I pulled in next to the van and we sat there for a moment. "Ah," I said stretching exaggeratedly. "Nothing like an afternoon at the polo matches." I tried to sound as distinguished as I could. I thought it might get a laugh.

Laura looked at me from across the seat. Her eyes were wide and as blue as her dress. She smiled. "Come on, slugger," she said, placing her hand gently on my leg, and suddenly I was sorry I'd gone back into the house before we'd left and put on a pair of jeans. "Let's go check this thing out. See what we've been missing."

We stepped out of the car and I looked across the roof at Laura. She stood there and held her head back a little, letting the sun hit her face. I watched her do that for a second or two. Then I glanced down and saw the sunlight skimming into the car from behind the row of trees in front of us. Some light caught the edge of my keys dangling from the ignition, and the sharp metallic sparkle registered in my mind just as Laura and I simultaneously swung the locked doors closed.

I stood there, my hands hanging down at my sides like dead fish. For no good reason I tapped the outside of my pockets in hopes that the keys would be in there as well. Then I tried the door handle again.

"What now?" Laura had walked several steps from the car before noticing I hadn't come around from the other side. She was in a hurry and a little aggravated by what she took to be my show of procrastination. "Are you coming?"

"Problem," I said.

She took a deep breath and let it out slowly, then closed her eyes. There was absolutely no movement in the air and when I turned away from her I realized that I still could see the sparkle of sun off the keys, which swung slightly back and forth in the ignition. "Problem," she said. "Tell me what the problem is, Zack. Hurry up."

I shifted my attention back toward Laura but I could still see the keys out of the corner of my vision, dangling there behind my reflection in the window. And at the same time I noticed that Laura was not carrying her purse. The whole thing kind of made me feel a little sick. "The keys," I said. "The keys are the problem. They're still in the car." I pointed then, as if for emphasis.

"Leave them," she said, and began heading toward where she believed the polo grounds to be. "Come on."

"We can't leave them," I said, louder than I needed to, really. I shifted my feet and patted my pockets again. "We can't just go without taking care of this first."

She stopped. "Why not?"

"Do you have your Triple-A card on you?"

"Where would I put it?" She held her hands out to her sides. "And where do you plan on calling them from, Zack?" She looked at her watch quickly, lowered her arm, then jerked it back up and looked at the watch again. "Please, Zack. Are you really going to do this now?"

I bent down and looked in the car; looking for clues, maybe. Then I heard talking and two people appeared from between the parked cars behind Laura. She did not turn around, though; she kept watching me. When the other people—a man carrying a paper bag and a woman holding on to the man's arm, both probably a little younger than we were—reached Laura they quit talking to each other and the woman said, "You guys going to this polo deal? We're so damn lost."

Laura kept looking at me. "That was the plan."

The woman giggled. "Well, do you know which way it is? We've been doing laps around here for, like, hours." She patted the man twice on the chest. "Give me a beer, hon."

The man unrolled the paper bag and pulled out a can of Budweiser. He handed one to the woman, took out another, and silently offered it to Laura. My wife swept her hands lightly across her upper arms, then reached out and took the beer.

"Laura," I said.

The woman popped open her can and held it up. "Cheers," she said.

Laura said, "You've never been to one of these either, I take it."

The woman giggled again. She and the man gave each other a confidential sideglance, then the man pulled another beer from the bag and held it out to me.

"No," I said, a little harshly. "We're in the middle of something here. Our keys are locked in the car." I tapped on the window. "I have to get them out."

The man replaced the beer and handed his bag to the woman. Then he walked over to me and peered inside the car thoughtfully. After a moment he said, "I'll be damned. Look at the bastards."

"Let me see," the woman said and skipped over to the driver's side. She moved in front of me and got right up against the glass, hands framed around her face. "Oh, shit," she said.

"Let's just go," Laura said. "It's probably halftime, or whatever they call it, by now." She took a sip of her beer. The way she held the can, standing there in the filtered sunlight, in her blue dress, made me want to smash the window with a rock.

"Can you get in, Bruce?" the woman said. As she turned from the car and looked right at me I noticed she had several freckles under each eye. "Bruce knows how to unlock cars," she said.

Bruce stepped in a little closer. "Not sure," he said. "This a ninety-one?"

I wanted Bruce and the freckled girl to go away. This was not how I wanted to solve our problem. I stared at the left front tire. "Ninety-two," I heard myself say.

"Well, see, that might be somewhat of a bitch." Bruce stuffed his hands in this pockets. "Ninety-two's when they started using the new trigger mechanisms in the locks, which I'm not very good at. This was a ninety-one I'd have the sucker open in no time with a stick."

"With a stick," I repeated, kind of stupidly.

Bruce shrugged. "Or whatever."

An expanding, swooshing sound rose above the trees then. It sounded like wind blowing and rustling leaves, only deeper, thicker, and I think all four of us realized at the same time that it was the sound of people cheering.

"Oh, see. Someone must've scored," Laura said. "It came from that direction. Are you coming, Zack? I can't believe this. We're here. We drove all the way here and now we're standing in the parking lot." She drained the last of her beer and looked around for a place to deposit the can. Finding nothing suitable, she stood there, holding it.

I said, "Laura, we have to get these keys out. We can't just let this go."

Bruce and the freckled girl still stood around the car, watching us, appraising the situation. Then Bruce said, "Man, if this were a ninety-one . . ." He shook his head slowly.

"Maybe," the freckled girl said, "up at the game—the match—one of the people there has a phone you could use. I'll bet you those people bring phones with them just about everywhere."

"That's a possibility," Laura said. "We could call from the . . . the field."

Laura stood looking down at the grass reaching up around her shins, holding the empty beer can in her hand. The sun was starting to go down now over her right shoulder and streaks of light skirted between the spread branches of the trees. She kicked timidly at something in the tall grass, and I remember thinking, *This isn't funny at all*.

Finally, I said, "So, what I'm hearing is, you want to go to the polo match, and ask one of the people there to borrow their cellular phone so we can call Triple-A to come get our keys out of the car. That's pretty much what you want to do, right?"

"Unless this was a ninety-one," Bruce said.

"No," Laura said. "I said it was a possibility. Which it is. What I'd really like to do is follow the sound of that cheering to the polo match. I want to watch the polo match without worrying about things we can't control. Then, when it's over, I want to come back here and the two of us'll deal with this . . . setback. That's pretty much what I want to do." She looked down at the empty beer can in her hand and I noticed the tiny muscles in her cheeks twitch upward a couple of quick times and her lips stretch out into something like a smile, but it wasn't a smile. Then she lifted her head back up. "Can we do that, do you think?"

Bruce cracked open another beer; I felt it spray lightly on the back of my arm. "Ninety-two's are a bitch, though. Never underestimate the stubbornness of a ninety-two. That's what I have to say about it."

"Bruce," the freckled girl said.

"Yeah?"

I was watching Laura—her skin had paled a little as the sun receded—so I couldn't know for sure, but the freckled girl must have given Bruce a look of some sort because without another word he walked quickly over to her. As he passed, Laura handed him her empty can hesitantly, as if it were a snake. He crushed it and deposited it back in the crumpled bag held by the freckled girl. Then he cleared his throat and stood with her. I tried the car door again. The chrome was hot.

"You guys married?" the girl said—I supposed—to whoever wanted to answer. When nobody did she said, "You look married."

Laura turned to her. "Thank you," she said.

"I could tell. I could tell from your, you know, your eyes."

My wife lowered hers. "Zack," she said, and I let go of the door handle. Applause roared in across the treetops again. Bruce and the girl turned toward the sound and, I swear, there was this feeling—I felt it, too—of being drawn to it. I walked over to Laura and stood with her, applause blowing through the leaves; then we felt the ground vibrate like the handle of a lawnmower, and we heard the swelling, palpitating thump-thump-thump of hooves. Many, many hooves.

"Well," Laura said. "It's about time."

Then that night, as we were getting into bed, Laura told me she wanted to have kids. Said she'd always wanted to.

Of course, I said. I know you do. So do I.

No, she said. I mean now. I want to start now. She stood at the side of the bed, as if to somehow prove that she was serious. Her hair was brushed out and hung weightless in front of her shoulders. She looked serious enough to me. I shifted under the covers. I'd been reading a magazine and I set it down on my legs. I looked at her face, which was shiny and pink from her having washed it, then at the inside of her bare, white elbow. I didn't say anything more, and to this day I'm grateful to Laura for not pressing it, not saying, Zack, did you hear me? Did you hear what I said? I've never told her how much I appreciated that gesture, or lack of one, but it made it a lot easier for me to finally laugh softly in the back of my throat, flip down her side of the covers and pat the mattress a few times (a rather weak gesture, sure, but—). Anyway, I don't know if I could've done that otherwise. All right, I said. Okay. Okay.

And afterwards, as we lay there, our bedroom window open, the smell of the grass I'd cut that afternoon and the murmurs of people leaving the Harrisons' party we weren't invited to floating in, Laura took her hand and put it on my thigh, and kept it there, and said: I need this.

Then she put her head down on my shoulder, and her hair spilled over my chin and collarbone and I felt as though I'd done something pretty terrific. Or, at the very least, that I was now capable of terrific things. She said, Why is it that men think they have to atone for every little wrong that crosses their lives? That if they don't, then they're not men?

I don't think that, I said. Do I?

She sat up on her elbows and looked at me. Light from the silent TV flickered behind her, darkening her face. Yes, she said. But you—you're fishing in an empty pond.

I waited for her to say more, and as I waited I knew this would be one of those conversations that we'd never touch on again, that in the light of day and with our eyes and throats exposed to each other and a baby in Laura's belly, between us, the words would somehow embarrass, make us cringe and turn away and cause one of us to suggest a movie, or a polo match. So for now I just watched the shadows bounce around her face, concentrated on them so hard I believed I could hear her heart pounding in her chest. And then I believed I heard another sound, a second set of beats. But that was impossible, I knew. How can a man hear what he doesn't *know* to be there? How can he ever be sure?

Hepatitis

SHE'S LATE AGAIN, and this time it's got me to wondering. The worst part happens when my little girl stands up on her own for the first time and Gail is not there to see it. I'm at the kitchen table going over some notes for a meeting in the morning and my daughter, who's been crawling around the linoleum, braces herself with the chair leg and pulls herself up. She holds it like that for a few seconds and then lets go.

"Jesus," I say.

She looks up at me, swaying, fingers moving all around, squeezing at the air.

"Holy shit," I say.

She keeps looking at me, a dark ring of grape juice around the neckline of her yellow shirt, her bangs cut unevenly. That was my fault. She looks so much like my wife, nothing like me. "Katie," I say to her. "You're standing. You're standing, aren't you?" But that sounds stupid, so I say, "Holy shit," again which is more what I feel like saying anyway.

Gail should have been home by now. I check my watch and then look out the half-moon window above the table with my chin in my hand. It's getting dark and I realize I should turn on some lights in the kitchen. The refrigerator starts to hum. Then I remember Katie and glance back down and she's still there, standing, staring at me. I don't know what to say to her at this point. She stares at me for another moment then tries to turn her head around, to look at something behind her I guess, and falls down on her padded backside.

"Boom," I say, and cringe. Katie crawls away toward the living room. A sock slips off her foot but she keeps crawling, unfazed.

I look at the papers in front of me. Some of them are stapled together and I flip through them because I feel like I should. My mind's not on it, though. When I picked Katie up at day-care earlier, one of the girls who works there approached me outside the school and said that Katie had not taken to the environment in the traditional forms that most children do. She actually said those words. I could tell the girl was nervous, frightened even, to tell me this. She kept pulling at the ends of her fingers and tossing her straight, red hair back over her shoulder. Her voice bounced around a lot, quavering. She doesn't cry, she told me. She expected crying. "It's not the crying," she said, looking past my face. She brought her fingers up to her mouth. "She just, well, she hasn't been . . . responding."

I held Katie on my hip. She grabbed at my tie. "Responding to what?"

"Well, to anything." She exhaled and looked down at the sidewalk between us. Leaves were actually in the process of falling, rocking back and forth on their way down. "Look," she said finally, "I don't want to worry you or anything. I don't want to do that at all, believe me. I mean, I haven't been here all that long so all I have to go on is instincts, along with what I've been taught. But," she looked at Katie, "it's like you're not even there. By now she should be demonstrating a little more awareness of the presence of others." She stopped and sucked her lips in. "She just seems very unaware is about the only way I can say it. Like, it's not at all uncommon for Katie to just sit for an hour or more. No toy or anything. She'll just sit there. And it's really difficult to get her attention. Usually children her age will be enthralled with anything you hold up to them: a toy, a shoe, a dish rag, a—" She stopped and looked back up at me, at my chest. She seemed exhausted. Then the nervousness came back, and I felt for her. "I'm sorry," she said. "I just thought it was something you should know. Maybe you were already aware of it."

I shook my head stupidly. "We've never done this before," I said.

"Well," she went on as if I'd interrupted her and now she had to find her place again. "Maybe . . . I don't know. Maybe it's nothing. That's all I wanted to say." She tried to smile but her face was tight. "Tell Gail I said hello."

But Gail is late. It is almost seven o'clock. Katie is in the dark living room and I haven't heard any sounds for the past couple of minutes so I get up to see what she's in to. I flip on the ceiling light and find her sitting in the middle of the floor. She has taken her other sock off and now she has one foot clenched in each of her hands. She's examining her toes or something. This seems normal to me. This is what babies do. She's playing with her feet, I tell myself, and this makes me feel a little better. Then I decide to do something. I turn off the ceiling light and leave it like that for a few seconds. Then I flick it back on. Katie is still looking at her feet. Not even a flinch. She's not wiggling her toes or anything, just loosening and tightening her grip, it seems like. I think about calling out to her. Katie, I want to say. Katie, honey. But I don't. I don't want to see what she does. She looks okay to me, like a baby, so I leave the light on and walk back to the kitchen.

Gail has never been this late before. Not without calling. She has been late pretty often the past few weeks. She says her company is in the middle of an audit and there is a lot of information gathering that needs to be done every day at the auditors' request. Sometimes they need it first thing in the morning, which means the work must get done the night before. She's never been this late, though. Not without calling; and for the first time I wonder about it.

I look back down at the papers for my meeting in the morning, which is not as important as an audit. The refrigerator motor shuts off and suddenly it is so quiet I feel a wrenching in my chest. "Katie," I say in the direction of the living room, so softly that I can barely hear myself.

* * *

Every morning is a test. We used to get up at the same time, Gail and me. Then, a while back, she started getting out of bed a little earlier each day. Just a minute or two. Barely noticeable at first. But this morning I sat up to find her fully dressed, sitting at her vanity table applying mascara while eyeing me in the mirror. As I checked the clock radio it occurred to me that I'd been doing the same thing each morning as her only in reverse, sleeping an extra minute. I looked at her in the mirror and saw myself behind her, smaller, creases all through my face, tangled in the comforter. She kept applying the mascara in smooth, even strokes, then switched eyes without taking them off of me. I felt like I'd been caught in the act of something.

"You think you can pick Katie up tonight?" she said. She looked away from me for the first time and examined her own reflection. She turned her head a little and looked at herself kind of sideways. "I'll take her on my way in. She has to be there soon."

I thought about saying *what for?* but instead I leaned back against the headboard and dragged a hand through my hair. "I can take her," I said. "Go ahead and go if you have to."

She examined her watch. "You'll be late," she said. "Just pick her up at five. Okay?" She selected a lipstick and twisted it up; she pushed out her lips, as if to kiss me in the mirror. When she finished she snapped the cap back on the tube and sat up straight in her chair. "Oh. I'm going to be late tonight, so don't forget."

"The audit?"

She stood quickly, fluidly, and checked the back of her leg for runners. "She's playing in her room right now. She's dressed. If you get up anytime soon, you could give her something to eat before I leave."

"I'm getting up," I said. I was thinking of a way to ask her to come back to bed herself.

She smoothed down the front of her skirt with her palms then looked around on the floor for something.

"What is it?" I said. "What are you looking for, Gail?"

She swung her hair over her shoulder and looked straight at me, without the mirror. I heard her take a breath. "Nothing," she said.

"Tell me."

"Five o'clock," she said. "Don't forget."

She turned and started putting stuff in her purse, makeup and other things.

"Gail," I said. "Let's go away this weekend. Let's go to . . . let's go . . . I don't know. Where? Where could we go?"

Her motions slowed. She held a plastic container of some sort in her hand for a moment, then lowered it into her purse.

"I'm serious," I said.

She lifted her eyes and regarded me in the mirror again. Suddenly I saw how pathetic I looked. My t-shirt was twisted on my body and I had made a disheveled mess of the sheets. Gail is a very well-mannered sleeper. She lies almost weightless, on her side or back; she hardly moves, never snores. It was obvious I had destroyed our bed single-handedly once she'd gotten out of it. She kept looking at me then turned to the door. Katie crawled in, mechanically, staring at her hands as she padded along. When she got to the middle of the room she stopped, as if she'd bumped into a wall with her forehead, and sat back on the carpet. She looked from Gail to me and then between us, at my tie rack hanging inside the closet door.

"Toronto. That's where we'll go. The drive up'll be magnificent." When I was done I heard the words I'd spoken. "I mean, it'll be a nice drive," I said.

Gail walked over and scooped Katie into her arms. She held her to her chest and tapped her back as if Katie were crying, but she wasn't crying. Without looking at me Gail said, "That would be nice, yes," and kept on tapping.

The refrigerator behind me clicks back on and the humming starts; rising in volume as if it were getting closer, sneaking up on me. I look at my watch but I can't see the hands because the kitchen is so dark. I can't wait for Gail any longer. It is late and Katie needs to be fed. I slide my chair out from the table and think about sticking my head into the living room, but I don't. When I open the refrigerator door to see what's inside, I notice that the refrigerator is vibrating more than it should. I can feel it in my hand. I stand there in the light it's giving off, squeezing the door handle, trying to make it stop. When we moved into the apartment we were a little confused to find that a refrigerator was not supplied. Gail was skeptical of this and was willing to bypass the apartment, even though we both liked it, in favor of a better equipped one. The last thing we need right now, she said, is to have to go out and buy a refrigerator. Something we know nothing about. But I told her not to worry. I'd take care of it. When we moved in she'd never even know the refrigerator in the kitchen hadn't come with the place, I said. So I went out and bought one. It was inexpensive because the model had been discontinued the year before, but it had an ice maker and big slots in the doors that could hold the gallon-size jugs of milk, so Gail was happy with it.

Now it's humming, moaning almost, and vibrating in my hand and I can't make it stop.

I stand there, concentrating, trying to pinpoint the source. Finally I realize it's the bottom section, where the motor is apparently, that's causing all the problems. I turn and examine the kitchen in the refrigerator's hazy yellow light. It reminds me of colorized black and white movies, where people say it looks like everyone's got hepatitis. I think, *My kitchen has hepatitis.*

I leave the door open and go to the hall closet where I keep my tool case. It is paralyzingly dark and I need to turn on the single bulb on the ceiling. From the tool case I choose a screwdriver, a hammer and pliers, since I have no idea what I might need. On my way back to the glowing refrigerator I stop across from the entrance to the living room and listen. I listen but all I hear is the refrigerator moaning.

There is a metal grille, about six inches high, that runs along the bottom of the refrigerator like a skirt. This needs to come off somehow so I can get behind it and stop the moaning, which keeps getting louder. I get down on my hands and knees and begin looking for screws. I run my fingers along the edges but I don't find any. It's still too dark down by the floor to see as well as I need to so I open the freezer for more light. There are no screws and I realize I'll have to pry the grille off somehow. Gail has never been this late before.

I take the screwdriver in my hand and slide it in between two of the slats in the grille. I maneuver the screwdriver up and down, twisting it, and then I hear a sharp snap. I know I've broken something but I have no idea what. The grille is still attached to the refrigerator and the refrigerator is still moaning and vibrating but now something else is broken, too. I sit back with my hands supporting me on the linoleum, which I know is blue but looks dull purple from the light, and wait to hear rattling sounds from some spot inside the refrigerator. The thought hits me that I should change out of my suit. There is a slimy coating on my hands from the floor underneath the refrigerator and I figure that this must be on my clothes as well. The word *tinker* comes to my mind. *I'm tinkering with the refrigerator.* I think of how I've never tinkered before—with anything really—and this makes me laugh out loud a little.

I sit there and laugh quietly for a moment then run a hand through my hair, and at that moment I remember the grime on my hands. "Shit," I say. I feel it all over. Then I hear the patting behind me. I turn awkwardly and see Katie crawling steadily into the light; steadily, hand over hand, eyes down. She looks so much like Gail, nothing like me.

"Sweetheart," I say. "Daddy's tinkering." This makes me smile again but I don't like it. Katie keeps on. It seems like she's not getting anywhere even though her hands and knees are churning at what I think is an incredible rate. When she reaches me her hand comes down on the pliers and her elbow buckles a little.

She recovers easily, though, and sits back. I try to remember when I changed her last, but can't. She looks at the pliers for a moment then reaches for them. She holds them between her knees, one hand tightly gripped around one of the handles. I can't tell if she's examining them or looking at something nearby.

"Those are pliers," I say. "Here, look." I take them from her and hold them up the way they're supposed to be held. Then I open and close them a couple times, making a clicking sound. "Watch," I say, and clamp down very lightly around the tip of her nose. I gently twist back and forth. "See?"

Katie is looking straight ahead at something in the freezer. Her arms are out at her sides, waving, as if for balance. Then she tries unsuccessfully to cross her eyes and look at what I'm doing to her. I can see the green of her eyes drifting inward and then snapping back into place. I quickly release her nose. "Anyway," I say. "Those are pliers."

I figure maybe I should drink something. I figure if Gail comes home and finds me hunched over a bottle of Jack Daniel's at the kitchen table looking morose, looking like I have hepatitis, that'd give her something to think about.

But we have no Jack Daniel's. In the cupboard over the stove where I used to keep that kind of stuff there is only grape juice (both regular and white), apple juice, nilla wafers and three cans of sliced pears. Even if we had any Jack Daniel's I know I wouldn't drink it. But just to make myself feel a little better I slide the cans over and check behind them. All that's there is a leftover jar of Gerber's blueberry buckle, Katie's favorite.

Katie is still sitting in front of the open refrigerator, my tools spilled around her.

One other thing Gail said this morning bothers me now. It hadn't before, but now it does. I was sitting up in bed, watching her, hands locked behind my neck. After she checked herself in the mirror one last time, she took her peach blazer off the back of the chair and slid it on. Her hair hung down half in front of her shoulders and half behind and her skirt shaped her in a way that made me remember other times. The top two buttons on her blouse were unfastened and I could almost smell the perfume there and I was awful close to begging her to come back to bed. But instead I said, "Gail, you look great."

Still looking in the mirror, she reached up inside the cuff of her blazer and pulled at the sleeve of her blouse so that just a sliver poked out. She said, "Thanks," and it occurs to me now, as I stand in my kitchen trying to decide what to do next, that she said it more or less the same way you'd thank the guy who just gave you your change at the newsstand: as courtesy only.

I used to say things like this to her all the time. I'd say, "You look beautiful today," or, "What a beautiful girl you are," or something like that, and she would actually blush. She would turn away and smile and press her fingers to her face and say to stop, that I was embarrassing her, which of course only made her look more beautiful. I can't say exactly what I got out of that. I don't think it had anything to do with ego. I think now it had something to do with comfort. It was reassuring for me to see her reassured, and now that her need for that has apparently gone away I wonder what will take its place.

The phone on the wall right next to my head rings and my body jumps so that I feel an aftershock running through my arms and spine. I find myself still holding the cupboard handle. The kitchen is yellow like chrome. Katie is sliding the pliers around in tiny circles on the linoleum. The phone rings again, not as loud this time it seems, and I pick it up.

"Yes?" I say. I've never answered the phone in this way before.

I hear a throat clearing. "Ms. Remick please." It is a male voice, very strangled and nasal.

"Mrs. Remick is not in," I say.

There is a pause. Then he says, "I see."

"Is there anything else?"

"Well," he says. "Perhaps. Is this Mr. Remick by chance?"

"Who is this?"

"Mr. Remick, this is Dr. Collins. Your wife scheduled an appointment for tomorrow morning and I'm afraid I have to reschedule. I left a note for my secretary to call earlier but she's gone home, and on my way out I just noticed my note to her still sitting here on the desk and it doesn't appear she's seen it. She hasn't called, has she?"

"Who?"

"My secretary."

"Oh." I look around me. The clock on the stove says it's after eight, but that clock has always been a little fast. "No," I say. "I think you're mistaken."

Dr. Collins is silent for a moment. Then I hear him breathe in deeply through his nose and let it out. "Your daughter's Katie?" he says.

I don't answer. I just wind the phone cord around my wrist.

"Mr. Remick?" He waits. "Mr. Remick, what exactly am I mistaken about?"

"I don't know." I feel completely silly in my suit. "What kind of appointment do you mean?"

I hear him moving the phone around on his end. "I'm sorry," he says. "I'm not sure I . . . I mean I didn't realize . . . You see, the appointment is for your daughter. Mrs. Remick thought maybe we should check her reflexes and hearing and related matters. Children her age should be checked for that kind of thing anyway. I'm sure she just forgot to mention it to you." I can feel my toes inside my shoes. After a minute he says, "Mr. Remick?"

"That's a good idea," I say. "Katie's fixing the refrigerator right now." I say, "She's working the front section off with a screwdriver. Soon as she gets inside she'll take care of it quick enough. She tells me the motor probably just needs cleaned out, or maybe there's a loose bolt or washer or something."

Dr. Collins chuckles clumsily on the other end. "Is she now?" he says.

"No," I say, "she's not. Actually she's scratching all hell out of the kitchen floor with a pair of pliers. Later on maybe she'll squeeze her feet for a while." I have no idea what's making me say these things.

"Well," Dr. Collins says, obviously uncomfortable, "please ask Mrs. Remick if next Monday is all right with her. Monday afternoon. If not, Wednesday is good, too. In the morning. Monday afternoon or Wednesday morning. Either one."

I hang up the phone and check for the Jack Daniel's again, this time thinking that I really would drink it if it was there. Katie stops with the pliers and looks up at me. I realize I'm getting used to the noise the refrigerator's making and wonder if anything is starting to melt inside. It also occurs to me suddenly, while I'm looking at my daughter, that Gail will not be home for a while yet tonight.

Katie is sleeping in the center of our bed, her t-shirt bunched up around her waist, when I hear the front door open at the end of the hall and Gail set her briefcase down against the wall. I hear her pause and slip off her shoes so as not to make a lot of noise on the hardwood floor. It is almost midnight, but I am awake. A little while after I hung up with Dr. Collins I fed Katie a boiled hot dog cut up into tiny pieces. I should have given her a bath, too—I really should have—but she fell asleep in her high chair, her chin tucked in against her chest; cold, mushy hot dog bits squeezed out between the fingers of her clenched fists.

Gail opens the closet door and hangs up her coat, quietly. I look around for those papers I'd meant to look at for my meeting in the morning and sit down in the chair next to the bed. The lamp on the nighttable at my side is the only light on in the room. The words in front of me make no sense. Katie is lying on her stomach at a forty-five degree angle to the rest of the bed. Her face is pressed awkwardly against a pillow and her diaper seems to have shifted on her somehow and I decide that at least she got her sleeping habits from me.

After a time Gail steps into the bedroom like she's trying not to wake anyone. I force myself to keep staring at the papers on my lap until she says something.

"Oh," she says finally, quickening her pace toward the closet, untucking her blouse from her skirt as she goes, "I thought you'd be sleeping."

"Well," I say, and then stop myself from saying something sarcastic.

Gail disappears inside the closet. "You know, Brian," she says, "I know it's tough sometimes, and you had work to do tonight and all, but you gotta watch Katie a little more closely. The refrigerator and freezer doors were wide open when I came in. I think a lot of the stuff in the freezer melted."

"I closed it once," I say. "I don't know how—"

"Well, obviously she got back into it. I don't know how she managed it, but—" She emerges from the closet wearing a teal sweatshirt and a pair of grey cotton shorts. "It's no big deal," she says. "I know, if you turn your back for even a second . . ."

"Did you get everything done at work?"

"My car's pulling to the left again," she says. "I can't stand that."

"We'll get it fixed then. And the refrigerator, too." I set the papers on the floor next to me.

"Don't give me that," she says. "I don't need that now."

"What?"

She leans over the bed and touches Katie with the back of her hand. "I didn't mean anything about the refrigerator. All I said was the door was open. That's all. You don't have to take that attitude."

"No," I say. "It's really broken. Something's . . . It really is broken. Did you get everything done at work?"

"You mean that humming sound it makes? It's *been* doing that. It's just not a very good refrigerator, Brian. We'll get another couple years out of it, tops. Haven't you noticed?"

"I guess not," I say. "It must be different, though. If you'd have heard it tonight . . ."

She goes into the bathroom and closes the door. I hear the water running. I hear things clanging against the sink and counter top. When she comes out I'll say something. I'm not exactly sure what, but I'll say something to her that will put things in the right perspective.

Katie snores softly, a hollow buzzing. She sounds like the refrigerator, only not as loud. I sit on the edge of the bed and watch her. Her lips are pursed together tightly and her eyes are just slightly open. Every so often they twitch and flutter.

Gail shuts the water off and then I don't hear anything for a minute or two. I am still in my suit; my shoes are still on. I try to think of what I've been missing, how I let so much get past me without my noticing. Then I wonder how many traits I've passed on to Katie that *can't* be seen; that can't be detected in the width of her nose or color of her hair or eyes, or even the beautiful sloppiness of her sleeping style. Things that won't show up till later. I think about what they might be and I'm not sure I want to know about them.

I get up and then decide to go back into the kitchen. As I'm collecting my papers from the floor Gail opens the door and comes out of the bathroom looking much the same as when she went in. Her face is redder, though, from her having washed it, and she has brushed her hair out, which makes me think of cotton. "Brian," she says, "you planning on going to sleep tonight?"

"In a minute," I say. Truth is, it's an option that hadn't really occurred to me. Then I say, "Gail—" and stop.

She is trying to turn down the covers without waking Katie. She puts one hand under Katie's chest and lifts up while gently sliding the covers halfway down the bed. It is pretty impressive.

I take Gail by the wrist. "Sweetheart, sit down for a minute." I guide her down next to me on the bed. We are both sitting there, knees together. "Listen," I say and rub my cheek and neck.

"What?" she says.

I realize I'm still holding her by the wrist. I take her hand and put it between my own. I pat it a couple of times. She looks at me in an important way. I know this. She wants to know what this is about. "Did you get everything done at work tonight?" I say.

She drops her eyes and looks at her bare feet on the floor. Then she takes her hand away and gets up. She goes to her vanity table and sits down as if she had a reason to and looks at something in the mirror. It is not her and it is not me. I wait for a minute and then realize she is not going to say anything. She gets up from the chair and shuffles over to the bed and lies down on the opposite side, behind me. I hear her pull the covers up over both her and Katie. "She can sleep here tonight," she says. "If it won't bother you."

"No," I say. "I mean it won't bother me."

"You should probably take your suit off before you come to bed," she says. "At least your tie."

I look down at myself. After a few seconds I hear the refrigerator click on and start humming in the kitchen. I'm not going to let it bother me. I take my suit off and fold it over the back of the chair and stand there in the swatch of light from the lamp. Gail is on her side facing the center of the bed. I bend down and flick off the lamp.

"Gail," I say. "Gail, Katie stood up tonight. In the kitchen."

It is dark and she doesn't answer. I feel my way into bed on the other side of Katie and lie there for a minute on my back, listening. Katie is snoring softly against my ear and I can't hear anything else. I reach across the bed until I feel Gail's hair. I stroke the back of her head until she sighs and I sense that she is somewhat awake.

"Gail," I say, whispering. "What should we do? We need to see someone about Katie. We need to do something."

Gail's legs move in the sheets. She shifts around some more and is still. Then she pulls her hand from the covers and reaches out and touches my hair. I remember the grime that is in it from the refrigerator, but she keeps her hand there. We lie like that for a while and then I feel like I should say something else.

I say, "Just listen, Gail. Can't you hear it?"

Ice Cream Headache

THEY EXPECT TO FIND Jarred and his friend in the lobby arcade. That was the plan going in, since the kids' movie was to let out a little before theirs. Wil and Nancy wanted to see the new Scorsese movie—a heavy drama with an R rating—but now, as they drift toward the beeps and squeals of the video games across from the ticket counters, Wil senses that perhaps the film has been a little more disturbing to his wife than she, or he, anticipated.

Jarred and Peter, a classmate whom Jarred has just recently begun to hang around with, went to see a comedy that, judging by the poster in the lobby, appears to be aimed directly at kids. But Jarred is at that age now—eleven—where thoughts of sneaking into a movie where excessive violence and gratuitous nudity might be witnessed actually seems like a good idea, and possible, especially when an accomplice is present, so Wil figures he really doesn't know *which* movie Jarred and Peter saw tonight.

Wil and Nancy pass in front of the poster for the Scorsese film and Wil intentionally looks away, hoping to divert Nancy's attention. In the movie, both the husband and wife characters engage in begrudged, mean-spirited affairs, and when this storyline was addressed on screen Wil could feel his wife shift in her seat.

"That Scorsese always has the weirdest music in his movies," Wil says. "Have you ever noticed that?"

Nancy glances at the poster, keeps her eyes there until they move past it. "No," she says. "I never have. But now that you mention it, that music was kind of weird."

"Intense."

"Yeah." She takes his hand, which surprises him.

They walk like that through the crowd of people heading in the opposite direction, those attending the nine-thirty show, toward the big glass doors at the front of the theater. Wil notices their reflection, their hand-holding, and it makes his breath a little short. It takes a couple of seconds to get it back.

In the arcade, a group of three teenage boys, shorts pulled down well below their hips, are crowded around a flashing, space-themed video machine; and, in the back, two grown men, one of them in his bare feet, aim plastic pistols at a screen and shout *blam!* each time a hit is scored. Jarred and Peter are not there.

"Hmm," Wil says.

Nancy takes an exasperated breath, releases Wil's hand.

"Not a problem," Wil says. "Let me ask the woman how long ago their movie let out. Wait here." He knows this will do no good, but it is an effort, something. He approaches the counter from the side but the white-haired woman selling tickets pays no attention to him. She just keeps taking money and punching out tickets through the computerized dispenser.

Wil clears his throat. "Excuse me," he says, but receives no response. She's heard him, though; she had to. "What time did—" Suddenly he cannot remember the name of the movie. He scans the theater lobby for the poster but can't spot it. He says, "That comedy. The one about the family that goes camping and something about a bear or something. Do you know how long ago that let out?" It occurs to him then to look up and scan the marquee above the woman's head for the title, but before he can find it she says, "About forty minutes," and hands out some change.

He finds Nancy sitting on a crimson cushioned bench near the front window. Her legs are crossed and her fingers drum nervously on her knee just below the hem of her skirt. He sits next to her, thinks for a moment. "Maybe they caught the end of another movie," he says. "On their way out. You know how that works." He lets that register for a second or two, and when he gets no response says, "Or maybe they went across the street for some ice cream."

Nancy keeps tapping. "Did he have any money?"

"I gave him a few bucks for video games."

She has nothing to say to this apparently, so they sit. Soon the line for tickets fades to an occasional straggler, usually a woman sprinting up to the counter, then being joined by a man who, Wil presumes, has been parking the car. Then activity ceases altogether, except for the buzzing and beeping of the arcade off to their left. The concession stand attendants begin closing up shop, tossing the leftover popcorn, cashing out the registers. It is obvious to Wil that all of the late showings are now in progress. He leans back onto the bench, stretches his legs out in front of him. "That kid," he says, and forces a laugh.

Nancy sits forward, unamused. Wil senses that she is waiting for him to suggest a solution. But the truth is he believes it would be foolish to leave this spot. Jarred knows where they are and if he and Peter come back to find Nancy and him gone, that would only make things worse. He wishes Nancy weren't so quick to detect tragedy, but ever since she found out about Wil and the waitress at the Pittsburgh Hilton, where Wil was staying while on business there, she has no composure, no imagination for anything. Or maybe it's too much imagination. In any case, the fact that she, not so long before, had a short-lived but completely effective affair with a mutual friend of theirs should have, he believes, put her in a position to be more understanding with regard to his subsequent, isolated slipup. But it hasn't. In fact, it seems worse; and Wil has been forced to admit to himself that, somehow, that makes sense.

The two men leave the arcade, one of them glancing down at what Wil is sure is his wife's legs as they pass. Wil says, "Let's have another one."

He finds that he quite possibly has confused even himself with this statement, but Nancy looks over at him unfazed. She squints and says, "Another one? Another *kid*?"

"Yeah. Another kid."

"Just forget about the one we've got and start over, huh?"

"No," Wil says. "We'll find this one. After all, there's nothing really wrong with it. It's not *defective* or anything." He hopes that will get a laugh, at least a smile, but all it does is deepen the lines of confused resistance around Nancy's eyes. He says, "It'll be like a new beginning. For us."

Nancy just looks back at him.

"Think it over," he says.

At about that time, Wil—and Nancy, too, he can tell—begins to suspect that something has happened to Jarred and Peter. Kidnapped. Hit by a car on the way over to Baskin-Robbins. Maybe they wandered too far down Cedar Road and got lost somewhere in Cleveland Heights. These possibilities flip through Wil's mind and collect, until he comes to the conclusion that one of them has to have happened. He puts his hand on Nancy's knee, examines her face. Her lips are dry and squeezed together, white around the edges, and he has to look away. The clock above the concession area reads 10:05. Wil stands.

"Okay, let's go find him," he says. "Something's happened."

Nancy unclenches her jaw, gathers her breath as if to say something, just as Jarred pushes open the glass door and enters the lobby.

"Jarred!" Wil calls out, as if in warning of something terrible. The boy jumps back, does some quick, startled movement with his shoulders that's kind of like a duck, and looks around. They are only a few feet from each other and Wil realizes suddenly that he must have startled everyone in the lobby. He adjusts his voice. "Where have you been?"

Nancy is up now, too. Jarred looks from his father, over to his mother, and back again. A ring of chocolate is around the boy's mouth and a single splotch the shape of Maine marks his yellow t-shirt. He takes two cautious steps toward them.

"Where have you been?" Wil says again. He finds now that his fear has turned to anger.

Jarred points a thumb back over his shoulder. "We went over to Baskin-Robbins," he says, and pauses. "Then we went to Revco."

Nancy takes hold of Jarred's shirt and examines the stain. "Where's Peter?" she says.

"He's still at Revco."

"Why?" Nancy loosens her grip on the shirt and focuses now on Jarred's chocolate-smeared face.

"Because," Jarred says. "He got picked up."

"He got picked up," Nancy says, as if simply to hear the words again, reconsider them. "Why? We told his parents we'd bring him home." Then she holds perfectly still for a moment, Jarred's yellow shirt still clenched in her fist. "I thought you said he was still at Revco?"

"Yeah," Jarred says. "He is."

Nancy's eyes freeze in her head. She doesn't know what to ask next, where to go with this information, and Wil, just as lost now, feels unable to help her.

"Son," Wil says finally. "What do you mean, 'He got picked up?'"

Jarred looks off to the side, over toward the fat, red, velvet-covered ropes separating the lobby from the theater screens. "He got picked up by the people at Revco. He tried to steal a pack of baseball cards and they caught him."

"Oh my God," Nancy says.

Wil waits to see if there is more. When he is relatively sure Jarred is through with his explanation, he says, "Are you in any trouble?"

Jarred shakes his head no.

"Did they call his parents?"

"Oh my God, his parents," Nancy says, suddenly realizing, Wil guesses, that they'll have to explain this to them, how their son came to get himself into legal trouble while in their care.

"I don't know," Jarred says. "They asked me who we were here with, and then told me to go and get you. They're holding Peter until we get back."

"Wonderful," Nancy says. "Just wonderful."

"All right," Wil says. "Let's go straighten this out," and he pushes open the glass door. "You're in big trouble, too, by the way, mister," he adds.

Jarred glances up at him, the idea of asking *why* perhaps playing around briefly in his mind. Wil waits for it, but the boy holds back, and as they step out onto the sidewalk, the muggy July air clinging to their skin, it occurs to Wil to ask, "So how was the movie?"

Jarred thinks for a moment. "Good," he says. "It was funny."

The manager is waiting for them as they enter through the automatic doors, standing off to the side of the checkout registers, near the Coke machine. He straightens when he sees Jarred. Wil notices the man's seriousness, his set lips and jaw beneath the unflinching mustache. But Wil is not intimidated, mostly because the man's red jacket is a size or two too small, forcing his arms to draw in close to his body and dangle there like those of an upright squirrel. The man takes a few steps toward them and extends his hand as best he can.

"George Mitchell," the man says as he and Wil shake. "I'm the manager here. I guess your boy's told you we had a slight situation here tonight."

Wil lets go of George Mitchell's hand. "He told us, yes. We apologize for that." For a brief moment he wonders if that will be enough, if they can just leave now.

George Mitchell nods. "Yes, well, we have to notify the child's guardian—it's store policy—and now that we've done that, he can go. Just so you understand what's happened and agree to take appropriate steps." He gives a little half-wave, slightly hindered by his tight jacket. "He's back in the office. Follow me, please."

They follow, single file, through the snacks aisle, past the beer and wine, to a copper colored door in the back wall marked "Employees Only." George Mitchell opens the door with a key and holds it for Nancy, Jarred and Wil. "After you," he says. They enter into a short hallway, at the end of which is another door. George Mitchell holds this one for them as well and when they enter they find Peter sitting behind a metal desk, reclining, hands locked behind his head. When he sees the others come into the room his eyes meet Jarred's and a smile that nearly envelops his entire face forms. It is so broad, so inherently proud of itself, that the sight of it makes Wil react before he can stop and consider it.

"Peter," Wil says, a little harsher than he believes he meant to.

Peter looks from Jarred to Wil. The grin has subsided somewhat, but still is there.

The office itself is silver and brown: metaled desk, dark paneled walls. There are papers and manuals piled on top of the desk, and the only personal item that Wil can see is a fraternity paddle nailed into the paneling. George Mitchell comes in and closes the door. Everyone is lined against the wall, facing Peter, as if the boy has called them all in. He sits smugly behind what Wil understands to be George Mitchell's desk, arms folded now across his chest. A thin sprout of hair stands straight up in the back.

Wil looks over at his wife. Her hand is on Jarred's head, holding him in place.

"Okay, Peter," George Mitchell says, moving over to the desk. "Looks like you're sprung."

Peter sits forward, pauses, as if he's just managed to make himself comfortable and now is reluctant to leave. Then the smile returns. Wil feels as though he has no control over what is going on around him. He's an observer. He watches as Peter slides

George Mitchell's chair out from the desk, stands, and walks around to stand next to Jarred. They both giggle and Wil sees Nancy tighten her grip on their son's head.

"We told him," George Mitchell says, addressing Wil, "that he no longer is permitted inside the store without an adult guardian. We tried to contact his parents but were unable to reach them. Since he was under your supervision at the time anyway, I'll leave it to you to notify them. If you have no objections."

Wil waits a moment, to see if Nancy sees fit to respond. When she doesn't, he says, "No. That's fine. We understand."

"Good," George Mitchell says, "because I'm not so sure Peter does." He glances over at Jarred's friend, who still is smiling. Wil suddenly finds that he is growing, quickly, to hate this little boy. "The baseball cards are fifty cents a pack," George Mitchell goes on, addressing Peter now. "Next time, ask your parents for the money. I'm sure they'd give it to you. Or, better yet, buy them yourself. There's a lot of satisfaction in that."

Peter giggles.

George Mitchell shakes his head disappointedly. There is nothing more he can do about this, and Wil suddenly feels for the man. "Peter," Wil says harshly. "That's enough." He takes a step forward, holds out what he hopes is an intimidating finger. "I won't have this."

Nancy puts her free hand behind Peter's head and, as if she's practiced this, guides both boys to the door. Jarred reaches out and pulls the door open, then all three are gone without saying a word. A few long seconds later, Wil says, "I'm sorry about all this."

"It's all right." George Mitchell goes behind his desk and examines it.

"Is anything missing?" Wil asks.

"No. There's nothing here a kid would want."

Wil feels himself take pause and consider this statement. "That doesn't mean he wouldn't take it," he says. Then, quickly, he says, "Okay. Well, thanks," and holds out his hand.

George Mitchell looks at the extended hand for a moment, then reaches out across the desk and shakes it. "Good luck with the parents," he says.

"Oh, yeah," Wil says. "The parents." Then he feels inclined to add, "We don't know them very well. My wife's talked to the mother once or twice on the phone. That's it."

George Mitchell nods.

Wil waits for something more, but nothing comes, so he turns and leaves the office. He walks back through the narrow hallway and out into the bright white light of the store. Up front, by the registers, he sees Nancy paying for something. When he reaches the magazine racks he is close enough to see his wife hand over two packs of baseball cards and Peter and Jarred happily tear away the wrappers.

The drive to Peter's house is a quiet one. Wil tries to put himself in the other position, that of a father being told the news he is about to tell Peter's father. He imagines Jarred being brought home like this. How would *he* feel? But that doesn't work. He doesn't know how he'd feel because that's not what is happening. Behind him, Wil can hear the boys flipping through their cards, using the light from the outside streetlamps to see the players' poses, read their stats. Nancy stares straight ahead, expressionless. She appears to be worried about having to tell Peter's parents, too, and Wil finds himself feeling strangely relieved. For the first time in quite a while he sees that the two of them are experiencing something important together. At least, he thinks, it's a distraction, a respite from what consumes them every day, every moment.

He drives down Green Road and makes the right onto Fairmount, both hands firmly on the wheel, trying to look in control. Fairmount empties into Warransville Circle and as he guides the car around counterclockwise, he glances over at Nancy. Light from the BP station hits her face and she stares straight into it. He hopes she will look over at him, so they can exchange some sort of facial expression, some kind of unspoken acknowledgment only they will comprehend; something with their eyes, a show of support for each other in the midst of this shared crisis, a smile that never actually forms but nonetheless is understood, fully developed below the surface. The turnoff from the circle is upon him, though, so Wil is forced to look away from his wife and veer the car back onto South Fairmount. This is Peter's neighborhood. Nancy shifts in her seat.

"Honey," Wil says, reaching across in search of Nancy's hand. Before he can find it, though, Jarred pokes his head between them from the back seat.

"Mom," he says, almost whispering. "Mom, my head hurts."

Nancy does not look at him. "It's from the ice cream," she says. "Mine hurts, too."

"But you didn't have any ice cr—"

"Sit back, Jarred."

Jarred sits back.

Wil makes the turn onto Ashurst, a usually quiet, residential street where the lawns are square and the houses, though on the larger side, are square and white and close together. This is no big deal, Wil thinks now. *They're* the ones who should be embarrassed. Orange light from the dashboard seeps into Wil's vision, soothing him, creating the sensation of rationality. He turns to Nancy, examines her fully—the thinness of her neck, her narrow shoulders and the brown hair, now short, that used to brush against them—and sees her as a nineteen-year-old girl, an Oberlin sophomore, a political science major, totally unaware of what was in store for her: an unfaithful husband who has yet to reach a semblance of his potential, the humiliation of apologizing to another boy's parents for failing to properly care for their son for a couple of hours, whatever else is to come. "This is no big deal," Wil says to her, and tries with everything he has to believe it himself.

Peter has to point out the house. Even though they picked

him up earlier that evening, in the dark and with the houses all looking so familiar, picking the right one would have been a crapshoot. They pull into the driveway and Wil kills the engine. He finds Peter in the rearview mirror, face bathed in shadows thrown from the porch light. "I guess we better come in with you," he says.

Peter shrugs.

"You know, Peter, we'd have *bought* the baseball cards for you.

"We did buy them," Nancy says, more correcting Wil than supporting him.

"That's right," Wil says. "See?"

"Yeah," Peter says. "I know." Then he adds, "Sorry."

They sit in silence for five, ten seconds. "All right then," Wil says, and opens his door. He leans over to Nancy. "You don't have to come in if you don't want to," he says. "I'll take care of it."

Peter and Jarred are already out of the car, heading up the walkway to the front door. They are giddy, bumping shoulders, trying to knock each other into the grass. Wil notices, though, that Jarred's enthusiasm seems to have dropped a level since the announcement of his headache. He seems slow, rubbery. The other thing Wil notices is that Peter is not carrying his baseball cards. Wil turns around and sees, illuminated by the inside dome light, both packs strewn across the back seat.

"I'll go," Nancy says then. She takes a breath and opens her door. "It's just so . . . I don't know." She swings her legs out and stands.

Jarred and Peter are already inside the house when Wil and Nancy reach the front porch. The boys have left the door open and cool air spills out. Inside, Wil can see the beige tile of the entryway, the hardwood steps leading upstairs, on which he can see thick tufts of dark cat hair. An umbrella stand holding a single umbrella sits next to the door, along with a ceramic Persian cat. At the other end of the narrow hallway he can make out part of the kitchen table. Wil takes Nancy's hand. "Let's make this a new beginning," he says. "Like I said before. We'll deal with this together, put it behind us, move on. Deal?" Then he says, "Okay?" and she looks up at him, and then the sound of adult footsteps tears them from that private and potentially hopeful zone Wil wants to believe they'd entered. Nancy looks away, clears her throat, gathers herself. A man steps from one of the side rooms into the entryway. Without looking at Wil or Nancy, he walks to the front door and pushes it closed.

Peter's father is several years older than Wil—early forties maybe—and stands with his shoulders pushed slightly forward. He tucks his t-shirt inside the navy blue bathrobe he is wearing and holds out a hand. A hint of a smile plays across his face that Wil believes he is supposed to interpret. "Rich Connelly," Peter's father says.

"Wil Ross."

They shake hands for several seconds, Connelly pumping again and again. Finally Wil breaks free and says, "My wife, Nancy."

Connelly shifts his hand over to Nancy, but she just gives a light, quick squeeze and pulls away before Connelly can get going. "It's nice to meet you both."

"Likewise," Wil says.

"So, how was the movie?"

"Fine," Wil says and prepares himself to say more, something about the music, but then doesn't.

"I understand Peter gave you some trouble tonight." Again the smile returns to Connelly's face, but Wil is unsure this time if it is meant to be shared, or if it is aimed at him. Connelly, even in his bathrobe, carries himself with an air of self-conscious, perhaps calculated, stateliness. His hair is prematurely white and his manner is precise, polished. He puts his hands in the pockets of his robe as if it were his suit pants, and Wil guesses he is either a higher-up at a corporation (a vice president maybe?) or a professor at the local college. "Peter just told us about it, leaving out a lot of the details, I'm sure, which we'll straighten out later. We were out for the evening. I apologize for sticking you with the mess."

"It was no big deal really," Wil says. "One of those things boys do. To see if they can get away with it. You know."

Connelly nods. "And they were—where?"

"At the Revco. In Beechwood."

"Ah."

Jarred emerges from the left, from what Wil now presumes to be the living room. He can see one corner of a piano in the darkness. The boy glances up suspiciously at Connelly and creeps around to Nancy. "Mom, my head really hurts," he says. "Really."

"Okay, honey."

"Why don't you go wait in the car," Connelly suggests. "Your folks will only be another minute."

Jarred glances up at his mother, who looks over at Wil. Wil doesn't know what to say. Finally he puts his hand on his son's shoulder. "Go on, Jarred," he says. "Climb into the back seat and put your head down, close your eyes. We'll only be another minute. I promise."

Reluctantly, Jarred slips out the front door, leaving it open. Wil watches him negotiate the front steps then stagger, as though drunk, along the walkway to the car. Wil turns back then and catches Nancy examining her fingernails.

"Now," Connelly says, as if calling a board meeting to order. "My wife's inside talking to Peter right now. We're not placing blame on anyone, and I'm not accusing you of anything. God knows we're at least just as much to blame. I want to make that clear up front." His hands are still buried to the wrists inside the pockets of his bathrobe. Every now and then he lifts up an inch or so onto the balls of his feet. But he does not rock back and forth on them, his voice does not waver and he looks from Wil's eyes to Nancy's and back again with the deft confidence of one who is used to having many people do what he tells them. "What we've decided, however, is that Peter will no longer have any association with Jarred outside of school. We're willing to let this one instance slide, but we'll take no chance of it happening again. I hope you understand."

Wil feels himself freeze up. His muscles lock and his vision drifts not exactly out of focus, but somehow out of specific definition. He sees Connelly smile congenially. He feels as though he has been inserted into a painting he's never seen before and now is expected to blend in and act natural. He wants to look over at Nancy, seek comfort in her returned glance, but he can't bring himself to do it. He just keeps hearing those words—or what he remembers to be the words—said over and over in his head: *We'll let this one slide.*

Let *what* slide? That's what Wil want's to ask. Just what exactly is this guy willing to let slide? What if he *wasn't* willing to let it slide? What then? What would the consequences of *that* be? Wil feels sweat suddenly flow down his back. The space behind his eyes grows hot and sticky. A funny taste, like aluminum, forms in his mouth. He points a finger at Connelly's smiling face. "Your precious little Peter is a monster," he says. "I'd rather our son wasn't exposed to him anyway."

Connelly nods. "That's fine. Everything works out then. A win-win."

"And I don't particularly appreciate having to bail out your delinquent son either. It was embarrassing and the least you can do is acknowledge as much."

"Absolutely. I'm quite sure it was embarrassing."

Wil pauses. "What?"

"I have no doubt that such an experience would be tremendously embarrassing."

Wil looks over at his wife then and is surprised to find her crying, silently, a single rivulet of tears extending from each eye, drops falling one at a time onto the beige tile of the entryway. Wil takes a step toward her. "Nancy. Sweetheart." He goes to touch her cheek with the back of his hand but he comes up an inch or two short and just brushes the air in front of her face.

"Thank you for getting Peter home," Connelly says. "It's late now, and we'd like to get ready—"

Wil's punch lands directly between Connelly's eyes. His fist seems to plant there and Wil watches as Connelly's irises draw inward, as if trying to count Wil's knuckles; then Connelly's head snaps back, his arms fling out to the sides, and he drops, casualty, to one knee.

Nobody reacts. Nancy wipes her nose with the back of her hand and looks down at Connelly, as if he were nothing more than another decorative object newly added to the stylish entryway. Wil holds both fists in front of him, like a boxer, until he realizes how he is standing and lowers his hands to his sides. He watches Connelly, who is positioned with one elbow across his raised knee, head resting on his forearm. The man looks as though he's a little winded and trying to catch his breath.

"Nancy," Wil says. "Nancy . . ."

She sidesteps over and puts her hand on the doorknob. "I don't want this," she says.

"What?" Wil says. "What don't you want?"

"My head hurts," she says.

"So does mine," Wil says, then, with an open hand, indicates Connelly who is still down on one knee. "So does his."

Nancy stops and regards both men. She is not crying anymore. Her eyes are red rimmed and swollen, but she is not crying. Wil wants to embrace her, to put his arms around her and shield her from what he's done, to hide with her, to disappear, so that they can start again together, start over, from someplace different, with clear heads and clean memories. But he knows he won't do that; he knows it is impossible. Every time he tries, the waitress from Pittsburgh pops into his mind and he feels a twinge of repulsion, a sudden sensation as though he might be sick. But then, as soon as the wave subsides it is replaced with something warm—longing—and just as suddenly he wishes with all his being that he were back in that hotel room in Pittsburgh right now, ordering room service, setting the alarm clock for one more hour.

Finally, Connelly lifts his head and looks up at them. Blood has spilled from his nose and now collects in the dimple above his mouth, and Wil notices a very small, almost ornamental, red puddle on the beige tile. Nancy releases a blast of breath that is something like a gasp but not exactly. Then she opens the front door and stops. She looks at Wil, wipes at her face with the tips of her fingers. Her eyes meet Wil's and he knows—there is no way to prove it to himself, but he absolutely *knows*—that she is right now feeling the same way he is, right now she is remembering her short-lived, guilt-ridden affair with repulsion and fondness. Despite the problems it's caused in her life, Wil knows it looks pretty inviting to her at this moment.

Connelly drops his other knee down to the tile and sits back on his heels. He looks up at Wil and Nancy with something like sympathy in his bloodstained face. His robe is partially open and Wil can see blue and yellow plaid boxer shorts showing through. Nancy pulls the door all the way open and walks out. Connelly then tries to lift himself up off the floor. He makes it halfway, then loses his balance and topples forward. Wil puts his arms out and catches him around the shoulders, and then they both fall back against the wall, knocking over the umbrella stand.

"Easy," Wil says.

Connelly finally finds his balance and rights himself. He dabs at the blood above his lip and then takes his nose between the fingers of both hands as if fitting it back onto his face. When he takes his hands away he says, "How's it look? All night?"

Wil leans forward, squints. "I think so," he says.

"Okay."

"Richard?" an unseen voice calls from somewhere in the back area of the house. "Is everything all right out there?"

"Everything's fine, dearest," Connelly answers.

Outside, a car starts. A few seconds later Wil watches from inside the front door as Nancy backs their car out of the driveway, pulls out onto Ashurst, and heads away down the street, headlights crawling across Connelly's front windows and spilling into the entryway.

"Uh-oh," Connelly says.

Wil feels himself go hollow. He actually feels this happen. Then he feels nothing. All that occurs to him is that now he has to find another way home. He thinks: *home*. Then he thinks of the damage he's done to Connelly's nose and of what Connelly will tell his wife, how he'll explain to her how it happened. Before he can think this through any further, though, he turns and takes hold of the doorknob. He says, "I'll see you," and looks up and to the right where he sees a nicely framed portrait photograph of Peter. He looks to be about four years old, wearing a neat yellow sweater over a white turtleneck; his hair is damp and perfectly combed, and he has a grin on his little face that is the obvious result of something extraordinarily funny being held up to him from behind the camera. Wil smiles. Sweet kid, he thinks, and then he lets himself out, onto the brightly lit front porch. Beyond is darkness, blocks and blocks of houses, inside of which, people talk, watch TV, eat, plan, make love, argue, sleep, dream, ignore, forget. He stands there for fifteen, twenty seconds, and then a little longer, breathing the summer air, feeling the throbbing in his knuckles, the numbness behind his eyes. He focuses on the Connellys' mailbox at the end of the driveway, the rounded edges, the empty space inside that will in the morning be occupied by a new batch of mail—or, as Connelly might say, correspondence.

Wil clears his throat as the porch light goes out behind him. He descends the front step, deeming it a beginning of sorts, and then, out of nowhere, Wil hears the roaring of what he immediately identifies as a lawnmower erupt down the block. The sound, though abrasive and out of place, is strangely soothing to Wil, and he stands there, somewhere in the Connellys' front yard, listening to it, trying to imagine whether the unseen person mowing his lawn can see each swatch of grass he's cut into the darkness, and whether he's cutting in strips or working inward around the perimeter.

The answer, most likely, is neither, because after only a minute or two—not nearly enough time to finish a lawn the size of those in this neighborhood—the mower shuts off suddenly, the sound evaporating into the warm evening air. Wil waits in the silence for what might come next. He decides to make a prediction: a garage door opening. He prepares to hear that sound, clears his mind so that he can decipher the motor and chains of an automatic garage door opening from somewhere off to his left, and as he heads across the Connellys' front lawn to the street, he's ready for it.

Passing Interest

Insomnia

Vogel dozed off in the middle of the weather report and jerked awake as the sportscaster with the plastic-looking face was saying his good-byes, shuffling papers. For some reason, missing the sports always irritated him more than anything else that could turn up during the day. "Goddamn," he said to the screen, then felt along between the cushions of the couch and under his butt until he found the remote. He aimed it at the set and flicked through the channels as if firing a pistol. The next news station was showing a commercial, and when he got to the third, the sportscaster and anchorman were stalling, making wisecracks about something Vogel could not understand since he had missed the sports report. "Bitch," he said and jammed the remote back into the cushions, then stood and absently scratched his crotch. Mike, Vogel's mutt, who stayed in the apartment illegally, lay motionless in the center of the room. He was a black, wiry-haired mongrel with huge, drooping balls that were more noticeable than if the dog had worn ice skates. To Vogel, Mike represented his marriage. After all, the grotesque creature was all Vogel received when it ended, and was, Vogel decided, equivalent company to his ex-wife.

The apartment was sticky and humid. Vogel had meant to buy a dehumidifier but now, as he loped across the living room carpet to the kitchen to fix his lunch for the next day, he realized it was one of those things he would never do. He took an open package of bologna from the refrigerator and sniffed it. Satisfied, he slapped three slices onto a hamburger bun and added mustard and some lettuce, then put it in a brown paper bag along with a handful of fancy pretzels and set the whole package back in the refrigerator. He stood for a moment in the kitchen's yellow light, staring at his bare feet on the linoleum, and thought of how Jenny always hated the looks of them. Fred Flintstone feet, she called them. Vogel wiggled his toes and went back into the living room.

This was the time of day Vogel was most wide awake. He forged through his job at the insurance company every day nearly collapsing, came home, made some sort of dinner, then watched TV the rest of the evening prone on the sofa, dozing frequently, usually missing the sports report, and thinking of how he really ought to go to bed. But come 11:30, Vogel was up; he was conscious and sharp. Sometimes he read. It was not uncommon for Vogel to consume an entire book about tropical rain forests or the Arctic Circle in one night, but usually he worked the remote control with rapid-fire precision, moving from talk show to talk show. And when they were over, he jumped from bad movies to music videos to documentaries to thirty-minute commercials for bamboo steamers and knives that can cut through paneling. Sometimes Vogel wrote down the tollfree phone numbers for these things, but he never actually called up and placed an order.

Standing in front of the sofa, Vogel picked up the remote and clicked off the set. If he didn't make a move now, he wouldn't go to bed all night.

"Hey," Vogel called to Mike. "Let's go. Bedtime." But the dog showed no signs of having heard, which was fine with Vogel.

In the bathroom, Vogel looked at his face in the mirror. He immediately noticed how sunken his eye sockets were. They were dark and deep and they made his nose and lips protrude outward. Then, in his mustache, Vogel saw grey. At first he thought it was the bathroom lighting, but when he leaned forward into the mirror, almost straddling the sink so that he had to look cross-eyed at his reflection, he saw the hairs interspersed throughout, mostly in the top half, near his nose. *Spattering* came to his mind. *I have a spattering of grey in my mustache*, he thought, and decided that was too much. At 31, any grey was too much. Quickly he lathered his upper lip. He picked up the razor and regarded his reflection for a moment as if it were another person. He heard the first stroke cut through the whiskers. It sounded loud—a crackling that echoed in the tiny bathroom—then he positioned for the second stroke. For some reason, this event seemed momentous to him. As he followed through with the razor, Vogel heard a series of quick clanks, like steel smacking together, outside his back door. Distracted, he felt completely stupid for having to reposition the razor on his lip. He heard the noise again, louder and more defined this time. Half-shaved, he set the razor down on the side of the sink and, leaving the water running, pushed open the back door of his apartment and stepped out onto the fire escape.

A story below, a rear end and legs stuck out of the building's trash dumpster, lit by the headlights of a running Cadillac de Ville. Vogel watched for a moment as the figure rummaged through the garbage. Then, as the figure—it was a man—apparently reached out for something, he teetered on the lip of the dumpster and fell in with a muffled crash.

"Hey," Vogel called out. "The hell you doing down there?" He obviously frightened the man and there was a flurry of rattling and scraping sounds from the bowels of the dumpster, then nothing. Vogel was positioned at too low an angle to see inside. He stood there, with shaving cream over half his lip, and waited. "You might as well just come out," he said. "I'm not going anywhere." In the alley, the Cadillac sat idling, lighting the scene. Vogel wondered if anyone else in the building was still up. Even though it wasn't all that late, he always had a peculiar feeling that he was the only one awake.

Suddenly Vogel saw a hat poke out of the dumpster. It looked like a Red Sox hat, but he couldn't be sure. Then the man stood. He stood slowly but, Vogel thought, confidently, with his shoulders thrown back. His beard was heavy in areas, but uneven, with thick sideburns and chin whiskers, but little if any on his cheeks. Vogel thought of his own face. The man looked to be in his fifties or thereabouts; he wore a dirty white windbreaker with a hood hanging in back and his round, bare belly squirting out the bottom. It *was* a Red Sox hat.

"Looking for anything in particular, buddy?" Vogel said.

The man squatted without taking his thick-browed eyes off of Vogel, then straightened. "Nope. Not really." Then he lifted a leg over the side of the dumpster and climbed out, carrying a garbage bag with very little in it, hanging long and thin, behind him. Vogel watched as the man carefully closed the lid on the dumpster then opened the door to the Cadillac, tossed the Hefty bag into the passenger seat, and got in behind the wheel himself.

"Hey," Vogel said.

The man cautiously backed out of the alley with his right arm up on the adjacent headrest, but still, somehow, looking at Vogel. When he was out of sight and the alley was dark again except for the streetlight coming in from Beechwood Avenue, Vogel walked the flight of fire escape stairs down to the dumpster. He looked around and saw nothing. Everything looked the same as when he emptied his garbage there days ago, and he wondered if the man had been there before. Probably not, he figured, since he was usually up and would have heard him.

The air, cold on the shaved section of Vogel's lip, felt huge and expansive around him. He heard the night's stillness and an occasional car moaning along the wet pavement at the other end of the alley. Slowly, Vogel lifted the lid of the dumpster and peered in. Blackness. Nothing else. Suddenly he was frightened, although he did not know of what. He released the lid and it slammed shut a little louder than he had wanted, then he hurried back up the fire escape to his apartment, where, once inside the bathroom, he shut off the water and wiped his face with a towel, leaving half of his mustache still unshaved. He walked into the living room and snapped on the light. Mike lay in the same spot. Vogel settled back into the sofa with the remote control and tuned to his favorite UHF station. He was pleased and comforted to find a feature-length ad for no-stick cookware just starting.

Protection

The next day, Vogel thought of calling the police. The image of that old bum fingering through his garbage, picking up God-knows-what diseases and spreading them who-knows-where made him angry, and then hateful. What right did he have? From his cubicle at the insurance company, Vogel called Jenny. He sat hunched over his desk to conceal his voice and fingered his now-shaved face while the phone rang on the other end. Vogel didn't like not having his mustache. Without it, his face looked emptier, less intelligent.

Jerry, Jenny's new husband, answered and Vogel tried to alter his voice in a generic, unfamiliar way when he asked for his ex-wife.

"Sure, Vogel," Jerry said. "I'll get her for you."

Jerry and Jenny: Vogel always got a little kick out of that. *Jerry and Jenny, Jerry and Jenny*, he'd say to himself sometimes, and then laugh. Jerry was some sort of computer consultant and worked out of an office in their house, so he usually was home. When they first got married, Vogel figured this would never work—too much of each other. But Jenny thought it was the most wonderful situation, frequently mentioning to Vogel in random conversation how nice it was that her husband was around every now and then.

Vogel had hoped to make a little small talk for a while, but his main intent was to tell her about the bum the night before. Jenny seemed rushed when she finally got to the phone, though, so he ended up getting into it sooner and more abruptly than he had wanted.

"And . . . ?" Jenny said once he did tell her.

"And I'm thinking of calling the police."

"The police? Whatever for?" Her voice faded out at the end, like she was doing something that did not require a telephone.

"Jenny, he goes through the *garbage*."

"Yeah, so?"

"Well, it's disgusting."

"But what business is it of yours? Hold on a minute." There was silence. Vogel tried to picture his ex-wife. What was she doing now? He tried to conjure up an image of her face, and when he couldn't he tried to visualize some of her eccentricities: The way she walked, the way she fluffed her hair with her hands, the way she slept (was it on her back or her side?), the way she used to kiss him—and he couldn't remember any of these things.

"Still there?" she said after a while. She was panting lightly.

"Yeah."

"Well, look," she said. "I have to go. But, hey, I don't know why you're getting so worked up about this garbage guy. I mean, what's the big deal? Let the poor guy live out of your garbage if he wants to. There's plenty of other shit to worry about. Like last week, you know our next door neighbors? The Wisermans? Their house got robbed the other night. While they were asleep. Can you believe that? Stuff was stolen right out of their bedroom. Talk about freaky. Now that's something to worry about."

"Jesus, Jenny. Why didn't you tell me this before?"

"I don't know. Why would I?" She sounded rushed again. Vogel could hear the receiver moving around.

"Well, this guy—this bum—he drives a Cadillac."

"That makes him dangerous?"

"I guess not. It's just, I don't know, like you said—freaky. Think about it. It's just not right. It's—

"I'm sorry, honey. I have to go now."

"All right." He didn't want to hang up. "But I think you should take some measures to protect yourself, Jenny."

"We're protected. I really have to go. If you get anything of value stolen from your garbage, let me know, okay?"

Vogel held the receiver in his lap and stared at the grey felt wall of his cube. All around him, insurance salesmen were on their phones, selling, haggling. He had not accomplished what he had hoped—whatever that was—by calling Jenny, but he now was sure of one thing: After work he would go out, although he wasn't sure where, and buy a gun.

Inside Clyde's Gun and Bow Shop, Vogel felt like an intruder at a family picnic. Everyone seemed to know each other. Groups mingled by the glass laughing and joking about different guns and telling stories of occasions when they'd used them.

"You ever fire a handgun?" the man behind the counter asked Vogel. He might have been Clyde. Two shiny black pistols lay between them. They looked thick and heavy.

Vogel cleared his throat. "Um, no."

The man picked one of the guns up and replaced it in the case. "This is the one you want." He nodded at the one still on the counter. "Light weight. Easy to shoot. Don't know what you want it for, but it'll stop just about anything."

Vogel looked up at the man, who was smiling under his bushy mustache, and ran an index finger over his own upper lip. Then he reached down and picked up the gun. It felt snug in his hand. Much more form-fitting than he remembered of toy guns when he was a kid. It was solid and powerful and Vogel felt a sourness rise in his stomach.

"Nice, huh?" the salesman said, still smiling, smirking actually, and Vogel thought that if the gun were loaded, he'd have shot him.

"Fine," Vogel said. "It's fine. Wrap it up."

"You'll need ammunition. That is, unless you already got some."

"No, I have no goddamn *ammunition*." Vogel's voice rose

and the conversations around him diminished slightly. "Just put some in the bag with it."

"Whoa there, partner," the salesman said. "There's this pesky little law in Pennsylvania. Called a five-day waiting period on the sale of all handguns, or something close to that anyhow. Maybe you heard of it?"

Vogel felt his face and neck go flush. "Yeah," he said. "Sure I have."

"Well, then. How 'bout you show me a driver's license. Preferably your own." The man smiled. "I'm sure whatever it is you're looking to shoot will still be there next week."

Morality

That night, Vogel watched out the window for the bum. The television played loud behind him, and every so often Vogel walked over to it and caught a few minutes of the network movie—it was an Indiana Jones film, although he wasn't sure which one.

Peering between the curtains into the dark alley behind his apartment building, Vogel thought of the bums he saw downtown on his way to work every day. Sometimes one sat next to him on the bus. They were revolting and they smelled and some had enormous scabs or sores all over their skin and hair the texture of something that might wash up on a New Jersey beach, but they were more or less harmless. Someone who had nothing could not harm you. But this bum—this vagrant—was a threat somehow. Maybe it was the fact that this guy was doing his scavenging right outside Vogel's back door. Or maybe it was the Cadillac. Vogel found it strangely immoral for someone riding around town in a machine he himself could never afford to be picking through his trash.

Vogel thumbed his upper lip and waited. Sometimes he pretended he had his gun, drawing back the curtains with the stiff barrel of his index finger and aiming at things: a neighbor's tire, a brick next to the chain-link fence, the base of a telephone pole, someone's cat. He imagined the cold iron in his hand and the kickback as he fired. He imagined the bullet itself, lodged somewhere, and he felt nauseous.

When Vogel was growing up, his family lived across a narrow stretch of woods from a rather wealthy neighborhood where the children all had the same haircuts and different shoes for different occasions and were taken every year to the Gulf of Mexico or some island off North Carolina that, if nothing else, was nicer than where the family down the street went for their vacation. The houses were big with proper names like Tudor and Colonial and the people who lived in them were doctors and lawyers and accountants or the bosses of such people, and sometimes Vogel played with their sons. These little boys laughed contemptuously and wore blinding white socks and, of course, it was a privilege for Vogel to be included among them from time to time. But what Vogel remembered now, as he waited by the window like a sniper in the dark, was Halloween. Every year, without fail, two or three of these children dressed up as what they called a hobo. Their mothers would take a pair of the kid's oldest pants and oldest shirt, and destroy them. They tore holes in the knees and cut strips up the pant legs and ripped the breast pocket of the shirt so that it hung by a single seam. Mascara was strategically smeared on the child's face to represent dirt and soot and the street and sometimes, if the right hobo materials were not accessible in the house, they'd go out and *buy* them. Vogel always dressed as something either scary or funny, and he was never sure how the children who went out dressed as these hobos interpreted their own costumes. No one ever seemed to be particularly frightened of them. And Vogel never saw them as funny; although, now, he figured that's what everyone else thought. He remembered walking around on Halloween night with these kids, answering all the stupid questions asked by the parents who opened the door and doled out the candy. "And what are *you*?" they asked. "A werewolf? Oh, how scary! And you. You're a hobo, right? How cute! Absolutely darling. Did your mother help you with the outfit? She did a wonderful job." Vogel remembered Mrs. Feeny saying that, almost to the letter.

When he saw the headlights pull into the alley, Vogel stepped out onto the fire escape before the car was even halfway back. The TV was so loud Vogel could hear it clearly even outside. The movie was ending and the Indiana Jones theme blared. Soon the news would be on. The Cadillac pulled up and swung around wide so its lights shone on the dumpster. It groaned to a stop and a moment later the man opened his door and got out. He walked over to the dumpster holding an empty Hefty bag which tailed behind him in the breeze. Never once glancing at Vogel, the man lifted the lid and, after quickly scanning its overall contents, raised one leg awkwardly over the lip of the dumpster and then the other.

"Why don't you get out of the garbage, you old fool?" Vogel called out. The pitch of his voice jumped a little. "What the hell's wrong with you?" The man pulled the brim of the Sox hat down over his brow and looked up at Vogel with what Vogel later decided was scornful compassion in his tiny eyes. "You drive around in a goddamn Caddy, for Christsake."

The man knelt slowly and put something in the bag. "You don't know anything about me," he said, almost under his breath. "You don't even know who I am."

The sound of the man's voice startled Vogel and he realized he had not anticipated any sort of interaction with him. "All right, then," he said. "Who are you? I'd like to know."

The man stood and looked right over the top of Vogel's head. "I'm that bum," he said. "The one who picks at your garbage and drives a Cadillac. That's all."

He's right, Vogel thought. He's exactly right. That's exactly who he is.

"I'm not even a real bum," the man went on. "I'm a notch below that. A bum with a Caddy—that usually makes me worth a second look. Passing interest, that's what I am."

"Yeah. Only you're in *my* garbage, which means you've gone beyond passing interest to real fucking nuisance."

The man shrugged. "I guess you're the one's gotta deal with *that*." He bent over and flipped something aside, then straightened again and stood motionless, as if in contemplation.

"Where'd you get the Caddy?" Vogel blurted.

"What's the difference?"

"I don't know. But there *is* one."

"My daddy left it to me."

"Why don't you sell it?"

"Then I'd have to walk."

"Well, how do you get gas?"

"What is this, Twenty Questions?"

"It's a damn good question's what it is," Vogel said, his voice rising. "How do you get gas?"

"A little at a time; with what I got. And not too often neither."

Vogel nodded.

"Now let me ask *you* something, mister." The bum leaned his elbow against the edge of the dumpster. "Why am I looking through your garbage?"

Vogel could hear the news coming from the living room. The sports would be on soon. "I don't know," he said.

"You know. You just won't say it. Why is some slimeball digging through your garbage? Of all people, why does it have to be you? What's wrong with this picture?"

Vogel shook his head. "I don't know."

The man pursed his lips and looked disgustedly at Vogel, like he'd spit at him if he were close enough. "Go to hell," he said and began climbing back out of the dumpster. "I don't want your goddamn trash. Fuck your trash. That's the problem with you people. Even your *garbage* is too fucking good. Well, I don't want it. Keep it. Choke on it, you bastard."

He lowered himself out of the dumpster and lumbered back toward his car. Suddenly Vogel realized that the man had had this same conversation many times before, with many other people just like himself.

"Wait," Vogel said. He knew he should say something; or do something. The man stopped with his hand on the door handle and turned toward Vogel. The sports report was on inside and the two men stood looking at each other, with the alley's huge, empty air piled between them like brickwork.

Additional Protection

Vogel's floor-length drapes were taking on a creased disfigurement from the five straight nights he had spent crouched behind them, drawing them closed, pulling them back. The bum never showed again, though. After the first couple of nights, Vogel had started wandering out onto the fire escape to wait, poised against the railing. He stood in the thin glow of the distant streetlight, listening to familiar dogs bark and blown leaves crinkle across the pavement and cars hum incessantly on the street at the end of the alley, and wondered where that bum was driving to now, and whose interest he had last piqued.

Vogel's intent, if the guy ever showed up again, was to offer him something, although he wasn't sure what at first. Then he had a notion to offer him insurance. Surely he could swing that, Vogel thought, and auto seemed to him to be the appropriate type. Vogel spent evenings nestled in the curtains trying to devise a plan to avoid the premiums, which obviously the guy could not afford to pay. Vogel himself would simply enter the man into his company's system as "approved," so he did not foresee a problem in that. But as he studied the blotched, haphazard pattern on the drapes, the thought made his mouth dry up just the same.

On the fifth night, Vogel drifted down the fire escape to the alley, and out to where it met Beechwood Avenue. It was raining lightly and traffic was sparse. Vogel had on a yellow slicker with the hood up and his hands in the pockets. He stood there at the corner and watched the cars, occasionally getting sprayed by one that drifted too close to the curb. His pants were quickly drenched, but still he stood planted on the side of the road, studying each car that skimmed past. I should stand by a stoplight, Vogel thought. That'd give me a better look.

"Hey, pal. You all right?"

Vogel turned and saw a City of Pittsburgh police cruiser idling several yards behind him on Beechwood. His first reaction was to wonder how he could not have noticed it pull up. "No, sir, officer. I'm fine. I'm just waiting for someone."

The headlights shone out into the street and the cop peered through the window, which was rolled less than halfway down. "Come here, please, sir," he said. Vogel walked over, feeling his thighs rub against the inside of his soggy pants. When he got over next to the car he saw that the cop was a black man, young. Late twenties, Vogel figured. He did not roll the window down any further. "Waiting on someone," the cop said, not quite looking into Vogel's face. "Out here in the street?"

Suddenly Vogel realized the absurdity of his actions and how sinister he must look. He felt rain run down his temples and chin. "Yeah, well," he said, "he was supposed to pick me up. But it doesn't look like he's going to show, I guess."

The cop turned toward the windshield. "No, it doesn't."

"I guess I should probably be heading back home now," Vogel said and turned to go.

"Hold on, sir." The cop's voice sounded more rigid to Vogel than before. "I'll take you home. Why don't you get in."

"Oh, no," Vogel said. "That's fine. It's not very far. Thanks anyway."

"Get in the car, please, sir. And I'll take you home."

The window was still nearly all the way up and the cop's eyes were still looking forward absently, but, for some reason, Vogel felt less of a barricade between them, protecting him. He glanced down at his sopping shoes, then opened the back door and climbed into the car.

"You know," the cop said into the rearview mirror as he pulled away from the curb, "it's not such a good idea to be standing out in the street alone at this time of night. Lots of undesirables around that have no regard to sex or size. They don't discriminate. If there's one thing I've learned on this job it's that. I don't mean to lecture or anything, but it just occurs to me that you should know better. But then again, I guess it's not really my place to say, now is it?"

"It's fine," Vogel said. "I suppose you're right." He listened to the wet sounds around him. "I've actually been meaning to take some precautionary steps, you know, to protect myself."

"Sir, that's up to you. I can't very well recommend such actions."

"I know. But, like you said, there's lots of undesirables out there. You have to be prepared, right?"

"Like I said, sir, I don't recommend it. One of the best precautions is not to be standing out in a street like that at one or two in the morning. You'd be surprised how far that'll get you in the protection department."

A few minutes later, the cop dropped Vogel off in front of a strange apartment building where Vogel had said he lived. Vogel trotted up the brick sidewalk and through the lobby door. The inside of the building was pretty ritzy, with turn-of-the-century furniture and high arching doorways, and Vogel wished he *did* live there. He waited at the front window for the cop to drive away, then he stepped back outside and walked home in the rain.

Vogel could not get out of work in time to get to Clyde's before closing. He took the bus into Bloomfield anyway, got off at the proper stop and walked past the glass door which was guarded by a lowered iron cage. A pistol just like the one Vogel had picked out sat in the display window next to a sign bearing the excited message, "Wow! A steal!" with an arrow pointed down at the gun.

Suddenly, Vogel felt oddly exposed. The pavement was wet and the sky was in a period between dusk and darkness. Across the street in front of a sub shop, two boys in camouflage pants and ratty jackets pushed each other around, lightly at first, then harder. They laughed, but it sounded to Vogel like a demonic sort of laugh. Vogel stood and watched as the cars and busses slid by between him and the boys. The taller boy, who had long, stringy hair and wore a brown knit cap, kept poking the shorter boy in the front of his shoulder in an annoying sort of way.

"Buzz off, dickhead!" the shorter boy said in a shrill, almost maniacal voice.

The taller boy kept poking.

"Lay off, I said."

More poking, then a soft head-slap. The tall boy bent over laughing.

"I'll fuck you up. As sure as I speak, I'll mess you good. Try me. Go ahead. Poke me once more, bad ass. You've had your fair warning now."

The boy was close to screaming and Vogel wondered why no one else was watching. The tall boy slumped to the ground, he was laughing so hard. Vogel looked over at his gun then back across the street.

"I'll give you to five to quit laughing. Then you're meat. One . . ." the shorter boy began.

Vogel turned away and headed down the street in the direction of his apartment. He could walk from here, he figured. It was close enough. Then, after a few steps, he broke into a hasty, awkward jog.

Matrimony, revised

Vogel's pulse began to race when Jenny showed up so soon after he'd hung up with her. He had called her upon his return from Bloomfield and the closed gun shop. Can you come over, he'd said. I need to see you. It's important. He figured she'd dawdle; come over when she found time, exhausted all other options. But she came straight away.

"I think I'm going crazy," he said after she bounced in, unannounced, and tossed her purse on the chair by the door. Her straw-colored hair was pulled back in a ponytail and her jogging shorts accented her newly developed calves. Vogel slouched on the sofa with a blanket around him and, as he spoke, he realized he didn't know what he wanted to say to her.

"You're not going crazy." She walked into the kitchen and Vogel heard her fill a glass with ice and water. She came back out with the glass half-empty and stood in front of him. "Is that what's so important?"

"Well . . ." Vogel shifted on the sofa, rearranged the blanket on his shoulders. "That's kind of it. I'm not sure."

Jenny set the glass on the coffee table and pushed up the sleeves of her sweatshirt. "You need to get out a little. You know, quit watching TV and bums going through the garbage. Lord knows you certainly got around enough when we were married."

"Jen—"

"Listen, I think I know what you're going through." She sat in the chair across from him with her legs extended and crossed at the ankles, calves exposed. "But you're just feeling sorry for yourself is all. I mean, it's been over a year now."

"It's not that," Vogel said, although he realized that it might be. "I bought a gun. After I talked to you last week I went out and bought a goddamn gun, I held it in my hand and told the guy, yeah, I wanted it."

"Jesus," Jenny said. "Can I see it?"

Vogel let out a long, breathy sigh through his nose. "I don't have it yet. They had to check me out first. Make sure, I don't know, make sure I'm the kind of person who should own a gun, I guess. I went to pick it up today but the place was closed. Then I . . . he looked over at Mike, sleeping on his back in the corner. "Then I came home."

"Is this what you wanted to tell me? Is this why I'm here?" Jenny picked up her water glass. When he didn't answer, she said, "Jerry doesn't know I'm here, and, frankly, I'm starting to think maybe I shouldn't be doing stuff like this anymore. I mean, I sort of feel like I owe you something, seeing as how we were married and all. But you know, you're not the same man I married. If you were, we'd still be together, right?" She got up from the chair and walked over toward the front window, keeping her back to him. "I just don't understand this. What are you doing with yourself? What happened to all those jokers you used to run around with?"

"They're all married."

Jenny turned and shuffled slowly, nonchalantly, over to the sofa. She sat next to Vogel, cuffed his head in her hand and pulled him into her shoulder. Smoothing his hair she said, "Sweetheart, you're embarrassing yourself. You're not this pathetic. Honest."

Vogel closed his eyes and hoped with all his being that she could not recognize his quickened, irregular breathing. "Jen, what do you think when you see some poor bum on the street?"

She stopped smoothing his hair. "Why are you doing this?"

Vogel pressed his head into her shoulder. He felt himself trembling.

"I suppose I feel sorry for him," she said.

"So do I. But I'm afraid, too. Why is that?"

"I don't know." She touched his hair again and he placed his damp hand on her hip.

"I can't sleep," he said. "I'm up all night and I'm frightened."

She took his hand and gently placed it next to her on the sofa. "I'm sorry," she said.

Fortune

Vogel went through all his drawers, tossing inappropriate clothing on the floor to keep from reexamining it. He settled on his oldest pair of navy cotton pants, a warped, ill-fitting flannel shirt, and a pair of old boots he kept only for shoveling snow off his fire escape stairs. He took a pair of scissors and cut holes in the knees and tore strips up the pantlegs. Then he took the shirt and yanked on the breast pocket until it ripped and hung there. He put the shirt and pants on overtop of his rattiest pair of long underwear. Before putting on the boots, he removed the laces.

As Jenny left his apartment nearly an hour ago, the last thing she said to him was, "And for Christsake, honey, get out and *do* something, would you please?" Well, he had decided he would.

The closest thing Vogel had to mascara was shoe polish, which he didn't even know he had until he found it. He mixed a little of the black and brown together and smeared it on his face, careful to make sure he got it around his ears and neckline. He did not wash his hands. He tried to mess his hair up but couldn't get it to look quite right, so he settled on an old Steelers tassel cap. Checking his look in the bathroom mirror, Vogel was satisfied with his authenticity. *I only wish I hadn't shaved this morning*, he thought.

He was the only person at the bus stop a block down from his building. The night was dark and damp; the streetlights threw streams of light in certain spots, but did not illuminate all that they should. The bus turned the corner on time and rambled up to Vogel's stop and the door swung open for him. At the top of the steps he put his change in the box and looked around; several people sat scattered throughout the bus, staring out the windows. Vogel walked about halfway back and sat across the aisle from a middle-aged woman wearing a silky red scarf around her head. She did not move toward the window, as Vogel had noticed most people did when a bum sat by them. In fact, she glanced in his direction and smiled. It was an impersonal smile, offered out of courtesy only, but a smile just the same.

The bus stopped four times on its way downtown. At the last stop, as the bus began to fill, a fat man with a briefcase asked to sit with Vogel. Vogel eyed him curiously for a moment, then slid over to the window. "Sorry for the inconvenience," the man said cheerfully. "The old arthritis is acting up in the old knee tonight. Didn't feel like walking all the way back to an empty seat. I'm getting off at the next stop, though. Be outta your way in a jiff."

Vogel said he understood. It was no problem. No problem at all. Then he looked out the window at the warehouses and storefronts. This is not the way it is, he thought.

He got off in Market Square, a busy shopping area where, nonetheless, the pigeons usually outnumbered the people. He stood at the edge of the square grass section in the center of town and watched the bus turn a corner and head toward his office building. The shops were closed now, but people were around, moving from their cars to restaurants or simply through Market Square on their way somewhere else. There were four benches—one on each side around the perimeter of the square grass section—and a homeless person slept on each one. Vogel didn't know what to do next. For a long while he just stood, staring straight ahead and trying to take in what was going on to his left and right and behind him and commit it to memory. *I should have worn gloves with the fingers cut out*, he thought.

The streets surrounding the square were brick, and Vogel spent a few moments deciding which one to cross, and what he'd do once he did. He chose one with some open space on the sidewalk where he could sit and lean against a building. But when he got there, it didn't seem quite right. Would a homeless man sit here? Then he decided it didn't matter. If he kept this up, he'd just wander around all night, and what purpose would that serve? So he sat. After ten long minutes, he picked himself up and crossed the street again. He walked by one of the homeless bums sprawled on a bench. The man was sleeping and Vogel stopped and stood over him, examining his face, his clothes, his body which Vogel could not describe in his mind, although he tried. The man's face was leathery and white like glue; the fact that he was a homeless bum was carved into it. The clothes he wore were essentially the same as the ones Vogel had on, but there was an inherent difference built in to them that seemed to radiate destitution. You could put this guy in an Armani suit, Vogel thought, and you'd still be able to tell. He looked down at his own getup then, and realized that there was a gaping difference between authenticity and reality.

"Get the hell away from him!"

Vogel swung around to the voice behind him, and the first thing he saw was the Red Sox hat. Then, shifting his eyes downward, he saw the garbage bag in that thick, grey hand, tailing long and thin.

"You," Vogel said.

"*You*," the man repeated. "*You.* You, you, you."

"No, you know me," Vogel said. "You remember."

"You, you, you, you, you."

"Hey," Vogel said. "Seriously. You know me. Really."

"Is that right? Well old Hobbs here sure doesn't." He pointed with his hand that held the Hefty bag at the man on the bench, who stirred and flipped onto his side, but did not wake up. "So leave him alone, why don't you. He's got diabetes now, poor bastard."

"So, where's your car?" Vogel asked, taking a step toward him.

The man opened his mouth, then stopped himself and looked Vogel up and down. "The hell's this shit you got going here?" He made a circular motion at Vogel with his free hand. When Vogel showed no signs of comprehension he added, "With the clothes. What's the deal? Just who are you trying to kid?"

"Nobody," Vogel said. "I was looking for you."

"So you're undercover?"

"What? No. I just—"

"Like hell."

"No, seriously. I was looking for you. I think maybe I can help you out with something. I can get you insurance for your car. Your Caddy. For free. So if you wreck it, or whatever, you won't lose it. You can collect money on it. That goes for if it's stolen, too."

Vogel waited a moment, then noticed that the man was smiling. "Looking to help me out, are you?" he said.

A couple walked by them on the street. They were tall and blond. The woman had her arm looped through the man's. "What's wrong with that, exactly?" Vogel said.

"Damn, man. You don't listen, do you? I didn't say there's anything *wrong* with it. Did I say there was anything wrong with it?"

"No."

"No. Exactly."

The wind had stopped blowing and the man's garbage bag hung limply at his side. Vogel wanted to get back to the insurance topic, but was hesitant to mention it.

"Look," the man said, a little irritably. I don't know what possessed you to come here looking like you do, but I guess you expect me to say something now. Right? Some words of wisdom or something? You got me. Maybe you want me to say something that'll set you straight, so you can go home and turn your sorry-ass life around—think, 'Well, at least *that* ain't me.'" He stopped and held Vogel's gaze for a long moment. "That's probably it," he said finally. "You younger fellas tend to do that a lot lately." Then he reached down to Hobbs, who slept silently next to them, and quickly slid the folded newspaper out from under Hobbs' head, which dropped and hit the bench's peeling wood with a thud. He put the paper in his Hefty bag and chuckled into his coat. "It must've cost you a fortune to look that way," he said, and turned toward the opposite side of the street.

Vogel wanted to leave; get as far away from there as possible. Yet his tiny apartment suddenly seemed vast and desolate somehow, and he did not want to return there. "What about the insurance?" he said to the man's dusty, hooded back.

"I'm covered."

Vogel watched as the man crossed the red brick street to where a split between two grey buildings formed an alley. The Cadillac sat there, backed in, like an abandoned wreck in the shadows.

The man squeezed in sideways between the car and the wall of the adjacent building, cracked open the passenger side door and slid inside, his Hefty bag following behind. Then he just sat there. Vogel wondered for a moment if this were one of the times when the man could not afford any gas. Then, before he could form an impression one way or the other, he began walking back toward the bus stop.

He had been standing there, alone, for about five minutes when the young man and woman who had passed by earlier approached from the opposite direction. Vogel studied them. They both had smooth, perfect skin and hair—him, confident and distinguished in his overcoat, and her, angelic and shy but fully knowing this, holding on to him for dear life. They were laughing nervously and, as they passed in front of Vogel, she stopped and said, "Oops. Hold on a second, honey." Then she bent over and reached into her purse, digging around.

"Come on," he said. "What are you doing?"

"Just a minute," she said. "Ah, here we go."

She pulled out a small wallet, unzipped it, and poured some change into her hand. Smiling, she stuck her closed fist out to Vogel.

Vogel looked into her face. Her blond hair was windblown around her forehead and there was a hint of pink in her cheeks. He watched her green eyes for a moment longer, waiting for something, a flinch maybe, that never came. Then he extended his hand to her, palm up.

The Farther You Go

ONCE, WHEN FLETCHER NASH was nine, his father kidnapped him and they spent a week together in Cincinnati. The event was fueled by an argument that had broken out between his parents over, to the best of Fletcher's recollection, his father's reluctance to replace the kitchen's linoleum. It was worn and cracked, his mother said; dark water stains all over the blessed place.

Somehow, apparently, words were spoken insinuating that Ned Nash was cheap. Then his trees were insulted. The man was always planting trees in the summertime. Not just trees with leaves; trees that grew things. Apples, peaches, plums, pears, whatever. Just think, Fletcher, he'd say. Next year at this time we'll be eating our very own plums.

Nothing ever grew, though. Sometimes he planted the trees in poor sections of the yard, sections that didn't provide enough sunlight, or had inadequate soil. Sometimes the tree's death was due to brutally cold Mansfield, Ohio winters. Sometimes, also during the winter, the thin saplings were gnawed by deer to the point of near disintegration. Sometimes they were just weak trees and never had a chance. But then there was the one time when Fletcher and a neighbor friend used two freshly planted future peach trees as swords during a particularly heated jousting match. That these two stems might ever bear fruit never occurred to Fletcher, and he knew his father would dismiss the tragedy as vandalism, which he did.

In any case, his mother's comment was something about her

husband spending more money on those pathetic sticks in the backyard than on his family's home. That's the way Fletcher remembered it.

When his mother retreated to the kitchen to finish washing the dishes from that evening's dinner, Fletcher's father took him by the arm and hoisted him up from in front of the television. "Come on," he said. "We're going." Fletcher put a coat on and followed his father out the door to the car.

They stopped at one of the interstate exits outside Columbus and Ned bought them a couple of changes of clothes, toothbrushes, all the essentials necessary for two refugees to survive comfortably for a week. He also made a phone call. When they were close to Cincinnati, Ned exited the interstate again, like he knew where he was going, and pulled into the parking lot of a Knights Inn.

They spent the next six days and nights there, watching movies and baseball on television and eating takeout pizza and burgers in their room. All in all, Fletcher figured his father'd spent more that week on the room and supplies than it would have cost to replace the linoleum.

On the sixth night Ned Nash, while lying on his back with the bed's Magic Fingers going, removed a bag of Fritos from his chest and sat up suddenly. "Well," he said, "guess we'll go home tomorrow. It's been long enough."

Fletcher thought he had the whole situation straight in his mind. Even for a nine-year-old, Ned Nash was easy to read: This was an act of spite, pure and simple, though, at the time, Fletcher didn't know the word for it. The only thing that confused him was: Why Cincinnati? Why not really make a statement and take off for California? Texas? At least get out of the state? Confident that he understood correctly—and actually enjoying the little vacation—Fletcher posed this theory to his father.

"You got a problem with Cincinnati?" Ned said, folding pizza boxes into thirds and mashing them into the waste basket.

Fletcher sat on the edge of the bed, flipping through channels. "No, it's all right," he said. "It's just, how come? It's still in Ohio even, right? Why didn't we go, you know, somewhere else?"

Ned stopped folding and stood up straight. "Well," he said, looking up toward the ceiling, "the farther you go, the tougher it is to get back."

The next morning they were on I-71, heading back to Mansfield.

Ned Nash wore a burgundy tux. He stood completely erect at the altar with a day-old beard and slicked, parted hair, tapping his heel nervously up and down and pulling at his fingers. He was pale and kept licking his lips. The lone organist began the bridal march and the thirty or so people in the church stood. Fletcher sat about halfway back with a pint of Canadian Club in his inside jacket pocket. Mary Bayne appeared at the rear entrance escorted by her brother, a squatty, toadlike man at least six inches shorter than his sister, and everyone but Ned and Fletcher Nash turned to watch. Ned continued his tapping and pulling, even more furiously now, as he stared toward the side wall at St. Joseph's feet, and Fletcher watched his father. The ceremony was performed by a lodge brother and poker partner of Ned's who happened to be a retired Justice of the Peace. When Mary got to the altar, Ned smiled and took her hand in his. She wore a white blouse and skirt with a quiet headpiece that hung about midway down her back. They had written their own vows, which they recited to each other. They spoke so softly, though, that Fletcher really couldn't understand them, except for the part where his father, voice vibrating horribly, said to his bride, "My love for you is a tall, sturdy tree, bearing the neverending fruit of desire." He also quoted Stevie Wonder—something about being the apple of his eye. Even then, though, Fletcher did not reach for the bottle in his jacket. But when the Justice of the Peace, whose name was Willie, coughed up a wad of phlegm and spat it dramatically into his handkerchief, Fletcher couldn't resist. He snatched it quickly, fumbling with the cap, and took a long pull while trying to keep his head down, then replaced it inside his jacket. He knew Mary's sister and brother-in-law, sitting just to his left, must have seen him, but he didn't look in their direction. He didn't recognize the people to his right.

At Fletcher's wedding, Ned had worn a powder blue tux. He was cheerful and boisterous, often seating guests himself and pausing to talk and laugh with them for a minute or two and reminisce about times he really couldn't remember very well. During the ceremony, Fletcher's mother had cried flowing tears of joy, as she routinely had done, and Ned could be heard above the minister tapping her shoulder and saying "There there," while chuckling blissfully.

But that was years ago and had no bearing. Fletcher drove himself to the reception hall, hitting the CC often along the way. His plan was to get himself drunk enough to be pleasant.

When he arrived, the hall was still nearly empty. A man in a green vest and chewing on a stubby cigar was setting up the bar in a corner, and Fletcher went up and asked him for an empty glass. The man gave Fletcher a knowing smile.

"I'm a little behind, I know. Bear with me," the man said, and then handed over the glass.

Fletcher found a chair and sat facing the door. He took out the bottle, which by now had only a couple swallows left in it, and drained the rest into the glass.

A woman in a hairnet and the same color green skirt and blouse placed covered plates out at the hors d'oeuvre table and the smell of the food began lingering in the air. Stuffed mushrooms, Fletcher thought. Always stuffed mushrooms.

The band, tuxedoed and balding, unpacked their instruments on the tiny stage. More greenclad workers filled balloons with helium, and Fletcher wondered how he could possibly be this early.

Soon, people filed in. At first, Fletcher took mental notes of who was ruthlessly overdressed and whether or not he knew them. But then he noticed that he was critiquing the attire of *couples,* and that he was the only person in the hall who was not a part of one.

Fletcher felt the space around him and the table he was sitting at expand. Suddenly he saw himself in the center of a huge expanse of emptiness. His glass was empty. Then Jamie walked in with Thomas, and Charlie tagging closely behind, pulling at his shirt collar. Fletcher noticed the boy's left shoe was untied, the laces flapping.

Fletcher stood quickly and had to steady himself with the back of his chair. Through some kind of magic that Fletcher was not aware of, the hall had filled up. All the tables were occupied and a line had formed in front of the hors d'oeuvres. Fletcher scanned the room for a familiar face, someone he could talk to. He started walking toward the bar, then remembered his empty bottle, still sitting on the table. He turned and took a step. Jamie, Thomas and Charlie were at the table, sliding out the chairs. Fletcher froze.

"Dad!" Charlie bounced out of his chair.

Fletcher watched Thomas pick the empty bottle up with two fingers and, holding it out away from his body like a dirty diaper, walk over to a trash can and drop it in. Charlie tugged on Fletcher's belt.

"Dad!"

"Hey, sport. How's tricks?"

"Good. Come sit with us."

"Okay," Fletcher said. "I'm just going to go get a drink first. Want anything? Shot and a beer maybe?"

"Da-ad." Charlie beamed up at him.

Fletcher turned. "Be right there," he called over his shoulder.

He took his time getting his drink, letting others order before him, then lingering in the crowd. When he moved to the side, Charlie called to him again and motioned him over.

Jamie leaned back and looked at him, too. Fletcher thought she may have made an attempt at a smile. She wore a sequined dress and her blond hair swept down across the scooped opening in back. Fletcher quickly collected himself and headed over to them. The glass in his hand, for some reason, felt huge and outlandish, like it was on fire.

"Sit here, Dad," Charlie said, patting the seat next to his.

"Hi, Jamie," Fletcher said. He set his drink on the table.

"Your father was looking for you at the church afterwards," she said.

"There were so many people," Fletcher said, sitting. "Figured I'd just see him here."

"I been practicing my chicken dance," Charlie said.

"You have?" Fletcher glanced at Thomas, who leisurely fingered a crack in the plastic tablecloth.

"Yeah. And the Hokey Pokey. They play that at all weddings, right?"

"Why'd you get your hair cut?" Fletcher said suddenly. "It's so short." He turned to Jamie. "Why'd you do that?"

"For Grandpa's wedding," Charlie said, fingering his bangs.

"Of course. Right." Fletcher shrugged, then set his chin in his hand and pretended to reexamine his son. "Looks good, actually. Now that I think about it."

"Here," Thomas said, reaching into his back pocket and pulling out a piece of paper folded into quarters. "Your father said to give this to you, if you're still willing to drive him and Mary to the train station next weekend." He unfolded it and scanned it briefly. "It's their schedule."

Fletcher reached out for it. "Why'd he give it to you?"

"Because," Jamie said, "we were there. He wasn't even sure if he'd see you tonight."

Fletcher read the schedule over.

"They leave at four-fifteen," Thomas said.

"I see that."

"Can I come with you when you take them, Dad?" Charlie said, tapping Fletcher's thigh.

"Well, I guess you'll have to. That's our day, isn't it?"

Thomas stood. "I'm going for drinks," he announced. "Any takers? Fletcher, how're you holding up?"

Fletcher looked into Thomas' eyes, which shifted once and then steadied, and willed himself behind them. He pictured the way they looked at his wife, what they saw. Then he glanced down at Thomas' fingers. He imagined them dancing across the shiny, white keys of his piano, what that felt like; he saw them, just as expertly, moving over his wife's skin, and what that felt like.

"Coke," Charlie said.

"You got it." Thomas pointed a finger at Charlie like a gun. "Jamie?"

"In a minute."

Fletcher picked up his glass and held it. Thomas turned and headed to the bar.

After a short moment filled only with the buzzing sound of wedding talk and the band tuning their instruments, Jamie said, "Your dad was really nervous. He was waiting for you to say something to him. I could tell."

Fletcher swallowed the rest of his whiskey. "Like what?"

"Anything. He needed you."

"Needed me."

"Yes. And you left."

Fletcher shook his head and looked down at his shoes. "You don't know what you're talking about."

"No?"

"No."

Jamie patted Charlie's hair down on top. "When are you picking him up?" she said.

"Next Friday, I guess. The fifteenth. That's the plan, right?"

"What all are we going to do?" Charlie said, leaning out from under his mother's hand.

"Lots of fun stuff," Fletcher said.

"Your father should be here any time now," Jamie said, turning toward the door.

"Maybe I'll get some mushrooms," Fletcher said, and pushed

out his chair. The band started into a bouncy fifties tune and one couple Fletcher did not recognize started dancing self-consciously. "I'll be back." Then he walked over past the rows of hors d'oeuvres with their bulging silver lids, and out the front door.

Outside the reception hall it was nearing dusk. Across the street and beyond a grassy field a row of evergreens diluted the late-afternoon sun. Fletcher stood and examined the cars in the parking lot. He wanted to see what he would do next.

Just then the hall door swung open and Charlie stepped outside. Fletcher ran a hand through his hair and straightened his jacket. He felt as though he'd been caught in the act of something.

"Hey," Fletcher said.

Charlie stuffed his hands in the pockets of his newly pressed slacks. The sleeves of his jacket hung down past his knuckles. "I don't like mushrooms," he said. "Yuck."

Fletcher smiled. "Me neither," he said. Then, "You better get back in there. Before your mother catches you."

Charlie looked down at his shoes. The piece of hair Jamie had been patting stuck straight up at the cowlick. Fletcher had a fleeting urge to pat it back down himself, but quickly thought better of it.

"Where're you going, Dad?" Charlie said.

Fletcher shrugged. "I don't know. California I think." He had no idea he was going to say that.

Charlie stared at a spot on the pavement next to the back tire of a Toyota pickup. "You think maybe I could come with you?" he said, keeping his stare. "I haven't missed any days of school yet this year. It would be all right."

The suggestion took Fletcher by surprise and he glanced over at the spot on the pavement Charlie had been watching, hoping answers presented themselves there. "You'd want to do that?" he said. "Come with me?"

Charlie nodded. "If you want me to."

"I'd love for you to come," Fletcher said. "That would be terrific."

"Really?"

"Really. Let's go. What do you say?"

Charlie lifted his head up and Fletcher saw the boy's eyes light a little. He tried for a moment to remember the last time he'd seen this, but couldn't.

"Let's go," he said again.

A stiff breeze swept across their pantlegs. Charlie stood and rubbed his upper arms. "I'm a little cold," he said.

"I'll buy you another coat on the way." Fletcher began walking toward his car. "We need to get you out of that monkey suit anyway." He listened for Charlie's footsteps behind him. For a brief instant, Fletcher held his breath. Then he heard his son's shoes shuffling on the pavement.

Neither spoke as Fletcher eased the Ford Escort—the first and only car he and Jamie had bought together—onto the state road heading back into town. Fletcher and Charlie spent every other weekend together, and a full week in the summer. On these visits, most of the catching up was done during their first couple of hours together, and then there was nothing much to talk about.

Fletcher wondered how long they'd stay away and what they'd do together, how they'd pass the time. He always had trouble packing the hours with meaningful activities. He felt pressured. Charlie always showed up eager and bouncing and it seemed to Fletcher that the boy's enthusiasm level gradually declined throughout the visit. But he did want to go to California with Charlie—more than anything. He thought this, assured himself of it. Then he reached down and turned on the headlights.

"Hungry?" he asked. "Want to get something to eat?"

"I guess," Charlie said, and craned his neck to see out of the windshield. Fletcher glanced over at his son. For some reason, the boy looked younger and even tinier than usual, all dressed up with the button on his sport jacket fastened, the bottom fanning out over his thighs. The top of his head was considerably below the seat's headrest.

"Pizza?" Fletcher said, focusing his attention back on the double yellow line laid out before him. Autumn corn fields receded from the road and grew darker. Every so often mailboxes on flimsy posts lined the roadside, but there were no houses in sight.

"Yeah," Charlie said. "Pizza." Then he sat up on his knees and turned around to look out the back window.

"What?" Fletcher said.

Charlie turned back around and regarded Fletcher as if he'd forgotten his father was there. "Nothing." Then he said, "Think I should start calling Mrs. Bayne 'Grandma' now?"

Fletcher looked over quickly at Charlie and reached out to softly stroke the boy's hair. "Not if you don't want to, Charlie. It's up to you. Don't do anything you don't feel comfortable with."

Charlie shrugged. "I don't mind," he said. "She's cool. She knows every player on the Browns. *And* their position, *and* their number."

"Mm."

"When they come back to visit we're gonna go to a game. She said so."

"No kidding?"

"Yep."

"Well good," Fletcher said. "That's real good. But, you know, right now we'd better think about getting you some new threads. Your mom pick that jacket out for you, I suppose?"

Charlie looked down at himself. "Yeah."

Fletcher nodded. "Well, we'll fix you right up. And me, too. I think I might look even goofier than you." He smiled.

After an awkward moment, Charlie smiled, too. Then Charlie unbuttoned his jacket, wriggled out of the sleeves, and tossed it, hard, in a balled-up heap onto the back seat. He looked up at his father.

"Right," Fletcher said.

*   *   *

They stopped at a discount clothing store in the Mansfield Shopping Plaza and walked hastily through the boys' section, Fletcher holding up items he found interesting and Charlie nodding or shrugging silently at each suggestion. They decided on a pair of blue jeans, a package of underwear and socks, two shirts (short sleeves, for California), a Browns jersey, and a red zippering sweatshirt with a hood (for the ride out).

They stood in the checkout line, still in their ties, holding Charlie's new clothes in their arms.

"What about you, Dad?" Charlie said, looking his father up and down.

"I'll be fine. I'll pick up some stuff later."

Charlie nodded, then looked away toward the women's shoes and began shifting his weight from foot to foot, anxious to leave. Fletcher remembered this feeling. He had it every week when he was a boy, after church, waiting for the old folks to hurry up and file out. And fishing. Oh, how he despised fishing. Planted there on the shore of a lake or stream, crouching, watching— that's all, just watching—a plastic red and yellow bobbin move lifelessly over the tiny rippling waves, Fletcher often felt as if the other end of the line was fastened directly and securely to his stomach. He'd sit, silent, fixed on the bobbin, feeling his father next to him, who never spoke when they were fishing other than to give instructions. Fletcher would wait and his thoughts would go. After long, still, mind-numbing periods, Fletcher would have himself prepared for when the hit would come, quick and sharp, yanking the bobbin under the glassy surface of the water and Fletcher's insides from his chest. He remembered wanting desperately to leave but being afraid to ask.

"We're leaving, son," he said now. "Hang on."

Fletcher paid for the clothes. On their way out of the store Fletcher pulled the sweatshirt out of the bag and suggested that Charlie put it on.

Walking through the parking lot, Fletcher was hit by a jarring recollection of the reception. What was everyone thinking?

He wondered if Jamie was in a state of panic, how Thomas was handling it, how he was handling her. He wondered what Jamie's first thought was when she realized what her ex-husband had done. Was she concerned for her son's welfare? This hurt Fletcher. He felt a hard, sudden twist inside him. That he could be perceived as a danger to his own son, by his wife, sucked the balance from his step. Suddenly Fletcher found himself standing next to his car. He put the key in the door.

"Dad." Fletcher turned and saw Charlie several steps back. His thin girlish hair danced over his face as he bent over, tugging on the zipper of his sweatshirt. "I need help. "

"Do it in the car."

"I'm cold." His bag was on the ground, propped up against his leg.

"Put your hood up."

Charlie paused, then reached around awkwardly and flipped the hood over his head. He stood there another moment, then picked up his bag and walked around to the passenger side of the car.

"Okay?" Fletcher said, and when he received no response, unlocked the door.

He drove aimlessly for several minutes before remembering the pizza idea. He wanted to change his mood. And he wanted some help entertaining his son for a while before heading out.

"Hey," Fletcher said suddenly, "wanna bring a couple pizzas over to Whippy's house? You always liked Whippy, huh? He'd enjoy seeing you. Wanna stop by there before we go?" He looked in Charlie's direction.

Whippy, a high school friend of Fletcher's, was a large, bearish man. He had gone on to play football at Ohio State and thus held a sort of elevated status around Mansfield and with Charlie.

"Sure," Charlie said, and then just as quickly added, "Maybe we should leave on Sunday instead? I forgot . . . I mean, I just remembered something."

Fletcher shifted in his seat and eased up on the gas pedal.

"What?"

Charlie sat on his hands. The hood was still on his head. "Thomas is performing tomorrow night, in Akron. And Mom wants me to go. I just remembered."

"Well, do you want to go?"

"I like Thomas," Charlie said, eyes forward.

"I didn't ask you that. Thomas is not your father. Even when they're married, he won't be your father. You understand that, don't you?"

"Yes."

"You even like that kind of music?"

Charlie shrugged.

"Well, you can't go. We have plans," Fletcher said, and then quickly caught himself. "I mean, we're going to have a really good time together, me and you. We should start right away. I don't want our time to get cut short."

"It's just one day," Charlie said, looking down at his loafers dangling above the floor mat. "We can go to California right after."

Fletcher considered this situation, and how, in the same month, he'd planned to attend the weddings of both his father and his wife. He almost laughed but swallowed down hard on it. "I'll think about it," he said.

Charlie looked out the side window. Fletcher, increasing the Escort's speed, pulled out into the left lane of the two-lane road and passed a red and white Agway truck. "I'll think about it," he said again.

Walt "Whippy" Fantuzo bred foxes, two different kinds, to be made into fur coats. That was his job. He lived in a trailer outside of Mansfield, sometimes alone and sometimes with various local women. Fletcher hoped he'd be alone at this particular time, for Charlie's sake.

When they pulled into Whippy's lot, the foxes, in cages stacked outside the trailer's front door, in the haze from the Escort's headlights, began yelping wildly. Fletcher and Charlie sat silently in the front seat for a moment, transfixed on the frantic animals, who slammed themselves against the wire mesh fronts of their individual cages and showed their sickly, rotting teeth.

Fletcher threw the Escort in reverse. "Let's scrap this idea. Just go have dinner ourselves, huh?" he said, as Whippy pushed open the trailer's screen door and stepped out. He wore a grey sweatshirt with the sleeves cut off, sweatpants pulled up above his knees, and flip-flops. His thinning hair was wild and he leaned forward, squinting to see through the Escort's windshield.

"Fletcher?" he said.

With the windows rolled up and the noise from the foxes, Fletcher only saw Whippy's lips form the word.

"Oh, well." Fletcher turned to his son. "We'll just say hi. Put your hood back up. And get out on this side; stay away from those dirty cages."

Charlie slid over and got out on the driver's side. Outside the car, the foxes were earpiercingly loud and maniacal.

"Fletcher!" Whippy shouted.

Suddenly, Fletcher did not want to be there. He felt a tightness in his stomach and an unpleasant certainty that this was a bad idea. He stood there with the foxes barking all around him, holding the pizzas in front of him and feeling utterly stupid.

"Fletcher, the hell you been?" Whippy held his arms out to the sides, as if Fletcher could have been anywhere on Earth. "Thought you died or something, you bastard. Barbara waited for you half the night, she told me. She thinks you're pretty much a shit and I can't say I blame her."

Fletcher nodded down at Charlie.

"Oops," Whippy said. "Sorry, Chaz-man. Forgive my vulgarity."

Charlie tried to smile, but was obviously still frightened by the foxes.

"Shut the hell up, you filthy sons-a-bitches!" Whippy walked over to the cages, his flip-flops snapping against his heels. He picked up a long piece of plywood from the ground and smacked it against the fronts of the cages several times. "Shut up, or I'll skin ya tonight!" he said, then turned to Charlie and gave him a confidential smile. "Pay no attention, Chaz-man. They're just a bunch of puppy dogs, really."

The sun was down now. Dark shadows from the outside light skipped unsymmetrically around the lot. Fletcher sighed heavily and saw his breath.

"Come on in, men," Whippy said. "It's almost their feeding time—that's why they're so uppity. But screw 'em. Come on, come on. It's cold out here." He waved his wrist to hurry them up.

Inside the trailer, the barks were muffled, but still audible. The smell was of fish and pine. Trophies and footballs with various scores and other writing on them sat strategically but often inappropriately displayed throughout the trailer. Whippy's obvious favorites enjoyed the prominent positions of the television top, coffee table, and homemade maple bookcase. Two balls and two trophies of apparent lesser importance lay on the floor against the wall, next to Whippy's gun rack, and Fletcher guessed there were others recklessly stacked in a closet somewhere.

Usually Charlie would head straight for one of the balls, feeling it in his hands and tossing it up in the air and catching it against his chest. Fletcher noticed that this time, though, the foxes had disturbed his son more than usual. Charlie seemed reserved, apprehensive to him. He stood inside Whippy's door, hood still on his head, and immediately began rocking back and forth on his feet.

"Take your hood off, son," Fletcher said.

Charlie lifted his eyes, as if trying to look at the top of his own head, then reached up and cautiously slid the hood off.

"So, where you been, partner?" Whippy said, his head in the refrigerator. "Looks like you're all duded up for something or another." He grabbed two bottles of beer and kicked the door shut. Then he said, "Barbara's pissed. Not to mention yours truly. I worked long and hard setting that up, you know. I was pretty goddamn proud of myself." He turned and lifted his eyebrows to Fletcher.

Fletcher decided to answer the first question and disregard the rest. "Weddings," he said. "Out the wahzoo."

"No shit? Hey, sit down. Chaz-man, you want a Coke or what?"

Charlie shook his head no.

"Geez. What's the matter, sport?" Whippy said. "You sick or something?"

"Nah," Fletcher said, walking over to the sofa. "He's just quiet today. Sort of a lull."

"Well pep up, killer. When's the last time you saw old Whippy anyway, huh?"

Charlie shrugged.

"Exactly," Whippy said, and cuffed Charlie behind his head. "Here's a Coke."

The boy reached up and took the glass.

"There you go," Whippy said. Then, "Pizza," and walked into the square living area. He handed Fletcher one of the bottles then grabbed a folding chair, spun it around and sat heavily with its back against his chest. "So what's this wedding shit? All's you gotta do is show up, right? Where's the hassle here?" He took a long, loud gulp from his beer.

"I don't know," Fletcher said, leaning back into the puffy, overstuffed sofa. He still had the pizzas on his lap. "It's like, I gotta psych myself up for them or something, you know? Something like that. Mentally prepare for it." He shrugged.

Whippy nodded knowingly, took another swig. "There is that, I guess." Then, turning to Charlie, who stood leaning against the kitchen counter with his untouched glass of Coke, "You see this yet, killer?" He pointed to a framed eight-by-ten photo nailed into the paneling. "You recognize those dudes? That's old Whippy there with Kevin Mack. Pretty neat, huh?"

Charlie set down his glass and walked over toward the wall, eyes on the picture.

"Yeah, they asked me to play in this golf tournament a couple months back. Some charity. And he was there, too." He turned back to Fletcher. "Golf's a stupid fucking game, man. Don't take it up."

"Grandpa and Grandma—Mrs. Bayne, I mean—they're gonna take me to a game," Charlie said, still examining the picture. "Soon as they come back."

"That so?" Whippy said. "What about Whippy here? And your old man? What about us taking you to a game? I got connections, you know." He winked at Charlie.

"You never asked me."

"Well . . ." Whippy scratched his stubbled cheek. "I guess it just never occurred to me is all."

"Tell Whippy about the spelling bee," Fletcher said quickly.

"Came in second," Charlie said.

"No shit?"

"Couldn't spell 'inclement.'"

"Well, Christ. What the hell's 'inclement'?"

"Don't know," Charlie said. "But there's only one 'm' in it." He glanced away from the picture and looked into his father's eyes.

"The hell's 'inclement'?" Whippy turned to Fletcher.

Fletcher felt himself sink into the sofa, its swollen insides engulfing him. They were both watching him. Wanting answers, it seemed. He ran his palms across the smooth top of the pizza box. On the lid it said "Fresh. Hot. Delicious" in swirling red script. Fletcher wet his lips. "Like, inclement weather," he said. "Cold. You know: bad. That kind of thing. Right, Charlie?"

Charlie nodded, then turned back to the picture and began rocking back and forth. Fletcher checked his watch.

"Inclement." Whippy made a sour face and looked at Charlie. "Screw it. It's a bullshit word. Trust me, you'll never use it. I know." He sucked down the rest of his beer and held the empty bottle up to show Fletcher. "Another?"

"One more maybe," Fletcher said.

Whippy picked himself up and walked past Charlie who sat on the floor now with his glass between his legs, digging his pinkie in his ear.

Fletcher leaned forward. He set the two boxes on the coffee table and flipped open one of the lids. "So what's the problem?" he said to his son.

The boy stopped digging and looked up at his father. "Nothing."

"You're awfully quiet."

Charlie looked directly at the tip of Fletcher's nose, shifted his eyes from left to right, then back.

"Hey, if it's that important to you, I guess you oughtta just go tomorrow, that's all. I mean, if you're gonna be in some kind of stupor anyway . . ." Fletcher leaned back. "Gotta do what you gotta do, you know? If you feel like you need to go to this thing tomorrow night, don't let me stop you."

Charlie watched his father for a moment longer, then lowered his eyes to the glass between his legs. Suddenly, Fletcher felt a wave of uncontrollable relief, like a fist loosening its grip around his gut, and he hated himself for it.

A loud belch echoed from behind the refrigerator door. "How you coming on that Coke, Chaz-man?" Whippy called.

Charlie waited a moment, softly cleared his throat. "Fine," he said.

Whippy lumbered back in with the beers and tossed one over the coffee table to Fletcher.

"Kid wants to go to the symphony tomorrow," Fletcher said.

Whippy sat and twisted the cap off of his bottle. "Nah. Not our Chaz-man. He's not into that fairy stuff."

"Ask him."

"I don't need to ask him." Whippy smiled at Charlie, who sat hunched over his sweaty glass, legs extended. "Do I, partner?"

Charlie looked up at Whippy and blinked.

"Oh, no." Whippy's chin dropped. He set his beer on the coffee table and fell to his knees. "Say it ain't so, Chaz-man."

He put a hand over his heart and swayed back and forth. "I can't believe it! Where have I gone wrong?" He gripped his chest with both hands and fell theatrically backward with a thud and lay spread-eagle on the floor. One flip-flop had slipped off and now sat upside down next to his knee. He lay there like that a moment longer, with his tongue hanging out the side of his mouth. Then a smile formed across his lips and he began laughing hysterically.

Fletcher and Charlie silently watched him.

Whippy laughed a while longer, legs curled up into him and holding his stomach, then sat up quickly. "What's on that? Sausage?" He reached for the pizza, pulled out a slice, and in one fluid, continuous movement, swung it up to his mouth. "Okay," he said, chewing. "We'll give it another shot. I'll call Barbara, set it up."

The foxes began yelping again. Fletcher emptied his beer, then twisted open the other bottle. He looked over at Charlie who just then took his first sip from the glass of Coke. He looks . . . what? Fletcher thought. More relaxed? Maybe, but that wasn't it exactly. Then it hit him: Finished. Suddenly his son was uninterested in all of this. He was washing his hands of it all.

Fletcher looked back at Whippy and shrugged. "Yeah," he said. "Okay. Set it up."

Whippy emerged from the back bedroom just as Fletcher and Charlie picked themselves up to leave. "Here," he said holding a fluffy, grey fur coat out to Fletcher. "Give this to Barbara when you pick her up. It should fit her fine."

"What?" Fletcher reached out and gently stroked the fur.

"I get these free all the time from the company I sell the skins to. I gave one to Peggy on our first date and she flipped. Go ahead."

"Jesus, man." Fletcher pulled his hand away. "I'm not giving some woman a fur coat on our first date. I don't even know her. Christ, I've never even met her."

Whippy draped the coat over his shoulder. "Suit yourself. But I'm telling you, she'll go nuts. I mean, it definitely would be to your advantage."

Fletcher looked down at the carpet, then over at Charlie, who stood leaning by the door. His hood was already on his head, tied in a little bow under his chin, tie poking out the bottom.

"Okay, well." Whippy tossed the coat onto the sofa. "Anyway, you're just gonna love Barbara. The stories I've heard. Mm—beautiful. I'll call her soon as you take off. Set everything up. Tomorrow night good?" He rubbed his hands together. "She'll be just what the doctor ordered."

"Yeah?"

"Beautiful."

"You said that already."

"Yeah."

"Jamie's wedding is in two weeks, you know."

Whippy looked down at his bare toes and made a face as though he'd just bitten into something rancid. "So the hell what?" he said and plopped down on the sofa next to the coat. "Don't start with that shit now, all right? Could you do that for me? For old Whippy?" He sat forward on the sofa and held his hands in front of him as if molding an invisible sculpture. "I mean, your chances with Barbara are *exceptional*, if you'd just let it. Don't fuck it up. That would be a shame."

Fletcher tried to muffle his voice with his hand. "You don't understand."

"Bullshit, I don't," Whippy said, almost shouting. "Listen, I'm not as dumb as I make out to be. I see what's going on here. But you gotta pull yourself up by the balls. Get on with it already."

Fletcher ran a hand through his stiff, jelled hair, then brushed some lint off the front of his slacks. "I can't go, man. I'm sorry but I . . . I'm not going to go."

"To Jamie's wedding?"

"No. I mean I'm not going out with any *Barbara*. You don't have to set it up."

Whippy nodded. "Mm."

"Sorry."

"Hey." Whippy held his hands up at shoulder level, as if in surrender. "No problem. Whippy understands."

"I got some things I need to take care of."

"Yeah. I know. It's cool."

"Dad." Suddenly, Charlie was at Fletcher's side. He was not looking up at his father, though. He watched something near the floor lamp next to the television. "Come with us tomorrow."

Fletcher looked at Whippy, who slid his hands inside the waist of his sweatpants and lowered his eyes. Then he looked down at the top of his son's head. The hood of the sweatshirt came to a point in back and poked upward. "I don't know, Charlie," he said. "I really wasn't invited."

"I just invited you."

Fletcher put his hand on the boy's shoulder. "Yeah, well, I know. But I mean by Thomas. Or your mother."

Charlie shrugged out from under his father's hand and headed toward the front door. "I just invited you," he said again, softly, as he walked away.

Fletcher guided the Escort past flashing yellow lights, through the Mansfield business district, to the west side of town. In the seat next to him, Charlie had his head propped up against the door and slept silently. Fletcher looked over at the boy, then back at the road. He had been thinking of Thomas' concert, but it was more of a conscious effort *not* to think about it. Now, as he watched his reflection in the windshield, he saw Charlie sitting in a plush, fold-up theater seat next to his mother, front and center, anxious, nervous for Thomas. The boy's hair is wet and combed back so perfectly it doesn't look quite real. He glances up at his mother and the two of them smile at each other as if in secret conspiracy. His brown shoes are freshly shined and Jamie has bought him a new sport jacket for the occasion. The lights dim and the crowd hushes. Charlie and Jamie take each other's hands and squeeze in giddy anticipation. The curtain rises presenting the orchestra, already seated. Charlie spots Thomas immediately and he quietly, excitedly, points him out to Jamie (he is easy to find, one of only two pianists, but Jamie acknowledges anyway: Oh, yes, there he is). Thomas, of course, is flawless. Jamie is so warmed with pride she has to hold back tears. This night, football does not even exist in Charlie's life.

Fletcher pulled into the driveway of his old house, shut off the engine and sat for a moment, examining the brickwork. For the first time he noticed that there was no For Sale sign in front. Would Jamie and Charlie be staying there to live with Thomas after the wedding? This had never occurred to Fletcher before and now it made him sweat. He remembered picking out counter tops, lighting fixtures.

Suddenly the porch light sprang on. Fletcher leaned over and woke Charlie gently. The boy rubbed his eyes and looked around, then the two of them got out of the car and walked up the front steps, Charlie in front, as Jamie swung the front door open and stood behind the screen.

"Hey there," Fletcher said, trying to look at her and avoid tripping on the steps at the same time. "We're not disturbing anything, are we?"

Jamie did not answer.

"Because if we are, you know, we could just come by another time. If it's a bother—"

"Come here, Charlie," Jamie said.

The boy quickened his pace up the front steps. When he got to his mother, she pushed open the screen door, leaned down to him, and whispered something in his ear. Charlie reached up then, quickly hugged her around the neck, and disappeared into the house. Jamie stood up straight. She folded her arms around herself.

"Jamie," Fletcher said. It was all he could do just to walk up to her. It seemed to take forever and his legs ached.

"Thomas is out looking for you," she said.

When he got to the second step, Fletcher stopped and looked up at her. Somehow he felt this was appropriate, her being above him. "I figured," he said, though this possibility had not crossed his mind. "Look, I'm sorry, of course. Very stupid." He watched her eyes. "Stupid."

Jamie pushed some hair away from her cheek and tucked it behind her ear. "I suppose I should yell at you now," she said—rather softly, Fletcher thought. "It probably'll be my best chance."

"Probably."

"Leaving the reception was cowardly enough, you know."

"Yes. It was."

She looked at him for a moment, into his eyes. Fletcher couldn't tell if it was with tenderness or some form of pity, but he didn't want it to end. "I hadn't expected this," she said. "I have to say that. This is something that just never even occurred to me."

Fletcher felt completely detached from himself, except for the pounding in his chest. "Did I frighten you?" he said.

She thought about this for a moment. She took a breath and let it out. "No," she said finally. "No. Not really. Not frightened. I just didn't expect it." She lifted her eyes then and looked over his head into the dark yard behind him.

"Jamie," he said, "could I come in? Just for a minute? We could talk about . . . something."

She took a cigarette out of a pack that seemed to Fletcher to have appeared out of thin air and tapped it. After a moment she turned and entered the house, holding the screen door open, just for a brief instant, then let it close behind her. Fletcher followed her. Inside, the house smelled so familiar it made his knees unsteady. He heard the water running in the upstairs bathroom.

When he walked into the kitchen, Jamie was already smoking the cigarette at the sink. "So what did you do?" she said. "Did you accomplish anything?"

Fletcher rested his elbow on the beige formica countertop he helped pick out. "Well," he said, "we were going to go to California. But then we decided not to."

Jamie raised an eyebrow.

"Charlie said he had prior engagements."

"That so?"

Fletcher nodded. He thought of the folded paper in his back pocket and of driving his father and new stepmother to the train station. "Where is Thomas?" he said. "I mean, where is he looking? I feel bad. I hope he's not—"

"Thomas," Jamie said quickly, then stopped and looked down toward the dog's bowl on the linoleum. "Thomas isn't out looking for you. He's at his apartment. He wanted to go look for you. But I told him . . . I told him you'd be back tonight."

Fletcher said these last words over again in his mind, considering them for other meanings. "Oh," he said. "I see."

Jamie looked up at him suddenly. She narrowed her eyes. "Have you lost your mind?" She said this sedately; she simply wanted to know.

"I don't know," he said. "I don't think so."

She watched him, waiting.

Fletcher cleared his throat. "Tell Charlie," he said, "tell him . . . Well, apologize for me for ruining his night. Or anything else."

Jamie began to nod, then closed her eyes and slowly shook her head from side to side. "I don't know what to say."

"Just tell him . . . tell him I—"

"I mean to you."

Fletcher looked up at her. Her jaw was tight, stern; but he thought she might be crying. He couldn't tell for sure, though. He never could. "Well," he said.

Jamie flicked her cigarette in the sink and washed it down the drain, following it with her eyes. She let the water run for a few extra seconds, then shut it off. Upstairs, Charlie rustled through drawers getting ready for bed. Fletcher could hear closets slam closed; he heard the floorboards creak and snap, straining under the weight of his son's footsteps.

About the Author

Chris Torockio earned his MFA from the University of Pittsburgh and has been awarded grants from the North Carolina Arts Council and the Vermont Studio Center. His fiction has appeared in *Ascent, The Dickinson Review, The Florida Review,* and others. He lives with his wife in Kalamazoo, Michigan, where he is a Doctoral Associate at Western Michigan University.